URBAN AMBROSIA

URBAN AMBROSIA

BY ROBERT SPRIGGS

To my wife Glynies who is so much more than
I ever dreamt a woman could be.

Made in Charleston, SC
www.PalmettoPublishingGroup.com

Urban Ambrosia

© 2020 by Robert Spriggs

ISBN-13: 978-1-64111-763-0
ISBN-10: 1-64111-763-X

1

HANK ROBERSON GLANCED over his shoulder as he walked
back from the corner store. His wariness had been in full force since he'd
returned to his East Oakland home a month ago. Tired of the street violence and noise surrounding his neighborhood, he had rented his home to
a Mexican family and then moved to a small town farther north. That was
over two years ago. He had a generous pension and was living comforta-
bly. He had come home to get closer to his grown children, who all lived
within thirty minutes. He hadn't talked to his eldest son much over the last
few years. The conversations had turned ugly, and they mutually decided
to avoid any unnecessary communication. Despite that, he felt good being
back in his hometown, where he had lived most of his seventy years. Strong
from years working at a local construction company, Hank still fancied himself a ladies man. Hell, he had most of his jet-black hair left, white teeth, and
his Eldorado.

Abruptly, a carful of young men sped past him with hip-hop blaring:
"Caught the motherfucka on the five-eight-oh…"

A shiver went through him. "Maybe I shoulda stayed up north," he
thought as he walked up his driveway and past the large magnolia tree cen-

1

tered in his front yard. He stopped to admire the new paint on his house. Light brown trimmed with dark brown and white. He made his way into his backyard, overgrown with weeds. He walked toward the oak tree he had planted at the back border of his fence over thirty years ago. It was just a sapling back then. Now it stood over forty feet tall with a girth of at least ten feet.

Hank sighed deeply, thinking of key events that had transpired since. He sat down on the old redwood bench underneath the oak. He tried to count all the women he had been with over the years. Before he was halfway through, he gave up and fell asleep in the shade.

His renters had cleaned the interior spotlessly, making the move back easier. He had placed a photo of Julia and himself on the mantel over the fireplace. Julia had been his one true love. He had loved her enough to marry her but regretted his affairs during their five-year union, which ended in her death from breast cancer. She bore one son and insisted they name him Hank Jr. She died when Junior was four. Junior rarely thought of his mother, and he had never forgiven his father for marrying a white woman. He had learned to hate his pale-yellow complexion and the negativity it brought. He was called "high yellow," "white boy with a tan," and "octoroon" by his predominately mid- to dark-complexioned classmates in East Oakland public schools.

As a result of that humiliation, Junior became increasingly introverted. He began avoiding social activities and parties. He spent most of his time alone reading and doing his homework. He became an honor student. The old insults were replaced with new ones: "sellout," "nerd," and "lame." Worse, he began to think people thought he was smart because he looked to have so much white blood in him. "That's crazy," Junior thought. His mother had never even finished grade school. He cursed his father and imagined a life being darker complexioned. Making matters worse, Junior had two younger siblings from a black girlfriend of Hank's, Nikira and Denard. Both were considerably darker, which he imagined made their lives easier.

By the time Junior turned twenty, he had dropped out of college and begun working for the county. Eight years later he converted to Islam, nam-
ing himself Rafiq Amin. He began to feel a sense of relief, having dropped
his father's surname. Two years after his conversion, he married a Nigerian
Muslim named Fatima, a graduate student in chemistry.

2

HANK CALLED HIS son for the first time since moving back home.

"I know we don't 'xactly see things the same way, but I've never met your wife, Junior."

"You must be losing your mind, old man. Don't you remember what we argued about the last time we talked? I told you to never call me Junior again. My name is Rafiq. I'm thirty-five years old. That's way too old for any man to be called Junior."

"You never used to mind being called that growin' up. Don't you remember Barbara? Your brother and sister's mother? She always called you that, and you would just eat it up. Remember? You would run over to her, and she would be ticklin' you. You acted like you really liked being called Junior back then."

"That's when I was five. Hadn't even started school yet. Listen. You don't have to call me Rafiq right away, but just don't call me Junior. OK?"

"I can't do that, son. 'Junior' is going to come out my mouth one way or the other."

"If you respected me, it wouldn't! I'm done talking."

"Wait—don't hang up the phone. I'll try my best to call you what you want. You got to understand that I didn't raise you to be no Muslim. You got to give me time to adjust."

"Time to adjust? You've had five years. That should have been more than enough."

"Son, please. Just come by for dinner on Saturday. Bring your wife, and let's just try to have a nice time. I'll be 'cueing some ribs and chicken."

Rafiq paused for several seconds. "I'll talk to my wife. If you don't hear from me before then, we'll be there."

■ ■ ■

Rafiq and Fatima sat in their early-nineties Honda and began the drive from their North Oakland home to East Oakland.

"I don't know why you are so worried about me meeting your fata. Many people in Lagos are not Muslim. I have not had a problem with them, and most of the people here are friendly as well."

"Fatima, you haven't been here long enough to really understand how afraid most Americans are of Muslims. Besides, you haven't had a problem here because as soon as people hear your Nigerian accent, you're pretty much OK with most of them. You've seen how bad some people respond to Rashida. She's a Muslim, but a black American one. Doesn't have an accent to protect her. She's a descendant of slaves, but Islam has given her an identity to kind of insulate her from racism. My father never had that. Many African slave descendants undervalue themselves, and my father's no different. He never was exposed to a religion like Islam or some other Eastern religion or philosophy that allows you to place yourself outside the self-hatred we've learned in the US. You'll see when you talk to him that he's much different than your non-Muslim elders in Nigeria. They weren't enslaved. At least not by Europeans."

The 580 was backed up. They exited on High Street and then drove south on East Fourteenth. Pulling up in front of Hank's house, Rafiq smelled the barbecue before he rolled up his window. They walked around to the side gate, where Hank was grilling what looked to be steak.

He turned toward them before they could speak. "I didn't see you standing there. How you doin', Ju...uh, son. This must be your wife," he said as he opened the gate.

"Yes. Fatima, this is my father."

"Just call me Hank. I hope y'all hungry. I made some cornbread and greens. I remembered you don't eat pork any mo'. I had thawed out some pork ribs, seasoned them and everything, then somethin' clicked in my brain. I forgot to thaw out the chicken, so I just threw on these steaks. Hope that's all right. Y'all eat beef, don't cha?"

"We try to stay away from beef most of the time, but yeah, it's OK," Rafiq said as the three sat in their patio chairs.

Hank turned to Fatima. "You a beautiful woman. If the rest of African women look anything like you, I think I better start savin' and make a trip over there."

Fatima smiled broadly as she and Hank exchanged glances.

Rafiq frowned. "African women aren't like the women you've met, Dad. You'd have trouble finding easy women like the ones you used to pull out of those bars downtown."

Fatima frowned at Rafiq and kicked his leg. They sat in awkward silence for some time before Hank got up and went into the house.

"Why did you say that to him? That was just mean."

Rafiq looked at his wife's watering eyes.

"You told me you did not talk well with your fata, but you are the one making trouble out of nothing, and we just arrived."

"I won't have anyone disrespecting you, especially not him."

"He called me beautiful. That is all he did."

"You don't understand. Whenever my father talks to a woman, there's always something sexual going on. That's the way he is. I watched him for years growing up. Even with his girlfriend Barbara, he was always trying to do whatever he could to get her into the bedroom. I think that's why she left him after my younger brother and sister were born. She realized he never loved her or even respected her. He treated her almost as bad as he treated those street women he used to bring home."

Fatima looked at him. "He brought women home when his girlfriend was here?"

"A couple times when she was out, but mostly after she left him."

"I don't think he meant anything like that by calling me beautiful. Why don't you give him a chance. Maybe he's changed."

"He hasn't changed. He hasn't had a steady woman in over twenty years. Why do you think that is? You see he looks good for his age. He's a womanizer."

"Shhhh," Fatima whispered as Hank came back outside with a huge bowl of collard greens and a pan of cornbread. He placed them on the table and then went back into the house, coming back in seconds with a large pitcher of lemonade.

"Y'all ready to eat?"

Hank placed the steak plates on the table. They each added vegetables and cornbread and poured lemonade. Hank took a forkful of greens and brought the food toward his mouth.

"Wait a second, Dad. We bless our food before we eat."

Hank looked at his son with a surprised expression and slowly put the fork down on his plate. "I'm sorry. I stopped prayin' over my food years ago, after your mother died. Go ahead, son."

"In the name of God, bless this food we are about to receive. Amin."

"Amen," Hank whispered as he picked his fork back up.

Fatima gazed at her father-in-law for a moment. "Hank, why did you stop praying?"

He gave his son a quick glance before answering. "I only did it for my wife. She was from a family of religious folk. She used to tell me they prayed at every meal when she was growin' up. She believed in Jesus and bein' saved and all that, but she said she hardly ever went to church after she left home. She didn't go to church at all after we was married, but she always wanted me to say a prayer when we ate. Understand, I never was a church-goin' man, but I loved my wife, so I did what she wanted."

Rafiq remembered a conversation he and Hank had years ago. "You told me my grandmother was a staunch Baptist. She raised you, and I know she took you to church. Why didn't Jesus ever take with you?"

"I never understood what it was all about. Lots of folks gettin' excited and sayin' 'Praise the Lord' all the time. Seemed to me they were just lettin' off steam. It never moved me like them. The preacher used to ask if anyone was ready to be saved, and it seemed to me he put pressure on folks to come forward. I don't know. I wish I could believe, but I don't. I just live day to day and do the best I can."

Rafiq suddenly felt a twinge of remorse. He remembered how Barbara had taken him to church regularly before she left Hank. He understood how his father felt, because he couldn't "catch the spirit" either. He looked up at his father. "You remember when I was about ten, Barbara used to take me to church?"

Hank looked up with embarrassment. "Yeah, I think I remember she took you a few times to that Baptist church she was a memba' of up in North Oakland. She told me all you did was sit there and be quiet. Wouldn't even sing the tunes." Hank chuckled, remembering he was the same way whenever he went to church.

"Yeah, that's right. I just sat there and watched Barbara. She almost couldn't control her body sometimes when she was singin' and shoutin'. I also remember she used to read her Bible all the time. At church and at home." Rafiq smiled at his wife. "Next to you baby, Barbara is the nicest person I've ever met."

Fatima gazed affectionately at her husband. "A person like Barbara—she sounds like a wonderful example of godliness. It seems you were destined to not be Christian," she said to Rafiq.

"She was wonderful. I guess I see how many of our people gravitate toward that kind of spirit. I remember the first time she took me there. The first thing I noticed were stained-glass windows. I looked up at the altar at Jesus. He was white. That sealed it for me right away. Nobody resembling Barbara or even me. Didn't feel right, so I—"

"Hey, Rafiq!" a voice called from the other side of the fence. They all turned. A dark, handsome man about Rafiq's age dressed in a multicolored shirt and a Kangol hat tilted to the left side of his head smiled broadly. "Bruh, I haven't seen you since you went Muslim. I see you still have that ol' raggedy Honda, though. You oughta break down and get you a fly ride like my 300, man."

The man looked over at Hank. "How you doin', Mr. Roberson? Hey, I'm sorry for interrupting your thing, but I was drivin' by and saw your son's car and got excited."

"Who the hell are you, and how you know my name?" Hank asked.

"Jimmy Taylor. I know your son from school and from when I used to work downtown at the county buildin'. I live a few blocks over on Nine-ty-Ninth. Me and Rafiq came by here long time ago to visit, but you wasn't home. He told me he grew up here, so every now and then I drive by, and today I got lucky."

Hank looked at Jimmy and wondered what kind of trouble he might bring. He decided to invite him in anyway. "You hungry?"

"Yes sir, yes sir," Jimmy replied.

"Come on in, then."

As he was walking around to the gate, Rafiq looked at his wife and whispered, "I've been trying to stay away from this guy ever since he stopped working downtown."

Jimmy walked over to the table and seated himself in the last remaining patio chair. "How you doin', man?" he almost hollered at Rafiq. "Last time I saw you was the day I got fired. Remember that? Man, that shit…" He looked at Fatima and then at Hank. "That wasn't right what went down that day."

"You want some greens and cornbread with yo' steak?" Hank asked gruffly.

"It don't matter. Whatever you want to put on a plate, I'll be happy with it."

He turned back to Rafiq. "They had just fired Jackson a coupla' weeks before me, and he was workin' down there for fifteen years. Never missed a day. Was always on time. Never talked back to the boss. In fact, he never talked at all. How you gonna ax a solid cat like that?"

Rafiq stared at Jimmy. "I thought you were going to talk about yourself. You worked with Jack in janitorial. You know why you got fired?"

"I got fired because somebody said they smelled alcohol on my breath after I came back from lunch. The boss called me into his office and axed me if I had been drinkin'. I told him the truth: no. I never drink at daytime unless it's a day off. Dude didn't even check my breath or anything, and you know I chew mint gum all the time. That can make your breath smell like alcohol sometime. Somebody else might have been drinkin', and the person who said it was me might have smelled it on somebody who look like me."

Hank interrupted. "What's your name again?"

"Jimmy."

"Listen, Jimmy. If you wanna stay and finish your food, you best tone down. You been gettin' louder and louder ever since you sat down in that chair."

"I'm sorry, sir. I get excited real easy, and sometime I don't know how loud I can get. But it ain't right, sir. They got a few white boys in janitorial be comin' in late, bein' lazy, not doin' they job, but they never think about lettin' them go."

Rafiq shook his head at Jimmy. "Listen, man. I believe what you're saying, but you got a felony on your record that goes back before that job."

Hank rose from his chair and went into the house.

Rafiq continued. "The Alameda County Parolee Job Placement Program got you that job. They did their part. You know you're even more of target for abuse by the man if you've got a record. How long did you work there? Six months? Management probably didn't want you there in the first place, so they took advantage of that."

"Yeah, I get it, man, but it still ain't right. Um tryin' to do right out here, makin' an honest livin', and that still ain't good enough. I got another job about a year ago at Parker's store up on Fifty-Fifth, but that's only part time. I can't even rent my own place for that chump change. I'm livin' with my sista', and that ain't hardly no fun."

Another car sped by, and a brief booming bass dissipated down the street.

Jimmy continued. "Rafiq, um off parole. Only been on probation for the last four years. I don't want to mess that up, but I sure am thinkin' about slingin' again." Suddenly he realized Fatima had been sitting in silence. He looked at Rafiq. "How come you didn't introduce me to this lady you here with? That's about some rude shit, Rafiq."

"This is my wife, Fatima, and I would appreciate it if you stopped the profanity around her. She doesn't deserve to be exposed to that kind of talk."

"I apologize," Jimmy said, smiling at her. "I'm from the street. That's just who I am." He continued to look at her.

"It's OK. I am from Nigeria and my parents sheltered me, but it is not the first time I have heard the word 'shit.'"

Rafiq's mouth gaped in surprise. He had never heard his wife utter a curse word. The sound was so utterly out of character, he struggled to fight back a laugh.

Jimmy rose from his chair. "I got to bounce. S'pose to be meetin' up with a partna' of mine. Thanks for the steak, sir," he said, looking at Hank. Jimmy went into his pants pocket and pulled out a small sheet of paper. He asked Rafiq for the pen protruding from the outline in his shirt pocket. He wrote down his telephone number and handed the paper and pen to Rafiq. "I know you got a different life now, bruh, and I respect that. But if you ever want to hook up or need me to help you with something, I'll be there."

Rafiq nodded as Jimmy turned and walked out the gate.

"That boy ain't nothin' but trouble," Hank mumbled to no one in particular.

Rafiq gestured with his head toward his wife that it was time to leave. Fatima did not respond.

Rafiq looked at Hank. "We've got to be going. I've got Arabic class at the mosque, and Fati—"

His wife interrupted. "I wasn't planning on studying tonight. I thought we were going to spend the evening here."

Rafiq gave her a stern look. "Baby, I told you Wednesday I have Arabic class at five every second and fourth Saturday of the month."

She did not reply. She looked at her father-in-law. "It has been a pleasure meeting you, but please, may I use your bathroom before we leave?"

"Do you want me to say no?" Hank smiled. "Go through the kitchen and turn left. It's the last door on the right down the hallway."

She rose and entered the house through the sliding patio door. Hank and Rafiq were silent during her brief absence.

When his wife returned, Rafiq rose before she could sit again. "Ready?"

Fatima looked at her husband with a sad expression.

Neither spoke as they walked toward the gate.

"It's good to see you, son, after all this time. Let's get together again soon and talk some more."

Fatima said goodbye. Rafiq looked back and nodded at his father as he closed the gate.

3

BARBARA JAMISON SAT in the store break room looking at the large digital clock glaring back at her. Her almond-shaped hazel eyes and light-brown braids contrasted against her dark-chocolate complexion. It was ten minutes before clock out. She hardly noticed. Thoughts of her late father repeatedly molesting her were never far from consciousness. She had been eight when he started. His assaults mercifully ended with a massive heart attack when she was twelve. She could still smell the whiskey he had panted into her nostrils as he took his last gasp and rolled off her onto his side. Her mother knew about his misdeeds but was too meek to confront him. She vowed to never be that weak. She had never disclosed that part of her past to anyone. Hank had never shown any pedophilic tendencies toward their children. If he had, Barbara knew she'd be in prison.

She snapped back to reality when someone activated the store paging system. The clock read 5:07. Her fifty-two-year-old arthritic knee cracked as she quickly stood and headed toward the time clock.

It was a hot Friday afternoon, especially for a late-autumn day in the East Bay. Barbara hurried toward her compact car. The excitement of driving a new car hadn't worn off even though two months had passed.

She had made arrangements with her boss last Monday to leave work early. Nikira was coming through. They hadn't seen each other for several weeks. Barbara was proud of her daughter. She had a decent job. She had never been married and had no kids. At thirty-two, she had time. Barbara was looking forward to an evening of shopping and dining with her. Barbara thought fleetingly about her only natural son. Both her children, Nikira and Denard, came from her relationship with Hank. Denard Roberson was languishing in San Quentin serving the fifth year of a life sentence. She remembered his preteen days when he was a sweet, thoughtful child—until he got older and the streets claimed him.

She entered the on-ramp to 880, with the freeway traffic immediately coming to a standstill. Barbara dialed her phone.

"Hello?"

"Niki, I'm just now leaving Hayward. It'll be at least a half hour before I can get home."

"That's OK. I'm just leaving Berkeley, so I'll probably get there a little before you."

"OK baby. Looking forward to seeing you."

She glanced at her watch: five fifteen. She turned on the radio and heard that a big rig had overturned just south of Broadway. Exiting the freeway at A Street, she drove the main thoroughfares through Hayward, San Leandro, and East Oakland until finally reaching her Lake Merritt apartment building forty minutes later. She entered the down-sloping entry into the underground garage and swiped her key over the electric eye. The gate slowly began to open.

"Momma," she heard coming from behind her. She turned her head and saw Nikira approaching the car.

Nikira Roberson had her mother's eyes and her creamy chocolate complexion. Her permed black hair and full figure contrasted sharply with Barbara's braids and angular form.

"How long you been waiting?" Barbara asked.

"Only about ten minutes. I thought you might get caught up in it. Should have told you to take 580 instead."

"That's OK. You know your mommy is patient."

They hugged for a long time.

"Hop in, Niki. We'll enter the apartment through the garage."

Barbara had to use her gate key again, as the lengthy greeting with her daughter had allowed the gate to close. She pulled into her designated parking spot, and they exited the car.

"What kind of car is that?" Nikira asked, pointing to a large, old foreign vehicle parked on the other side.

"Oh you talkin' about that beat-up thing there? That's Kenny Johnson's old Citroen. Kenny lives in the apartment at the end of my floor, right next to mine. I've only seen him drive it once, and the thing was sputterin' somethin' terrible. I was amazed it even got up the slope of the driveway."

They both laughed as they exited through the rear garage door and ascended up to the first-floor landing. Kenny came out of his apartment just as they opened the back door to the first floor.

Kenny was tall and overweight, and he always seemed to have a cigarette dangling from his thumb and index finger. "Hey, Barbara. Who's this? Oh, this must be your daughter you've been tellin' me about," he said as he looked the full-figured, shapely younger woman over.

"I was just headed out to the store to get some fresh vegetables. Going to fry some catfish when I get back. By the way, my name is Kenny. I was waiting for your mother to introduce us, but I know she doesn't like me much because of the noise I make in my apartment. I like to have friends over and throw down on weekends."

"Hi. I'm Nikira."

"A beautiful name befittin' a beautiful woman. Hey, why don't the two of you come over to my place. I'll be back from the store in twenty minutes, and I'd love to cook dinner for you both."

Kenny took his eyes off Nikira and turned back toward Barbara.

"No thanks, Kenny. We have other plans."

"Well, OK. But I hope to see you again soon…Nakari, is it?"

"No, it's Nikira." She gave him a long, warm smile.

"Oh, yeah. You would think a man wouldn't forget a name like that so quick, but it's a different kind of name. If Nancy was your name, I woulda remembered. But your name is ten times prettier than that. I hope you won't hold that against me."

Nikira said nothing, and she and her mother walked to the apartment next door. Barbara's place was small but immaculately decorated. A thin multicolored drape served as the partition into her doorless walk-in closet. Ornate planters flanked the entry into the kitchen. Nikira sat on the light-brown leather love seat next to her mother's small mahogany stereo console. Barbara sat down in her favorite rosewood chair. She had the kind of serious expression she typically carried just before counseling one of her children.

Nikira noticed. "Oh oh, Momma. What is it?"

"I'd advise you not to have contact with Kenny. He's thirty-eight years old and works security down at the Coliseum. The manager says he's been here for ten years and doesn't always pay his rent on time. You saw that cigarette in his hand. I have yet to see him when he wasn't smoking. Probably going get cancer at some point."

"Momma, you know I'm not looking for a man. I enjoy teaching and have a lot of friends I go out with. Besides, Howard killed my appetite for any sexual relationship."

"You talkin' about that almost-white man from Frisco who doesn't have a clue who he is? I never understood why you got involved with him in the first place. He acted strange to me from the get-go, like he was on drugs. Had that glazed-eyed look about him. Like the time you invited me to join you and him for dinner. He looked absent almost the whole time. Just a dead man look. What did you see in him anyway?"

"He has the type of allergies that make his eyes water. He was very sweet and kind to me. He had a good job working computer programming. Plus, he knew how to bring me to orgasm. I have slept with four men in my life, and he was the only one who took his time and knew what he was doing."

Barbara frowned at her daughter. "I have never met a man who was so confused. Talkin' about he's biracial. Man's got lips so big that if you stuck one of them with a pin, he would probably bleed to death."

Nikira chuckled. "Momma, you know you ain't right."

Barbara stayed dead serious. "He definitely has nappy hair, even though it's kind of blond. Ain't nothin' white about that head of hair."

"He suffers from what many light-skinned black people suffer from. He feels like he's caught between two worlds."

"Two worlds? Nikira, you know that just about every person in this country who has any visible black ancestry has suffered some form of direct racism. If you don't know you're black before that happens, you should know it after, regardless of how white lookin' you think you are."

"Yeah, I know you're right, but that man was good to me. I was just shocked when I found out he liked men too."

"Girl, you'll be lucky if you don't have AIDS. You know San Francisco has a reputation for homo- and bisexuals making up a big percentage of people living there. Did you just choose to ignore that man's homosexual side because he was making you happy?"

"No. I quit him as soon as I found out. We had gone to a Halloween party. We were having a good time until I realized I hadn't seen him for a while. So I walked into the kitchen, and he was kissin' this man dressed up as a cowboy. I screamed and just ran out the apartment and took a cab back home. He called a few times after that, but I never answered."

"You know what you need to do right away? Go get a total STD screen done. They do that confidentially at the free clinic across the lake."

They both sat on the plush sofa in the apartment and were silent for a time.

Barbara looked over at her daughter. "You don't like women, do you?"

Nikira looked at her with shock. "What?"

Barbara smiled. "Let's get out of here and go get something to eat. Where would you like to go? My treat."

"I don't care, Momma. Just pick a place."

4

BARBARA DROVE THE car up the on-ramp and out of the garage. She decided to take the downtown route to Jack London Square in order to avoid another freeway gridlock scenario. Dusk had settled over Lake Merritt as they drove up Grand toward downtown. The purplish reflective hue off the water gave it a pristine look compared to the brownish-green color typically seen during daylight. They headed up toward Broadway. A crowd had already gathered outside the Paramount Theatre as they passed.

The O'Jays, the Whispers, and the Four Tops were the headliners.

"Sad that all the great soul groups I grew up listening to are going by the wayside. The sixties and seventies had the best soul music ever made. I saw the Temptations and the Four Tops years ago at the Oakland Auditorium when they were in their heyday. They brought the house down."

"Oakland Auditorium? I never heard of that."

"They call it the Kaiser Center now, baby."

"Oh. I didn't know that. Did you forget that you and Daddy used to play all that soul stuff before we moved out? I know the music because y'all used to play it all the time. Especially Daddy."

Barbara didn't answer. She didn't want to think about Hank just then.

They continued up Broadway, crossing under the 880 and entering Jack London. A twenty-four-hour diner appeared on the right, and Barbara pulled into the parking lot. They exited the car. As she was locking the door, a ragged man ran toward her from the nearby sidewalk, struck her across her shoulder with a large, blunt object. He snatched her purse, and ran down the side street. Both women yelled for help, with Barbara's voice in obvious pain.

Two young men exited a car parked on the street and began to sprint after the attacker. Barbara slumped to the pavement holding her shoulder and moaning.

Nikira screamed, "Don't move, Momma. I'm going to give you something and get you to the hospital."

"My shoulder feels like it's broken. "

Nikira frantically dug in her purse and pulled out a prescription vial. "I forgot I have these Tylenol 3s in my purse. They've got codeine in them."

"Is the car locked?"

Nikira checked and saw the driver's door was still ajar. "It's open."

Some diner patrons had seen the commotion and gathered around the two women. A light-skinned man approached them and spoke with an accent. "I have pills for your pain. Do you know Norco?"

"No. But if it's strong, I'll take it."

The man ran to his car and returned with a vial of unmarked medication.

"Is that the medicine?" Nikira looked at him suspiciously. "There's no label on the bottle. My momma ain't taking that."

At that the man said nothing, backed away from the scene, and walked back toward his car.

"Baby, pop the trunk and get that water bottle out so I can take those Tylenols."

After giving her mother the medicine, Nikira helped her off the ground and around toward the passenger side of the car. At that moment, the two men who had chased the attacker returned with her purse.

While they were handing her purse back to her, the smaller one spoke to them. "We beat the shit out that dude once we caught him. Glad OPD wasn't around."

Barbara smiled at the two young men. "Thank you both for helping me. I've got to go to the ER for this pain, but I already feel better because you got me my life back. No telling what he might have done. I'd love it if you'd let me give you both something."

The larger of the two spoke. "Lady, we 'preciate you offering us something, but we don't need any. We ain't no angels out here, but we make a good living. Truth be told, all of it ain't...well, most of it ain't legal, but we just ain't gonna let nothing like what just happened to you go."

"Thank you again so much."

They women watched as the two men made their way back to their car and drove off. Nikira started the engine and headed toward East Oakland.

5

THE TRIP TO Highland Hospital seemed to take forever. Good thing it was just off the 580. The Tylenol/codeine had little effect on Barbara's pain. They finally pulled into the parking lot not far from the ER entrance. A row of ambulances were parked in designated spots. A good sign. Maybe it was too early for any wound trauma victims. She might have a chance to be seen right away. It was a good place to come for trauma, especially if you had marginal insurance coverage. Barbara walked toward the emergency room entry with her daughter nearby. She felt relieved when she saw most of the ER chairs were empty. They continued to ER admissions.

"I need your health insurance card and ID," the clerk said.

"I need some stronger pain medication right away. Feels like my arm is broken," Barbara pleaded.

"We'll take care of that soon as you complete these forms."

They walked over to the first row of chairs. The left-handed Barbara couldn't write, partly because of the pain and partly because it was her writing arm that had received the trauma. Nikira did the writing, and Barbara managed an uncharacteristic scribbled signature.

Fifteen minutes passed before they were called to a waiting room. A nurse entered within a few minutes and briefly examined the badly bruised shoulder. "What is your pain level on a scale of one through ten?"

"It's a nine right now," Barbara replied as she flinched.

"Have you taken any medication?"

She turned to Nikira. "I forgot what you gave me, baby."

Nikira looked at the nurse. "Two Tylenol 3s."

"How long ago?"

"About forty-five minutes," Nikira said.

"We'll have to wait another three hours before we can give you anything else. In the meantime, I'll run and get an ice pack. The doctor should be in soon."

With that the nurse turned and left the cubicle, returning five minutes later with the ice pack, which she handed to Nikira. The nurse turned and left the room without another word.

"Why didn't she put this thing on you herself?" Nikira frowned as she stood up to apply the ice pack. "I guess that nurse would rather have me hurt you."

"Baby, put the thing on my shoulder. It can't hurt me any more than I already am."

Nikira gently lowered the bag to her mother's shoulder.

"Oh, shit. Take it off."

"I'm sorry, Momma. You told me to do it."

"I didn't know it was gonna be that heavy. Felt like somebody dropped a vase on my arm."

She looked at her daughter and kind of chuckled under her breath. "I'm gonna lay down on this bed to take off the weight." Barbara slowly stood from the chair and sat on the edge of the ER bed.

Nikira assisted her with her upper body as she lay down on her back. "Whew. OK. Put the bag on top of my shoulder."

Nikira did as before. After adjusting the position of the bag, Barbara seemed comfortable.

"How's that, Momma?"

"Better. Feels like it's starting to get numb already."

Moments later the ER doctor entered the room, a black woman under five feet tall with a scowl on her face. "I'm Dr. Davis," she said in a soft voice belying her rough expression. "What is your name?"

"Barbara Jamison."

"I understand you were struck earlier tonight in the left shoulder with a blunt object you cannot identify. Is that correct?"

"Yes."

"Does the ice seem to be helping your pain at all?"

"Yes, it's beginning to feel better."

"Good. The next step is to get x-rays to see if you have a fracture. I'll have an attendant bring a wheelchair to take you to X-ray. After, I'll come back and discuss the results with you. OK?" The doctor managed a weak smile.

"OK. Can my daughter come with me?"

"She may, but she'll have to stay in the waiting area until you've had your x-rays." Dr. Davis turned and left the cubicle.

Minutes later, an Arab-looking man without a name tag came into the room with a wheelchair. Barbara turned her head away after noticing deep red scars on the left side of his face. "Are you Mrs. Jamison?"

"Yes," she replied, with her head still turned away from his voice.

"I'm here to take you down for your x-rays."

The man locked the wheelchair and stepped toward her. "Let me help."

"No, no. That's OK. My daughter can help me get up."

Nikira stood and gently assisted her mother to standing.

"Hold on a second, baby. I'm dizzy. Let me just stand here while you hold on."

After a few seconds, she said, "OK, I'm fine now."

Barbara turned and walked the short distance to the wheelchair, still with her eyes positioned away from the scar-faced man. They wheeled a long distance down the hallway leading out of the ER treatment area before making two turns down shorter hallways. They stopped in front of a double door with a neon sign overhead: Radiology.

He turned toward Nikira. "You'll have to wait here, ma'am. Only patients are allowed inside the x-ray area. You can sit over there until she comes back out."

The man motioned to chairs that were positioned against a blank wall several feet away. Nikira walked over and sat. She turned and watched the double doors close behind her mother and the large man. She examined the surrounding area. On the wall to the right of x-ray, there were two long, vertical black marks six to eight feet above the floor. She looked at them for an extended time, trying to figure out how such distinctive marks could have happened that far off the ground. Her thoughts were broken as the large man came back out of x-ray with the wheelchair. He stood by the doors with a bored expression.

"You don't have to wait. I can take my mother back."

"No. I have to do it. Besides, how do I know you won't get lost?"

"I know the way. You go back down that hallway, make a right, make another right, and go straight down a long hallway."

The man looked at her for several moments as if battling back and forth in his brain. "OK," he said, wheeling the chair over to Nikira. "There you go."

He locked the chair and left without another word. Several minutes later a pale, underage-looking woman exited from X-ray. She gazed around with a puzzled expression before finally training her eyes on Nikira and the empty wheelchair next to her. She walked over.

"What happened to the man who came down here with the patient?" She was clearly angry, her face turning from white to bright pink.

"He left and went that way," Nikira said, turning her head to the right.

"He knows better than to leave like that."

"It's OK. I can take my mother back. I told him I knew the directions. He seemed satisfied with that and left."

"That's not the point. It's against regulations for anyone but hospital staff to transport patients. Ahmad knows that."

Nikira noticed the x-ray tech's Highland name tag: Anna Vonovich, Radiology.

"Anna? Really, there's no problem with me taking my mother back. I know the way, and nothing will happen."

"You don't understand," the still-pink-faced tech repeated. "The hospital has liability if anything should happen to one of our patients. If the wheelchair were to turn over and she got hurt, the hospital could be sued for thousands of dollars. I'll have to take her back." With that, Anna angrily unlocked the chair and wheeled it back through the double doors into X-ray.

Minutes later, the doors reopened with Barbara seated in the wheelchair and a smile on her face. She kept the smile all the way back to her ER cubicle. Anna locked the chair. Barbara stood easily, as though she had renewed energy. Anna turned without a word and wheeled out of the room. Nikira noticed her still-smiling mother had a fresh ice pack on her shoulder, compliments of X-ray.

"Momma, what happened in there? I see the new ice pack. Your pain must be a lot better."

"Yeah, baby. That Anna was really nice when I first went in there. She gave me this fresh ice pack I never even asked for. Then she was real gentle with me getting on and off that hard table. Funny thing was, I was still thinkin' about that scary-looking man the whole time I was in there. I never looked at him after I first saw him down in my room. Then, when she was the one who came back in with the chair, I figured the man had left. She sure changed after she went out to get him, though. Got real short with me to get off the table and into the chair. Her face had changed too. Did you notice she had turned all pink? Plus, her lower lip was puckered out. Funny. She had turned mad, but I turned happy knowin' I wouldn't have to see that ugly man's face again."

"Momma, you know that ain't right. That man probably couldn't help what happened to his face. Maybe he was trying to save somebody and got cut up. That's what it looks like. Like somebody gashed his face with a knife. I don't understand how you can be so nice to me and other people but so mean sometimes."

"I can't help it, baby. You know your Uncle Willie. I love him too, but I can't stand to look at him either, with his bug-eyed self. I just can't stand some things that other people seem to be able to ignore. Scarred faces, big wide ears, and a whole lot of other things. Some of them have nothing to do with faces. I can't stand a lot of stuff, like textured ceilings, rocky hills—stuff like that. Your grandma Bessie and grandpa Rupert told me they went across the bridge to Frisco one time when I was two. They said I started screaming and crying. Didn't stop till they were on the other side. They told me they thought it was the overhead lights that set me off, and you know what? Those lights still bother me today. Not that bad, but I still try to avoid lookin' at 'em.

Dr. Davis reappeared. "Your x-rays didn't show any fracture. You're very lucky. You just have a very badly contused deltoid. I'm going to give you an exercise sheet, and you should continue icing it several times a day. I can prescribe a narcotic short term for pain. Norco is highly addictive. I'll give you a thirty-day supply. What kind of work do you do?"

"I do inventory and stock the shelves at a department store."

"You won't be stocking shelves for at least another two to four weeks. I'll sign a light-duty work form. I want to see you back in my office in two weeks. Pick up your prescription and light-duty form at the desk on the way out. Here's my card. Any questions?"

"No. Thank you, Doctor."

Dr. Davis turned and left the room.

"Momma? You OK to walk to the front desk?"

"Uh huh. Those Tylenols have worn off, though. You got any more?"

'I don't know if enough time has gone by for you to take more." Nikira looked at her phone. "Twelve twenty-seven a.m."

"I think it's safe. It's been at least three to four hours."

They walked out of the cubicle and picked up the items at the front desk before walking the short distance to the car. Fifteen minutes later they pulled up in front of Barbara's apartment building.

"You gonna be OK, Momma?"

"I'll be all right, baby. Don't think I'll get much sleep tonight, but I'm sure it'll get better. I'll take my medication at about nine tomorrow morning and make myself an ice bag. Good night, Niki. Love you."

"Love you too. Oh. Are you still going to the women's discussion group tomorrow night?"

"You think I would miss that? They could have broken both my arms, and I would still go."

Nikira laughed as Barbara turned and walked into the apartment building. She watched until her mother safely entered her apartment. Then she drove off.

6

RAFIQ AMIN DROVE back to his office at the downtown Oakland County Building. He went a bit out of his way to pass what was formerly the old Swan's department store building on the corner of Eighth and Washington. He felt mixed emotions whenever he passed Swan's. It saddened him whenever he thought about how much downtown had changed. His mood improved when he remembered Barbara taking him to Swan's for his school clothes and for groceries. She would talk to people in the store and strangers on the outside. "Times sure are different," he thought.

He recalled the parolee he had had coffee with last week. A three-strike drug offender who had recently served twenty years of a twenty-to-life sentence.

Ruben Scott was fifty years old, estranged from his family, and struggling to find steady work. He had been trained to make and assemble furniture at San Quentin. He even earned money doing that while on the inside. He had long stopped using cocaine. He smoked weed on the inside, but he stopped that too, knowing it could've squashed his chances for an early parole. Now he sometimes wished he was back in. He had gotten a job at a thrift store in Berkeley. The store insisted he work as a volunteer and stay clean for six weeks. After, he could be hired and make a regular wage. Ruben still had about $200 left of his parole money. He made it a point to avoid West Oakland. Some of the streets—and Ruben remembered them—were drug corners. As a condition of his parole, he couldn't go back there. Most the time he felt lonely, tired, and discouraged. But somehow he had managed to not violate the terms of his parole.

He had to find a way to at least talk to his two estranged daughters. He knew he had grandchildren. He just didn't know their names or where they were. They were all born when he was on the inside. He wrote his daughters, but his letters were never answered. His brother had written him from San Diego but had stopped four years ago after remarrying. Ruben sometimes teared up, knowing how much of a hill he had to ascend to get his life back. The kind of life where he meant something to somebody. He had found only one friend since his parole, a Muslim named Rafiq Amin. Their meeting was a chance encounter. Both were in Berkeley at a music store. Rafiq accidentally stepped back into Ruben as they were both examining CDs.

"Excuse me, brother," Rafiq said.

Ruben turned around and stared for a moment. "No sweat, man."

They both turned back and continued their perusal on opposite racks. Rafiq finished his rack, turned, and walked over a few feet from Ruben. Ruben stopped his search and looked at Rafiq suspiciously. After a few moments, Ruben turned back to the CD column he was on.

Rafiq looked over as Ruben picked up a CD and began to check it out. "I see you like jazz," he said to Ruben.

Ruben looked back over and paused. "Yeah, man. My father used to play piano at some of the clubs around the Bay. You into the music?"

"Most definitely. My father didn't like jazz much. Preferred blues and soul. I picked up the music from a musician friend of mine. You play piano?"

"Not a lick, but I did start diggin' the music early on. Never wanted to learn to play, though. Whenever I had control of the stereo or radio, it was always jazz. My mother liked R&B, so that's what the house music was. Pops couldn't play jazz around moms. She was home a lot more than him and just basically took control of the stereo."

Rafiq laughed but stopped abruptly when he noticed the still-serious look on Ruben's face. Rafiq turned and extended his hand. "Rafiq."

Ruben looked at the extended hand and obliged a restrained, brief handshake. "Ruben."

"So, Ruben. I'm into jazz piano."

Ruben looked back over at his new acquaintance.

Rafiq continued. "I've got a lot of CDs by pianists that I've accumulated over the years."

"Hmm. OK."

"Lots of them, including a few bad white cats. I never listened to white jazz pianists until just recently. Give those cats a solid drummer and bassist, and they can swing."

Ruben stared at him for a good while. "You think white cats can play anywhere near as good as the top brothers?"

Rafiq hesitated before responding. "Yes. Just depends on the rhythm section. You give a white dude a couple of solid brothers on bass and drums, and they can swing at a level that's the same as the top brothers on piano."

"I've heard a buncha white cats play, and I don't agree. Matta a fact, I can tell if a dude's a brother or not just by listenin'. Doesn't matter who the bass player or drummer is. Brothers have that soul thing that's hard to touch. I can hear it even if I don't know the name of the dude playin' the tune. There's only one cat I've heard where I thought he was a brother and found out later he was white."

"Who's that?"

"Victor Feldman on piano when he played with the Cannonball Adder-ley Quintet. That cat has as much soul as any piano player I've ever heard. Plays with feelin'. Big fat chords like Red Garland, but faster."

Rafiq wrote Feldman's name down as Ruben continued.

"When I found out that he was white, I damn near fell out on the floor." Ruben smiled at Rafiq for the first time.

"Brother. You drink coffee?" Rafiq asked.

"Hell yeah," Ruben responded loudly.

"Why don't we go across the street and continue the conversation over some java," Rafiq said.

"I'm up."

They jaywalked across Telegraph toward the coffee shop. It had been overcast and cold for several days. Rain threatened as the outdoor ceiling began to darken further. Just as they reached the entry, the skies opened up.

"Timed that one just right."

"Yeah. I hate the rain," Ruben muttered under his breath. "And I don't care if they say it's good for the drought and all that shit. I do a lot of work outside, and all rain ever done is help me not get paid."

"You work construction or something?"

"Man, I do any kind of work they pay me for. Construction, landscapin', haulin'. Shit. Right now I got an indoor job, but I don't start gettin' paid until I show them what I can do."

Rafiq paid for the coffees, and they made their way to a corner table. Rafiq began to sit in the chair facing the street window.

"Wait a minute, man. What you say your name was?"

"Rafiq."

"Look here, Rafiq. I don't mean to start no shit, but I always sit facing the window wherever I am."

Rafiq looked at his new acquaintance and took the wall chair, which had a peripheral outside view. They sat in silence for a few minutes, with Ruben looking nervously outside and around the room.

Rafiq abruptly broke the silence. "You say you're working but not get-ting paid. I never heard of anything like that that wasn't part of a parole or probation program."

Ruben suddenly jerked his hand across the table, nearly toppling his coffee cup. The scowl returned to his face. "Yeah, man, I been in the joint. More than once. Ain't you ever met anybody that's been inside before?"

Rafiq hesitated before answering. "Of course. My half broth…my broth-er's been in Quentin for seven years."

Ruben's angered expression began to soften. "Quentin's where I spent twenty years altogether. I probably know your brother. What's his name?"

"Denard."

"Denard what?"

"Roberson."

Ruben tapped his fingers on the table and thought. "Nope. Never heard of him. That's crazy. I know most of the brothers that come in and out of there. At least the mainline ones. If they there long enough, I meet 'um out in the yard sooner or later." His eyes and mouth opened wide simultane-ously. "Your brother must be in a lockdown cell. That's it, ain't it?"

Rafiq nodded and slowly spoke. "To answer your question further, it's not just my brother's situation. I'm a probation officer for Oakland."

Ruben abruptly stood up. "I'll be back." He turned and rudely walked past several tables of bewildered-looking customers and approached the counter. "Where's your bathroom?"

The tall Asian barista replied, "To the right and at the end of the hallway. You'll need this key."

He snatched the key off the counter and moved down the hallway. Fif-teen minutes passed before he reappeared. He slowly walked back and sat. He looked intently at Rafiq. "You sure you not tailin' me? You probably knew who I was the whole time you was bein' friendly in the CD store, right?"

"Man, that's nonsense. You aren't one of the parolees on my list, and even if you were, what harm do you think I would do to you? If you're complying with your parole, you've got nothing to fear from me or anyone like me."

Ruben slowly looked down at his coffee cup. "Man, it's a struggle out here. I don't know how long my money's gonna hold out. I feel like now I got a chance to find out where my kids at, but don't know where to start. I ain't taken a toke for almost two years, and sometimes I feel like I can't hold out. Somehow I get the strength from somewhere to keep from doin' it because I know that as much as I want to go back to the pen sometimes…if I ever go back, I feel like I'm gonna die in there, and I'll never have a chance to find my daughters."

Rafiq was silent as he watched Ruben's eyes redden and glisten. "Nothing wrong with expressing what matters to you, brother," he offered. "I'm happy I met you. A lot of the brothers I know—some are my assignments and some aren't—express similar concerns. We have a support and discussion group at the mosque. It's for adults only. Ex-cons, Christians, Muslims, atheists, fathers, mothers, brothers, sisters, wives, angry girlfriends…"

Ruben looked up and laughed.

"All are invited to intend."

"I don't know. I don't like talking much, and 'specially not around people I don't know."

"The only way to get to know people is to be around them," Rafiq said. "Come and just sit if you want to. There are a few people who attend who only do that. We encourage but don't insist on participation."

Ruben looked at him but had no reply.

"Let me give you my phone number and the address of the mosque."

Rafiq pulled out one of his city probationer business cards, wrote the information down, and handed it to Ruben. Ruben gazed at the card before putting it in his front jacket pocket.

"I hope you'll show. It can help you feel less alone."

Rafiq rose out of his chair, went around the table, and shook Ruben's hand. Ruben's grip was stronger than the first time. Rafiq walked out the door and down Telegraph toward his car, leaving Ruben sitting over his almost-empty coffee cup thinking about this Muslim he had just met. He had met some Muslims at Quentin. He thought they were too high-minded and serious. This was the first one he had met outside. He began to trust him a little.

7

ALMOST TWO WEEKS had passed since Rafiq encountered the stranger at the CD store. He had known right away Ruben was likely on parole. He had dealt with enough parolees to recognize common traits: the tattered clothes and purposeful aloofness. Expressions of fear, anger, or suspicion whenever eye contact was made. The mosque meetings allowed for a freer flow of communication. Rafiq could speak and listen at a venue where the participants were confident he would not share sensitive information. Conversely, tension was always present whenever he met with a parolee in an official capacity. In fact, many of his parolees resented being monitored, and that resentment came through clearly in their facial expressions if not their voices. But the mosque meetings were different. Attendees came of their own will, with the main conditions being their verbal consent to be searched at the door and the willingness to remove their shoes. Security was composed of a few dedicated Muslim men who intervened only if discussions turned heated, threatening physical violence. This was a rare occurrence. The four men were large, muscular, and expressionless. They wore the required mosque security garb of black suit and tie and were positioned several feet away on each wall, within earshot but unobtrusive.

They did not speak casually to the participants. Nor were they spoken to. A mutually silent understanding. Whenever trouble did occur, security acted by immediately removing the offenders from the premises. Those removed had to write a statement of appeal and talk to Rafiq. If approved, they were allowed to rejoin the group.

Meetings were scheduled every second and fourth Thursday of the month at 2:00 p.m. It was 1:47 when Rafiq pulled up. He made his way to the main entry. Sister Amina was standing on the left side of the double doors, with two of the security men standing on the right. This was traditional Nation of Islam (NOI) protocol for searches back in the less trusting days before Orthodox Islam began to gain traction in African American communities. Sister Amina had just finished searching one of the female participants.

"*As Salaamu Alaikum*, Brother Rafiq."

"*Wa Alaikum As Salaam*, Sister Amina. Is your husband coming today?"

"No, he's busy completing his doctorate at Cal State. You'll only be seeing him at Juma for a few weeks."

"The future Dr. Yusef Rashid. Has he decided what the next step is?"

"He's got an offer to teach as an associate professor at Cal State Dominguez Hills."

"That's down near LA, isn't it?"

"Yes, Brother."

"That's wonderful. Got to get inside."

Rafiq entered the large linoleum entry room. This was the site of instruction in Quranic Arabic. Folding chairs faced a chalkboard, which bordered the entry into the mosque proper. Entrants were required to remove their shoes at this point, prior to stepping onto the larger, carpeted prayer area. Rafiq removed his shoes, placing them in the cubicle to the right. He walked toward the center of the carpeted area. Five participants were already seated on the bright-red carpet facing one another. Four of the six people were returnees. A Chinese man named Eugene Jew, who owned a few corner stores in East Oakland, had a perpetual scowl on his face. His conversational style was animated, often devolving into a combination of Chinese and English when he became angry or excited. Forty-two years old, he had inherited his late father's stores and had been working them since finishing high school.

To Mr. Jew's right sat Ricky Green, an ordained Baptist minister who led a small church a few blocks away. Reverend Green had a cherubic, engaging smile that never seemed to waver regardless of the seriousness of the conversation. He looked much younger than his fifty-four years suggested. He had a full head of hair, no facial hair, and bright teeth that contrasted against his dark complexion. To Mr. Green's right sat Cora Johnson, an attractive, middle-aged, medium-complexioned woman. She was the one whom Sister Amina had searched at the door. Unbeknownst to Rafiq, Cora was also a member of Reverend Green's church. She had entered minutes after Reverend Green. Hamid Shahid was a Lebanese immigrant. Fluent in both English and Arabic, he was the third returnee of the present group. Rafiq knew from prior meetings that Mr. Shahid had more of an interest in black culture than anything connected to religion. He had lost his wife a year earlier, and even though he gave only subtle clues, Rafiq suspected he had come to the meetings, in part, to look for a new mate.

Rafiq introduced himself to the two new participants. David, a twenty-something black man, wore hip-hop type attire: earrings, baseball cap on backward, white T-shirt two sizes too large, and several tattoos. His friend, Shameka, a light-skinned woman with reddish-colored hair mixed in with her natural dark brown, nose ring, large earrings, and bright-purple lipstick, sat close to him. Both looked friendly and confident as they chatted with each other openly, clearly indicating they weren't concerned about others listening in. Over the ensuing fifteen minutes, six other participants entered the mosque, all African American, including a Muslim couple. The remaining four were East Oakland residents, including one city council-man, Nate Harrison.

Rafiq called the meeting to order. "Those of you who are returnees know the rules. This is a house of God. We do encourage you to not use profan-ity, understanding the discussions sometimes become heated. We want to conduct this meeting and all meetings here with respect for God and one another. Our security"—Rafiq pointed out each the four men positioned around the mosque—"will act decisively to remove anyone who is overtly disrespectful. Any and all topics are open for discussion, but we always have a starter topic written on the board."

He pointed toward the front of the mosque, at a large portable chalk-board that read, "Ways to improve our community through improved col-lective character."

"Can everyone read and understand tonight's beginning topic?"

Some participants nodded. Most had no response.

Reverend Green started the conversation. "My name is Ricky, and I'm a pastor at All Baptist church near here. The key word up there is 'character.' Let's face it. The reason people have poor character is because they don't believe in Jesus."

The young black man, David, groaned and shook his head but said nothing.

Mr. Green looked at him and continued. "If Jesus hadn't done what he did, none of us would be sitting here right now. He sacrificed himself so that mankind could go on. All of us should be grateful for that. That's the key emotion to improve character—gratitude for being alive for what Jesus did for us. Without loving Jesus, you can't really be grateful."

Young David spoke. "Listen, uh…what's your name again?"

"Just call me Ricky," Mr. Green replied with a smile.

"Listen, Ricky. I been lisnen' to that stuff since I was three. Seems like all Jesus ever did was make life worse, 'specially in Oakland. I got two brothers dead. Ain't seen my father since I was five. You trying to tell me Jesus gonna make my life better? I can't get a job just because I'm black, and damn near every time I walk down the street, some white man with a badge be stopping me. Pattin' me down. How Jesus gonna change them racist police and just let me live?"

Hamid Shahid began to speak. "I am not a Christian. I revere but do not worship Jesus. The most important thing is to be grateful. Grateful for as much of your life as you can. If you do not believe in God, be grateful for waking in the morning. Be grateful for your mother who bore you. Be grateful for your next drink of water. Many people in the world do not have water at this moment. You," he continued, looking directly at David, "already have an advantage over them. It is best to believe in God and be grateful for him. But if you cannot do that, find something else to be grateful for."

"Amen" Mr. Green said.

The Muslim man sitting next to his wife spoke. "My name is Rashad." He looked and spoke to David. "Brother, I don't know your situation. I do see anger and negativity coming out of you, though. I used to be like that. Had a sense of hopelessness. Just wanted to strike out at everything, especially the police. I was fortunate enough to find God and be granted peace. Does that mean I think you should become a Muslim or even a Christian? No. Only God can do that. What I am saying is that Hamid has made an important point: If you don't give regular thanks for something or someone in your life, you're likely to have a bad attitude. That anger will continue to eat at you until you are either dead or no one wants to be around you. So my advice is, think of something you can give thanks for, and do it several times a day."

The man's wife said, "My name is Isha. I found God through my husband, but I understand from talking to a lot of people of all faiths that life isn't easy. And if it is, it won't be for long. I know from my own life that the next challenge to overcome is usually just around the corner. But most of the brothers out here haven't discovered their own value yet. They chasin' after the world thinkin' that's the answer to their problems."

"Wait a minute," David said. "You sittin' here lookin' pretty comfortable to me. I saw you and your husband get out of that nice car you was in. You both dressed nice. Bet you have your own house, don't 'cha?"

"We rent a house," said Rashad.

"See? That's what I'm talkin' about. You and your wife come in here talkin' about being grateful and having value for yourself. How in the hell you gonna be grateful when you barely have a regular place to sleep?"

Shameka rubbed on her companion's shoulder to calm him down.

"Damn. It's just hard out here tryin' to get by day to day." David's eyes began to glisten. "I had a good job out in Contra Costa. It was at a shoe store. They wanted me to wear a tie to work every day, and that was OK. I didn't mind. The store manager acted rude to me a lot, but I didn't even mind that. But some of those white people would come through there with they kids and act like they didn't want me to touch they kids' feet. I know I have a lot of tattoos, but that shit wasn't about that."

"David, I'll ask you to not curse again," Rafiq said.

David looked over his shoulder at security and then back at Rafiq before continuing. "I asked to be transferred up to another store, but they didn't have nothin' open, so I just quit."

"Do you regret not keeping that job?" Mr. Green asked.

David paused and looked at Shameka. "Yeah. Sometimes I do, but I couldn't deal wit' it anymore."

There was silence for several moments. Rafiq looked at David. "Have you lived in Oakland most of your life?"

"All of it."

"Was that job your first outside Oakland?"

"Yeah, man. But it ain't about going outside Oakland. It's about bein' around a lot of white people. Sooner or later you gonna be dissed in that situation, and I don't want to be around nothin' like that. Not comin' from them, anyway. I never did anything to deserve bein' treated the way I was treated out there. I been dissed by some white teachers before who didn't like black people but had to be there because they didn't have no choice. They was assigned to an Oakland school. That didn't bother me 'cause they wasn't just dissin' me. I never been the only one like I was out there. Couldn't deal with it."

Rafiq said, "Listen, brother. It's not too late for you to learn how to interface with the outside world. You have to deal with a whole variety of folks in order to function. You darker than I am, so some of them are going to like you even less than they like me."

David shot a half smile at Rafiq.

"How many of us are blessed or talented enough to have jobs or careers where they're dealing primarily with black people their whole lives? Not many. But it has to be about who we are. Who we become. I'm going to say something I've never said before in public. I used to hate my own pale skin. Couldn't stand the white blood running through my veins. Hated my white mother. Hated my father for marrying her. Hated my darker brother and sister, who have a black mother. Race was turning me into an angry schizoid. I found something to believe in that made all that less important. Race no longer consumes me. Is it still important? Yes. Always will be, as long as there are people. The point is, each of us has to determine our own value. If you're letting something or someone outside yourself do that, you've already lost. Brother David, you let those white people assign a value to you because you didn't have value assigned by yourself for yourself. If you did, you would still be working there until that transfer to that other store came through."

David's eyes turned softer and clear. He was thinking about what Rafiq had said.

Rafiq looked around the group and noticed everyone looking at him, as if expecting him to continue. He smiled briefly. "Life is challenging, especially for black people in this country. We have all been assigned an institutionalized value that's below the majority. Many of us, maybe even most of us, buy into that assigned value, which prevents us from fulfilling our potential. Potential as what? As human beings."

He looked directly at Reverend Green and continued. "I found a faith that puts me outside—no, that isn't right. It neutralizes the self-hatred and replaces it with an informed awareness of my value."

Reverend Green spoke. "You believe in God, but what you are lacking is the love that only Jesus can give you. You have to accept that he saved all of us from sure death. I can tell you that when you do that sincerely, you're consumed by his love like…well, like you're in a cocoon. You have the awareness that there is a place better than this earth, and Jesus guarantees you are going to that place at the end of this life's trials. That is the most precious gift a human being can have—the knowledge that God loves you so much, he is offering you paradise. All you have to do is accept him as your savior, and that promise will be granted."

Cora Johnson nodded approvingly throughout Mr. Green's commentary and uttered "Yes Lord" and "Praise Jesus" throughout.

Rashad spoke. "I was raised a Baptist but left the church for a lot of reasons. The main one was not being able to accept Jesus as being God in the flesh. Seems to me you might as well accept Santa Claus or the Easter Bunny as the truth. Too much of a stretch for me. I needed my faith to be more reality based, so I turned to Islam. Look around here in this mosque. You don't see any human images in here, because it's not allowed. The church I was raised in had stained-glass windows with angels, and they all were Caucasian. This was a black church I'm talkin' about. Does that sound like an expression of God to you?" Rashad looked at Mr. Green, then Cora.

"I mean I was eight years old and could see there was something wrong with that. The preacher drove a Cadillac. Don't you think a religious leader should have a humbler car? I've studied the life of Jesus and know comfort and style weren't his priorities. Shouldn't the preacher reflect the values of Jesus? So these are just a couple of hypocritical things I became aware of. I got tired of going and told my mother I was done. I began to study Islam and found it to be more compatible with reality. Something I could grow into and believe in."

Reverend Green was shaking his head while Rashad was speaking. "You don't understand the beauty of God's grace through the life of his Son Jesus Christ. All that stuff you saw in that church doesn't matter. This life is just a trial of belief. It's an illusion. You look at all the mess happenin' around you and in the world. It's all going to come to an end. The only thing that's going to matter is the condition of your soul when we all get taken. You Muslims and Buddhists"—he glanced at Mr. Jew—"have it all wrong. You're focusing on the wrong thing. Until you have accepted Jesus, you have no hope of heaven. That's the Word of God."

Isha said, "Does that sound like God to you? You think the creator of the world would have a condition that narrow for the hereafter? This is why so many of our people have left the church. It may be rooted in miracles, but it lacks rationality. You think that because of scripture, you have a lock on heaven that excludes people of all other faiths? You believe that God is going to extend that privilege to one religion? No. Doesn't jibe with the nature of God, who is merciful, forgiving, and inclusive. Your religion puts too much stake in heaven and not enough of how to live on earth. You accept Jesus, and you think 'I'm in.' Do you know how dangerous that is? It's like the hard blue-collar worker who suddenly inherits enough cash to set him up for the rest of his life. What does he do? He stops working hard. Sleeps late. Gets fat. Buys unnecessary things that actually take him further from God. Why? He figures he really doesn't have to work hard anymore in this life."

Mr. Jew finally spoke. "You are right. My brother won the lottery ten year ago. He stop working at our store. He get fat and die from heart attack last year. Leave his wife and child with no father. They have money but no father. He not like that before he get all that money."

"That's the point. The tendency is to relax too much if you think you have it made," Rashad said. "That's one issue with Christianity. At least it is in the black community. Go to one of our churches and look at our people. Too many of them are overweight compared to white churches. Of course, our people struggle with our self-image and most other aspects of living more than white folks. So when our people get saved, some of them just throw their hands in the air and say, 'Oh well. I can't get any further in this life, so I might as well lay back and wait for heaven.' That's sounds like an oversimplification, but it's definitely a tendency. It's an all-too-common consequence of getting 'saved.' Subliminal, but real."

"In our church, we have nutritional and exercise classes all the time," Reverend Green said.

"Is it working?" Isha asked.

Mr. Green was silent for a moment. "I can't say that it is. I think too many of our old habits get in the way. After service or Bible study, people go out to eat, and I don't think they pay much attention to what or how much. But we will continue to emphasize what we're teaching."

Everyone turned quiet.

David broke the silence. "Look. All this talk about Jesus and eatin' too much ain't got nothin' to do with me. Do I look like I eat too much? I barely get enough to keep the little weight I have on. That's not what I think about. I think about how am I gonna walk down the street without a police stoppin' and searchin' me? Last week, I took a bus downtown to look for a job. Got off the bus, and soon as I went two blocks, I got stopped. Um just trying to go look for a job, and one of them motherf…one of them stopped me for no reason other than I'm black. Let's talk about what can stop that."

"You can change what you wear," Councilman Harrison said. "You've got your cap on backward, that big untucked T-shirt, earrings, and I saw your shoes before you took them off. Bright-red high tops? Young brother, you are like a big neon sign that says, 'Stop me; I'm a criminal.' You can't get a job dressed like that. Even black-owned businesses won't hire—"

"Wait a minute, man. I didn't dress like this that day. Had on a blue dress shirt and left my hat at home. Even put on some dress slacks and wore my black tennis shoes."

David's companion laughed at his comment.

"What chu laughing at, B?" he said, staring at her menacingly.

She looked away and barely whispered, "I only laughed because it seems crazy to go for a job in tennis shoes when the rest of your clothes are more formal."

"That don't have nothin' to do with the police stopping me, Shameka. I ain't on parole or probation. They ain't doing it for no other reason than to keep me down and because they can. Happens whether I'm lookin' hip-hop or not."

Ricky looked at David as he spoke. "Listen. I grew up in West Oakland on Seventh, just a block off Adeline. It was tough, and I was angry like you. Used to wear my chains, hats, and bright bell-bottoms. Got stopped a few times in my car and on the street. Mother sent me to the Hall three times for fighting. I'll never forget she told me I looked the way the devil must look. Said my face was twisted, and it scared her. Spent a year in the penitentiary for selling drugs. In jail I met a preacher who used to come every Sunday. Name was William Scott. He asked me if I wanted to change my life. I began to study the Bible in his classes, and the anger just began to drop off me. I changed. Stopped wearing all that hip stuff I was wearing. Started talking to people more—white people too. Took the furniture assembly skills they taught me and opened up my own business. You have to want to change, because anger is the emotion of death. If you don't find how to get rid of it, or at least contain it, you either gonna be dead or end up spending your life in prison, which is the same thing."

"You tryin' to get me to change the way I look?" David said. "You said yourself that you used to wear chains, and I bet whatever hat you wore was tilted to the side. The stuff I wear, the music I listen to, just reflect what's happenin' in Oakland. Most of Oakland, anyway. Life is hard out here, and hip-hop dress reflects that. I'm not changin' that for nobody. Even if I wanted to change it, brothers out here would know I wasn't down. One of them would just fire a cap in me, and it would be over. So I survive because of the way I dress. It tells other dudes I'm not a sellout. Brothers who dress like you…you say your name is Richard?" He was looking directly at Ricky.

"Ricky," Mr. Green said.

"Brothers get shot sooner or later if they start lookin' like you look… if they was hip-hop before that. You have to leave the hood if you gonna change like that."

"So why don't you?" Isha asked.

David stared in disbelief at Isha. "Where I'm gonna go? Don't have a job. No money. I sleep at my auntie's house, but she gettin' tired of me. She go to church and 'spect me to go wit her. I go only 'cause she say if I don't she gon' kick me out the house. I put on them same clothes I wear to look for jobs, but that ain't really me. I hate it. All them people shoutin' in there. Most of 'um fat and smilin' all the time. They talk to me all nice, but I think that's only 'cause they want me to be like them, all Jesused up and sh…stuff. Always puttin' pressure on people to come up to the front of the church and get saved. I know some of them people that go up there don't really believe. They just go up there to get the pressure off. That ain't God. That's politickin'."

The councilman, Nate Harrison, half smiled at David. "I understand how you feel, young brother. I was raised a Catholic, if you can believe that. Went to Catholic schools and graduated. Formal religion never took with me. I was a good student, so I got a scholarship to go there. You could say that politics became my religion. That and the need to try to make East Oakland a better community to live in."

"You can forget about that," David said. "How you gonna make it better when there ain't no jobs here?"

"I agree. There aren't a lot of jobs in private industry, and honestly, we haven't been able to do much to change that. We do have some high-tech companies that offer training for promising black students, but not nearly enough of them for the need. A lot of the problem here is a poorly funded public education system. We have statistics that show over the last several years, many of the people who have left Oakland did so because of poorly performing schools, especially high schools. Would you say you got a good education at your high school?"

"Man, listen. Wasn't nothin' wrong with my high school other than the dudes I hung with. All us knew we wasn't ever gon' get out of Oakland. Not one of us even knew they daddy. But if you asking me if the teachers was tryin' to teach, hell yeah. Every year some of us went on to college. Most of them girls. I was never very good in school, so by the seventh grade, I pretty much gave up. When I was little, my momma would come home from work and be so tired, most the time she just fall sleep on the couch. She would wake up later and try to read me a story. I couldn't pay attention for long. She got mad, but I couldn't help it. Just didn't like it. I wanted to play with my toys or do somethin' with my hands. I always been good fixin' and buildin' things. But book learnin'?"

"Do you have a high school diploma?" Nate asked.

"Yeah."

"You should think about joining the military."

"What?"

"The army and navy have programs that can train young men such as yourself in mechanics."

"You mean a car mechanic? I already know how to work on some cars."

"Well. I was referring to an aircraft mechanic. You sound like you already have some mechanical ability. The military could train you and pay for your training."

"But they might not take me 'cause of my tattoos. Besides, I know a brother who signed up with the army. They told him he would get the kinna training you talkin' 'bout, but he never did. He got sent to 'Ghanistan twice, and the second time he came back home, his head was all fu…messed up. I would go over to his house, and he be just sittin' front of the TV. Barely look up when I talk. His girl say he never leave the house, and he downin' forties like they was water. Man, I ain't gonna let that happen to me."

"You have to make sure you get a contract that guarantees you will be trained at some point during your enlistment."

"Whoa. Hold it right there, Mr. Harrison," Rafiq said. "I've worked with parolees for a few years now. Some of them served in the Middle East. I've seen copies of the contracts they signed, some of which stipulated they would receive various types of vocational training paid for by the army. One of them received Jeep mechanics training during his third tour to Iraq. When he tried to get a job after, no one would hire him. Not even at a Jeep auto dealership or private repair shop. The other five or six parolees with contracts never received any of the training promised. This tells me the contracts aren't worth the paper they're printed on. The one vet was fortunate he got any training at all. The army conveniently either ignored or canceled the other contracts, probably for reasons of 'combat necessity.' That is, having more guns in more hands for longer periods. There are no guarantees. Not in the army, at least."

Mr. Green continued. "What you say might be true, but at least he'd be gettin' paid. Look around the streets outside here. You go six blocks, and you'll see five or more young black men like him on the street. You think their chances are better out there or in the army? I know a coupla boys who joined, and they came back upstanding men. One of them became a deacon in my church. Name is Randy. He's a manager at a grocery store. I met him years ago at a church picnic, and he looked just like David here. A little younger. About sixteen. I encouraged him to come with his mother to church, but he never did until eight years later. He had grown into a man. Still had tattoos but looked clean, sharp. Came to church with a suit and dress shoes, and he was friendly. Could barely get him to talk eight years earlier."

"Sounds to me like he just got lucky," David said.

"That wasn't luck. That was the blessing and grace of the Lord. He told me he met a soldier. The man led prayer for his platoon and had Bible study. Randy told me he was scared the whole time he was over in Iraq. Even after he accepted Jesus right there on the battlefield, he was still scared. He said if he made it home alive, he would change his life, and he did. Went and got his AA. Got hired not too long after that."

"You tryin' to say that Jesus saved him from gettin' offed over there?"

"No, I'm not saying that, because I don't know. I do know that I hadn't seen him for eight years, and when I saw him again, I didn't recognize him right away. The anger he had as a teenager was gone. I didn't know who he was because his face had changed so much. The Randy I had known was gone. There was peace on his face. A look of quiet confidence, and it's still there today."

"Yeah, well, maybe he changed because he was happy he made it home."

"He changed because he found Jesus even before he came home. He became a grateful human being. Just like we were talking about before: when gratitude replaces anger, what you come out with is a changed human being."

David looked at Ricky for a long time.

Rafiq adjourned the meeting. "Very stimulating discussion. Our time has run out for today. We'll be back in two weeks at the same time. Spread the word."

With that the participants rose and walked over to the entry room to put their shoes back on.

8

BARBARA WOKE IN her apartment for the third time in six hours. She looked over at the bedside clock: 9:18 a.m. She knew Nikira would be picking her up later tonight. The discussion group started at 7:00. She groaned as she rolled out of bed and walked to the bathroom. Opening the medicine cabinet, she removed the bottle and took her medication before returning to bed.

"Forget that ice bag. Don't feel like messin' with that right now anyway," she whispered. Within minutes, her shoulder pain had eased, and she fell back to sleep. At 11:43 her cell rang. She slowly sat up. "Hello."

The exuberant voice of Stella Young answered back. "Barbara! How you doin', girl? Nikira called me a little while ago and told me what happened last night. No need for you to try to make the discussion group. You just need to rest and get better."

Barbara groaned again, but more from sluggishness than pain. "Hi, Stella. How are you?"

"If I was any better, I'd be suspicious. Charles and I had our five-year anniversary yesterday, and we couldn't be happier. Barbara, I don't want you coming tonight. You must be in pretty bad pain. You taking any pain medicine?"

"Oh, yes. Got some strong stuff from the doctor. Really cuts into the pain a lot. I can take one every six hours, so I'll be OK to make it tonight."

"OK. You know I love to have you in the discussion with your crazy sense of humor. I'll let you go and get some more rest. If you change your mind, I understand."

She eased back into bed while trying to avoid taking any pressure on her left arm. She had just begun to drift off when she heard a loud knock on the door. Lifting her head, she glanced toward the door and then immediately placed her head back down on the pillow. Several seconds passed. The knock came again, but louder this time.

"Who is it?"

"It's Kenny from next door."

"I don't feel very good right now. You having some kind of problem?"

"Yeah. I locked myself outta my apartment. The manager ain't here to let me in, so I thought you wouldn't mind if I waited with you. But if you feelin' under the weather, I understand. I'll just walk down the hill to the lake and hang out there till he gets back. Hope you feel better. Bye."

Barbara did not answer.

"What next?" she thought as she eased out of bed, took a few steps over to the dresser, reached behind it, and unplugged the phone. Back in bed, sleep returned minutes later.

She awoke at 2:25 p.m. Her shoulder was throbbing. She struggled to sit up, draping her arm across her body in a sling-like position. Dizziness returned. She sat for several seconds before noticing rain pelting against her bedroom window. The dizziness gradually subsided. She stood, supporting herself on the nightstand. Only five hours had passed since her last pain dose.

"Supposed to wait another hour," she muttered. "Don't think I can take the pain for that long."

She slowly ambled toward the bathroom and took another dose, went back, and plugged the phone in. Nikira had left a message: "Momma, I won't be able to take you tonight. My friend called and said she's moving to Atlanta next week. They're having a farewell party for her tonight up in Richmond. She wasn't supposed to leave until next month but said the house she's gonna rent came vacant, and she'll get about three weeks of free rent. Call me."

"How am I supposed to get to the meeting? Can't drive with one arm, and my head swimmin'." She dialed her daughter.

"Hello. Momma? You get my message."

"Yes, baby. This must be a special friend for you to not pick me up. Who is she?"

"You remember Danielle. She used to come over to the apartment a lot."

Barbara paused for long time. "Whose apartment?"

"Yours. Danielle was my classmate at Tech. Remember?"

"You mean the one with the braids hanging down over her eyes? I never liked that, but I liked her. What happened to her? She stopped coming by after a while."

"She got a scholarship to UC San Diego. Then she came back and moved to San Jose to go to graduate school. She's a computer systems analyst for a Silicon Valley company. She comes to Oakland on the weekends to visit, and we get together sometimes. Now she's got a similar opportunity in the ATL."

"Well, I understand, baby. Maybe Stella won't mind picking me up, or I might be able to drive. It's only about five minutes away."

"Don't you even think about driving. I know how much you love those get-togethers, but you can go next month. You'll feel better by then anyway."

"I know you right, baby. I won't drive."

"OK, good. Love you."

"Love you too, Niki."

Barbara sat in the chair near her window. The rain was coming in torrents. Three hours later she began to get dressed. Her blue velvet sweat suit would do nicely for the casual affair. She slipped on the pants. Her full front-button blouse presented no difficulty. "Hmm," she whispered as she lifted her sweat jacket off the bed. "Forgot this only has a couple buttons at the top. Not even going to try to put it on."

She hung it up in the closet and replaced it with her navy raincoat. She called for a taxi. It was 5:45.

"Be there in twenty to thirty minutes, ma'am," the cab dispatcher proclaimed.

"That'll get me there in plenty time," she thought confidently. No cab came. It was 6:35. She redialed. The same dispatcher answered.

"You said the taxi would be here by six fifteen at the latest," she said angrily.

"Hold on a moment, ma'am. Let me dial the driver."

She held on another five minutes. The man came back on the line. "I'm sorry, ma'am. That driver had a mechanical problem with his cab. They're supposed to call us whenever something like this happens, but he was trying to fix it himself. I sincerely apologize. We'll have another cab there inside of ten min—"

"Oh no you won't. How do I know the next driver won't have another 'mechanical problem'?"

As she disconnected, she whispered, "Calm down Barbara; calm down."

She retrieved her purse off the nightstand and walked swiftly toward the door.

"Ooh, almost forgot."

She went to the medicine cabinet for her prescription bottle. She walked down the back staircase to the garage and entered her car, surprised at how good she felt. Only a little pain, and if she needed to, she could take another in a few hours. As she drove up the ramp, she suddenly became dizzy. The garage gate was lifting. Her vision blurred, it looked to her that a second gate was following the first. As the first gate completed its task, the second one disappeared. She did not move the car forward. She blinked and moved her head side to side as the dizziness gradually began to subside. Feeling normal again, she moved the car forward and out into the rain. The ten-minute drive to the meeting was uneventful. She stayed in the right lane the entire time, just in case. Nothing happened. She parked just down the street from Stella's apartment.

"Barbara?" a surprised Stella said as she answered her doorbell. "What in the world? I didn't expect you. Where's Nikira?" Stella reached out for a hug.

"No. No hugs for a while." Barbara extended her right arm to inhibit Stella's forward motion.

"Sorry. Forgot about your arm. I'm just so happy you're here. Let me guess. You took a taxi."

Barbara smiled one of her wry half smiles with a glint in her eye.

Stella shook her head. She recognized the expression—Barbara's usual look after one of her jokes.

"Nikira's not here, is she? I bet you drove yourself. Whatever. Come on. Let's get started."

Stella led her from the entry into the living room. Four women were sitting around the room. Two were on the expensive leather couch. The other two sat in chairs opposite the couch. They all greeted her as she moved toward a vacant chair. Stella was the last to sit, in her usual chair. The most comfortable. It also provided the best vantage point to see the other women.

"OK. Here we all are again. At the end of our last meeting, we were discussing men, as usual. Romella, you were concerned that your boyfriend doesn't treat your kids the same as his own."

Romella Thompson was the youngest of the group. She had two boys in their early teens, both in middle school. Romella always dressed elegantly, even with casual attire. She wore a blue-green jean outfit with matching blouse and shoes.

"As I said last time, my boyfriend, Anthony, and I have been going together for three years. He has a daughter and son about my kids' ages. We've gone on outings several times. He talks to his kids a lot more than mine. I make an effort to not be partial toward my kids when we're together, and I expect the same thing from him. We've discussed this several times, and he says he'll do better, but nothing has changed. I'm thinking about breaking it off because my kids already feel like he doesn't really like them. It's hard because he's wonderful toward me, but that's not good enough."

"Have you told him that you can't accept that?" Stella asked.

"Yes. I've told him."

"You need to tell him point-blank that if he can't treat your kids equally, it's over," Stella said. "That ought to light a fire under his butt."

The women laughed. All except Barbara. She waited for the laughter to subside. "I had a boyfriend about twenty years ago. You met him, Stella. He had a daughter about Nikira's age, and every time we got together, he almost ignored my kids. I gave him two chances to start doin' right, and when he wouldn't, I sent him walkin'. You got to let these men know right off the top that if they want you, they have to take the whole package."

Romella continued. "He keeps telling me he only gets his kids every other weekend, so he feels rushed to catch up with them. I love this man, but I'm not going to take…"

The tears began to flow down her cheeks. She sobbed. "I really don't know what I'm going to do."

Stella rose from her chair and knelt beside Romella. Barbara's phone rang. She looked at the screen.

"Excuse me," she whispered as she quickly stepped to the back of the room.

"Momma?" Barbara heard the grief behind Nikira's troubled voice.

"What's the matter, baby?"

Nikira answered, but her mother couldn't make out any content as the crying became more profuse.

"Baby, just calm down and talk to me."

A long pause followed.

"Nikira? You still there?"

"Daddy called me just now. He said the prison called him earlier today. Denard got into some kinda fight. Daddy said he's hurt real bad, Momma. They had to send him out to the hospital. They told him he's in a coma and might not live."

Barbara fought back the tears. "Oh God," she whispered into the phone. "Where are you?"

"I'm still up at the party in Richmond."

"You think you can drive over to my place?"

Nikira was still sobbing but not as profusely now. "I'll be OK. I'll head out in a few minutes."

"OK, baby. Just go slow. I'll tell the group I have an emergency, but I'll see you when you get there. Be safe."

"Bye, Momma. Love you."

"I love you too, baby."

Barbara slowly returned to the group. Romella had recovered, for the most part. Pronounced mascara tracks were showing on her cheeks.

Stella was the first to notice Barbara's pained expression. "You look like you just saw a ghost. What happened?"

Barbara's voiced cracked. "I have a family emergency to take care of. I have to go right now."

Stella came over and lightly embraced her. The other women followed. "I'll call you later," Stella said.

"No, don't. I'll call you as soon as I know more."

With that, she quickly exited the apartment and drove home.

9

TWENTY MINUTES AFTER Barbara arrived at her Lake Merritt
apartment, the doorbell rang. She looked out her door down the long hallway. Nikira was standing at the front entry. Barbara buzzed her in. Nikira
ran down the hallway into her mother's arms. They both cried, embracing
for several moments before going inside.

"You want something to drink, baby?"

"You have some ginger ale or 7Up? I feel sick to my stomach."

"I've got some Sprite." Barbara returned with the soda and a glass.
Nikira's hands shook as Barbara gave her the drink.

"Did your daddy give you any other details about Denard?"

Nikira took a sip before answering. "He only told me the name of the
hospital they took him to." She reached in her purse and pulled out a small,
torn piece of paper. "Marin County Hospital." She handed the paper to her
mother.

Barbara dialed the number.

"Marin County," said the operator.

"Yes. My son was admitted to your hospital earlier today. I understand
he is in a coma, and I would like to speak to his doctor."

"What is his name?"

"Denard Roberson."

"Hold, please." Several minutes passed before the operator returned. "Ma'am? Our doctors are currently unavailable, but I can connect you with his nurse."

"OK. Wait. Wait, please. Can you tell me which room he's in?"

"Ma'am, we can't do that. Your son is an inmate. We are required by the California Department of Corrections to keep that information confidential. I'll connect you with his nurse."

The phone rang several times before being answered. "Nurse Fitzpatrick. May I help you?"

"Yes. I understand you are my son's nurse."

"What's your son's name?"

"Denard Roberson."

"I'll need your name, relationship to the patient, and phone number."

Barbara supplied the required information. There was a pause for several seconds.

"Yes. What would like to know?"

"I was told he's in a coma. That true?"

"Yes. I'm afraid it is. He's breathing on a respirator and receiving tubal nutrition and hydration. His face is swollen, and he has lacerations in the head and neck area."

"I want to come visit him tomorrow with my daughter. Can you tell me what the procedure is for that?"

"Visiting hours are twelve to six p.m. You will need to check in at the front desk downstairs. Security there will conduct a search before you are allowed to enter his room."

"Thank you. What's the address?"

Barbara jotted it down on the piece of paper Nikira had given her.

They left the next morning for Marin County, taking the Richmond Bridge. After exiting, they passed San Quentin on the left and proceeded straight to the hospital. They were early by almost an hour. A blonde woman at the information desk did not look up at them as they approached. "May I help you?"

"Yes," Barbara replied. "We're here to see Denard Roberson."

"One moment." She scanned a sheet of paper which was out of view. There was a long hesitation before she abruptly rose from her chair and exited through a nearby door without saying a word. Mother and daughter looked at each other with a kind of implicit understanding.

The receptionist returned five minutes later.

Barbara spoke. "You know, that was very rude of you to just get up and leave without saying anything. Do you treat all visitors like that?"

The woman glanced up briefly, not replying. She ran her index finger along the sheet of paper. "I need to see identification from both of you."

The women retrieved their driver's licenses, handing them to the clerk. She studied the licenses for what seemed to be an unnecessarily lengthy period before handing them back. She wrote the women's names on separate ID cards before placing them on the counter.

"Pin these on to your blouses or coats. You must have them visible at all times. You'll have to wait here until noon before you will be allowed entry into the main corridor," the woman flatly said while turning her head in the direction of a door where a female security guard stood.

"Britney will conduct a search prior to your entry. You will be allowed a maximum of two hours for your visit. During that time you will be under surveillance by cameras and a correctional officer. You may not touch the patient or approach the bed without permission of the officer who is on duty in the hospital room. The information I have just told you is in writing along with other hospital visiting regulations. Read it over and sign the bottom. If you have any questions, I will answer them if I can."

The woman placed the form on the desk while continuing to avoid eye contact.

Barbara's anger finally boiled over. "Listen here, whatever your name is. You have no right to treat visitors with the kind of disrespect you've shown us, and don't think I don't know why. I don't give a damn if you're having a bad day or whatever your excuse might be. What's your name?"

The clerk was looking directly at Barbara and replied impassively, "Joan Davidson."

"Why is it you don't have a name tag, Joan Danielson?"

"Davidson," she replied under her breath.

"I want you to show me some ID so I know you are who you say."

The woman opened a drawer, pulled out a name tag, and handed it to Barbara. "Joan Davidson" was etched in red.

"Joan Davidson, you'll be hearing about this. Maybe before the end of the day."

Joan rose out of her chair and disappeared through the same door. Barbara and Nikira sat and waited. Joan did not return. A man in a suit and tie replaced her at the desk. Promptly at noon, the man called their names. They approached the front desk.

"I'm am so sorry for Joan's behavior. She's just cranky in the morning sometimes, and she was called in today at the last minute. Sunday is normally her day off."

"That's no excuse," Nikira said. "She barely even looked up from the counter at us, then just left without saying anything. You can't treat people like that."

"I agree, and I know what you're thinking. Joan is not racist or biased about inmates or their families. She spent two years in Africa working with the Peace Corps. She is a staunch Democrat who voted for Obama both terms. I talked with her just now, and she feels very badly about her behavior. She also told me she's grumpy because…well…because it's her time of the month. She would like to apologize to both of you."

"Who are you?" Barbara said.

"James Bennett, the assistant human resources director."

"Human resources?" Nikira asked. "Why would you be here on a Sunday?"

"I had to catch up on some work."

The two women glanced at each other but did not speak.

"Would you like Joan to apologize, or would you prefer to proceed to your relative's room?"

"We've gone through enough already," Barbara said. "She can apologize later if she wants. She can send it in writing to my address in Oakland. That won't be all, though. I'll be speaking with someone in a position of higher authority than you seem to be. Whether that woman is a racist or not, she needs help, and shouldn't be allowed to front your hospital until she's ready."

Bennett nodded and began walking over to Britney, the ground-floor security guard. The women followed, were searched without incident, and were escorted to the fourth-floor hospital room by Britney. The door to room 4216 was open.

A burly guard stood just outside the doorway. As Barbara and Nikira approached, the guard spoke. "Good afternoon. Do you understand the rules once you enter the room?"

"Yes. We think so. Are we allowed to touch my son?" Tears began to flow down Barbara's cheeks as she laid eyes on her motionless son.

"Of course you can touch him. Just don't remove anything from your person to place on the bed."

With that, the women slowly approached Denard's bedside. His face and neck were half covered with gauze. The respirator mouthpiece protruded from the side of his mouth. His lips and gums were dark blue and swollen. Two teeth were missing from the upper right side. Caked blood showed on his lower lip below the missing teeth. A nurse entered the room. She changed his near-empty IV bag, emptied his urinal bag, and then took his vitals.

"You two must be family," she said. "The doctor says your son is stronger than most and will likely survive. The relief doctor is here now, if you would like to talk to him."

"Yes. Thank you. Will you please tell him we need to talk to him."

"Of course." The nurse smiled pleasantly, touching Barbara on her arm before exiting.

Barbara and Nikira went to opposite sides of the bed, lightly stroking Denard on each arm. Barbara lightly sang "Amazing Grace" over and over until the doctor finally arrived.

"Hello."

He immediately withdrew his micro light and examined both eyes thoroughly. "No response," he whispered. He then turned and faced the women.

"Please tell me everything you can about my son, Doctor."

"Well, obviously he's comatose. That's the bad news. You never know how long that can last or whether he will ever regain consciousness. The good news is his reflexes are still intact, indicating no spinal cord damage. Most of the trauma was inflicted in the head area, so we think no vital organ damage occurred. To this point he has no brain swelling we can detect, but sometimes that takes a few days to develop. He's getting range of motion by nursing three times a day to keep his arms and legs supple. We also routinely turn him to keep bedsores from developing. Other than that, we just have to wait and see. He's a strong man. When you come in, the most important thing to do is talk to him."

"Momma just sang to him," Nikira said, holding back more tears.

"That's just as good. Maybe better." The doctor smiled. "Does he like music?"

The women smiled back in recognition of the doctor's kindness.

"He definitely does. Too Short, Jay-Z, and Drake."

"Who?" the doctor frowned for a moment.

Nikira chuckled. "Rap music. Hip-hop, Doc."

An embarrassed half-grin appeared on his face. "We have rules against music for patients while in a coma. You see, music is only allowed if the patient can operate the controls themselves. Sorry." With that the doctor started toward the door, turning back when he reached it. "Do you have any more questions?"

"No. Thank you, Doctor, for your information and kindness," Barbara said.

The doctor smiled, nodded, and then disappeared down the hallway. The women said nothing for a long time.

"You ready to go, Momma?"

"I guess," Barbara replied as she stood and kissed Denard tenderly on the cheek. Nikira dropped her mother off at her Lake Merritt apartment, then drove home.

10

"MOMMA, DADDY SAID he found out what happened to Denard," Nikira said sadly.

She heard a long pause on the other end of the line. Her mother finally replied, "I don't think I care, baby. Unless it was the guards. But if it was, we wouldn't know about it anyway."

This time it was Nikira who paused. She had tried off and on for years to reunite her mother and father. She saw her brother's hospitalization as a chance. At least for them to talk to each other. Hank Roberson had regularly tried to call Barbara after she left him. His calls were never returned. He had sent Barbara birthday and holiday cards to no avail.

"Daddy's sorry for everything he ever did to you. He says he only wants to apologize to you face-to-face. I don't think he wants to get back with you, but he really regrets the way he used to be."

"Listen, Niki. I love you and it know how much it would mean to you if your daddy and I were to meet. I've told you before, once he broke my trust, he broke it completely. There's really no way you can understand how that feels unless it happens to you. He was the only man I ever gave myself to completely, and he used that."

65

"But he's not the same anymore."

"How do you know?"

"He's never had a steady woman since you left him. I know because I can see the change on his face. He tries to put on a happy front, but that's all it is, Momma. A facade. Rafiq really doesn't want to have anything to do with him. His brother and sisters are dead. I'm the only one in the family who talks to him regularly, and now this thing with Denard. I'm not asking you for him. I'm asking you for me. Just call and talk to him."

Barbara frowned and said nothing.

"Momma?"

"OK, I'll talk to him," Barbara said brusquely. "He still have the same phone number?"

"He's only got a cell phone now. Here's the number."

Barbara jotted it down. "Talk to you later," she said.

"Bye, Momma. Love you."

"And I love you too. That's the only reason I'm doing this."

Barbara dialed Hank's number, which went straight to voice mail. "Hank, this is Barbara. Nikira told me you have some information about Denard. We're going back out to the hospital tomorrow. Should be there around one. Maybe we can sit down and talk. Call me back."

Her phone rang a few seconds after she disconnected. "Hank Roberson" appeared in the window face.

A strange sensation of fear and sadness overtook her. She let it go to voice mail. Hank's voice on the recording sounded much older than she remembered. It was still deep but had kind of a crackling quality. "Thank you for calling, Barbara. I'm so mad I feel like I could hurt that warden real bad. He tryin' to tell me Denard had gotten some drugs from somebody and started actin' crazy. Says he went out for yard time and got beaten up out there by three dudes. That don't sound like my boy, provokin' somebody. I can't get to the hospital until about two. Got to go to the doctor myself and been waitin' a long time to get in there. Hope you still at the hospital by then. Bye."

She thought about Hank and how different he sounded. It had been almost twenty years since they had spoken. Hank was almost eighteen years older than her. She began to suspect that his loose lifestyle was beginning to take its toll. She was surprised to discover she really felt nothing about it. Hank had wronged her. She began to replay the time he had brought one of his holes home late one night. Both of them drunk.

"Why am I replaying that madness in my head?" she thought.

She stopped thinking about Hank, turned on an Anita Baker CD, and then went into the kitchen.

Barbara and Nikira arrived at the hospital around 12:40. The rude woman from their first visit wasn't there. A Latino woman greeted them with friendliness. They completed the sign-in and security requirements without incident before taking the elevator to Denard's floor. The same security guard manned the entry. "How you two holdin' up?"

Nikira said, "We've been better. Just trying to hang on. How's my brother?"

The guard shook his head slowly side to side. "I've been on duty since he's been here. Wish I could tell you he's better, but I haven't seen any change."

"Thank you, Officer," Barbara said.

They looked into the room and saw Denard lying on his side. The respirator caused his chest to gently rise and fall. His face was a blank slate, unchanged from before. At the nurses' station sat two nurses, both doing paperwork. One of them lifted her head. "May I help you?"

"Yes. I'm Denard's sister, and this is my mother. We would like an update on his condition."

The nurse responded with a dour expression. "He's stable. Blood pressure, heart rate both good. Physical Therapy has started trying electrical stimulation on him, but he hasn't responded as of yet."

"Can you tell us anything else?" Barbara asked.

"Well, they did a brain CT earlier today, which showed hydrocephalus."

"What's that?" asked Nikira.

"Swelling of the brain. You should talk to his doctor about that."

"Thank you, Nurse," Barbara said. They turned and walked down the hallway into Denard's room. Barbara stroked his legs and sang gently to him. After a time, they both sat and waited for Hank.

Hank came out the elevator at 2:00 p.m. sharp. Barbara was the first to see him walking down the hallway toward them. She shuddered. He looked good, though, walking straight and purposefully. "He definitely looks better than he sounded," Barbara thought.

Hank slowed down and quietly walked into the room. He smiled at the women, showing pristine, white teeth. His tight black T-shirt read "Don't do nothin' I wouldn't do" and revealed a muscular physique not typical of a seventy-year-old. He hugged Nikira warmly before walking over to the other side of the bed to greet Barbara.

As he came closer, she abruptly turned away. "I think I can do without a hug."

There was a chill in her voice Nikira had been hoping she wouldn't hear.

"OK, then," Hank said, walking back over to the other side of the bed. He looked down at Denard. Hank slowly shook his head. "Damn shame this happened to my boy. Damn shame."

"Nurse said he may have some brain swelling," Nikira said.

"I know. I talked to his doctor yesterday. Say they might have to take the fluid out his head 'cause it could cause perm'nent brain damage. They say you have to give permission, Barbara, since you have medical power ova' it."

She looked over at Hank, "I'll talk to his doctor about it."

Without warning, tears began to stream down her face. Nikira, seeing her mother crying, began to cry as well. She walked over to her mother and hugged her. After a short time, the tears ceased. The three of them sat quietly, listening to the sound of the respirator and the occasional muddled conversation coming from the nurses' station.

Hank broke the silence. "I'm hungry. Think I'll run down to the caf'teria and get me somethin.'"

Nikira and Barbara looked up at Hank and then at each other.

"You go ahead, Daddy."

"Barbara. I would 'preciate it if you came with me, I have somethin' important to tell you."

She looked up with a shocked expression. "Now, what could you possibly have to tell me that Nikira can't hear?"

"Please. I got a good reason. I need for you to talk to me. I'm not lookin' to get back with you in any way. I just need to fo' you to know some important stuff."

She stared at him suspiciously for a moment. "All right. I'll listen for a little while, then I'm coming right back up here."

Nikira watched as her parents walked briskly toward the elevator. As the elevator door shut, she smiled.

The cafeteria was empty except for two nurses drinking coffee. Hank led Barbara to the opposite side of the cafeteria.

"You want me to get you somethin'?"

"No. You go ahead." She pulled out a chair and sat.

Hank returned with a sandwich and a bottle of juice. He sat down opposite Barbara, taking a couple sips. Barbara watched him nervously.

"I know how you feel about me, and I don't blame you at all," Hank said. "I was a stone dog when we were together, and I know I don't deserve forgiveness."

"You brought me down here to tell me that?"

Barbara could see him squirming in his chair, nervously trying to frame what he was going to say next.

"I went to the doctor earlier today."

"I know. You left the message on my phone. Remember?"

Hank nodded.

"Are you sick? You don't look sick. Matter of fact, you look much healthier than I thought you would by how feeble your voice sounded." Barbara surprised herself at the utter lack of feeling she had for Hank.

Hank looked at Barbara and began to laugh. "You probably thought I would walk in here with a cane and all hunched over. I get a ratchety throat sometimes. You know I smoked for years. Gave it up 'bout eight years ago, but still got some issues from it. You ain't even heard one of my coughin' fits yet."

Barbara listened and watched stoically as Hank took a bite of his sandwich. She was becoming increasingly uneasy being alone with her former boyfriend. "What is it you want to tell me? I want to get back upstairs and be with my kids."

"They my kids too, Barbara," Hank blurted out.

"They're a lot more mine than yours," she said calmly. "This is feeling like a waste of time. If you're not going to tell me what you brought me down here for, I'm going back upstairs."

Hank looked across the table. "Doctor says I got cancer of my prostate. Says it's spreading in my blood, and it's pro'bly too late to get rid of it."

Barbara sat a bit closer to the table. She felt something stir in her that surprised her.

Hank continued. "I just want to get things straight. I don't think I want to do any of that radiation or chemical stuff. I heard all your hair falls out, and you get real weak, and most the time, it don't help for long anyway. I don't wanna to go through all that. I came back to Oakland to get closer to my kids. Since seeing the doctor this mornin'—that's mo' important to me than eva'. That's why I don't want Nikira to know. Me and her already have an understanding, and I can feel that she love me. She gonna find out sooner or later, but I don't want her to be hurtin' right now over me. She got enough pain with her brother layin' up there. Not much chance of me closin' the gap with him, and Junior ain't never forgave me for gettin' with his momma. You know he a Muslim now, but I think he still hate himself some 'cause he so light. I want to try to get closer to him if I can.

"In the meantime, I'm gonna get my will done. Got a real good pension. Own the house on Hundred and Fifth. Don't owe nothin' on it. I don't want nothin' from you except maybe to forgive me sometime befo' yo' life end. Um givin' everything to you. You probably won't believe me, but I ain't had a steady woman since you left. Pro'bly lucky for her."

Hank smiled at Barbara. He noticed her eyes had reddened since they had been sitting. "Doctor says I got maybe six months without the treatment. Already told him I don't want it, so that's it. Says he'll give me drugs when the pain get real bad. Told him that's what I want. I ain't afraid to die, but I ain't never been good with bad pain."

Tears flowed down Barbara's face for the second time that afternoon. She got up out of her chair, went around the table, and bent down to give Hank a long hug.

"I forgive you right now," she whispered in his ear.

"When we were together, I prayed everyday your goodness would come out. God doesn't always answer when we want him to, but he does answer." She kissed Hank on his cheek. They got up and walked down the cafeteria hallway to the elevator.

11

RUBEN SCOTT HEARD the tune "Lovely Day" playing on his tiny clock-radio: "…wake up in the morning, love, and the sunlight hurts my eyes."

The volume seemed to get louder as he gradually woke up. He let the tune play for a time and then reached over and turned it off. He looked around his new sleeping quarters. Big water heater in the opposite corner. Boxes piled next to his cot on the right. Clothes hanging on a portable rack just beyond his feet. For a moment, he had forgotten how he got there, in that warm basement. Hell. He didn't even need the blanket Josh Portman had given him.

"This shit here definitely warmer than Quentin," he thought.

He threw the sheet off and sat up.

Ruben had met Josh at a Bible studies meeting in Quentin. Not that he was ever committed to religion at any time in his life. He had gone there because he had been told they served doughnuts and coffee, and he went back a few times for the same reason. During the second session, Josh approached him. Ruben tried in vain to ignore him. No white man was to be trusted. He had never talked to a white person who wasn't in a position to take something from him. At his parole hearings. The guards in his cell-block. And the supervisor at the furniture store, who fired him at the end of his nonpaid six-week probation period for "refusing to talk to other workers about work-related matters."

"Motherfucka," he muttered. "Just 'cause I wasn't skinnin' and grinnin'…did my work as good as any of those other fools there."

Ruben already knew the real reason: "That chump was gonna find a way to not pay me."

He heard footsteps upstairs and looked over at the clock: 6:27 a.m. glared back at him in big, red figures. He heard a knock on the basement door.

"Ruben, you awake?"

"Yeah."

"I'm making some breakfast. It'll be ready in about twenty minutes. Come up when you're ready."

"Aw-ight."

Ruben dressed and then walked over to the toilet in the far corner to his left. He did his business and then washed at the adjoining sink. He thought how lucky he was to have kept Josh's number. Josh had paroled a year before Ruben. He had done some business-related crime that Ruben knew little about. Josh had taken a plea and did two years out of five to ten. He told Ruben to contact him if he ever needed a place to stay.

Ruben finished in the corner and then walked upstairs to the main floor.

Josh was sitting at the breakfast nook window with his back to Ruben. Hearing footsteps, he turned to greet his guest. "Man, you were out of it. You crashed at about seven last night, and it's about seven now. You sleep all that time?"

"Yeah. I guess so."

Ruben looked over the shoulder of the pale, pony-tailed man. Hanging down and partially covering the window was a rendering of Jesus. Josh noticed him staring at the image but said nothing. Ruben had seen plenty of

Jesus artwork before, but none like this one. Curly black hair covered the sides and back of Jesus's head. The nose was curved in a Semitic manner, but the lips were full and medium brown, as was the face. Dark-brown eyes glowed in a slightly exaggerated manner, and the white robe contrasted against the predominate sepia tones.

Finally, Josh spoke as Ruben sat in the chair next to him. "Well, what do you think?"

Ruben hesitated for several seconds as he pondered the image further. "I feel the love, the power coming out from his face. Never saw any Jesus lookin' like that."

"I know from our prison sessions you're not yet a believer, so you probably don't know passages from the Bible. They don't fully describe Jesus, but they give a solid idea how he might have looked. I met a Christian minister from Venezuela who also happens to be an artist. That's his painting," Josh said, gesturing toward the window.

"Well, it's actually a lithograph of a painting. I liked it, so I bought it from him. He told me he tried to paint a historically accurate image of Jesus based on what scripture says. I think it's pretty close."

"Yeah. That was Malcolm X's point when he was in prison. At least that's how he said it in the movie. You know the one with Denzel playin' Malcolm?"

"Yes, I saw the movie. The prison chaplain had a portrait of Jesus as white skinned and blue eyed. Kind of like me."

They both laughed. "Yeah," Ruben said. "A lot like you."

Ruben briefly scanned Josh's blond ponytail, beard, and creamy white complexion before turning back toward the painting.

"How come you didn't have someone bring it to the prison chapel?"

"I had it there for a while, then I had my sister bring it back here on one of her visits."

"What for?"

"A couple of white guys at Quentin complained about it, so the associate warden in charge decided it had to go."

"That's a damn shame. I notice you didn't have any Jesus pictures in there during the times I went. So was this one the only one that was ever in there?"

"No. There was one like me in there when I first came, but I managed to take it down after a Bible session one day. Had one of the prison guards hide it in a storage room. It's probably still there."

"Yeah, but you trying to tell me nobody missed it?"

"Nobody mentioned it except the same two white guys. I told them someone must have taken it. I let several months go by before I replaced it with this one, but like I told you, that didn't last long."

Ruben continued to sit as Josh brought over breakfast. Ruben gazed at the portrait and thought about what Josh had said.

"This dude just might be all right," he thought.

12

HANK WAS OUT in his backyard tending his garden when his cell rang.

"Hello?"

"Dad?"

"Hey, son. How you doin?"

"I'm all right. Nikira called and told me about Denard. Do you have any more information about who did it?"

"I told her to not tell you 'bout that," Hank said angrily. "Told her you got enough goin' on to not be worrying about Denard right now. Um definitely gonna be talkin' to her 'bout that. Damn."

"Calm down, Dad. You're overreacting. Besides, I didn't call you to talk about Denard."

"Oh, shit. She probably told you about what's happening to me too. Girl can't keep her mouth shut for nothin'."

"I'm glad she did tell me. You just going to give up and not get treatment? She told me you don't want radiation or chemo. I can understand that, but there are holistic practitioners who can fight cancer with herbs, meditation, healing imagery. All kinds of stuff."

"That ain't gonna help nothing. The cancer spread. Too late for any kinda hero stuff from anybody. Doctor say it's in my whole pelvis. My lower back. I really don't feel no pain except if I bend over to pick somethin' up. Look here, I've had a good life. Done some stuff I regret, but at least I got some money and this house I can pass on to Barbara. Everything I put her through, she deserve it and more."

There was a long silence as Rafiq's mood began to sadden. "Dad. I'm sorry..."

"Now, don't go there, son. I'm cookin' dinner this Friday night. Gonna fry up some snapper, make some gumbo and cornbread. Come on by about seven with your wife. Barbara already told me she would come. I'm gonna call Nikira and invite her. First thing um gonna do is tell her about her big mouth. By the way, Ricky Green told me he went to yo' meetin' at yo' church. He's comin' by too. I worked with his father, Charles, in construction for years. Ricky used to come along wit' him sometimes when he was little."

"I didn't know you knew Reverend Green."

"Yeah. I ran into him downtown. Hadn't seen him for years. We got to talkin', and he told me about the meeting he went to. Said it was the first time he ever went into a Muslim church. Told me you led the meetin'. When he said 'Rafiq,' I told him you were my son. You know what he said?"

"What?"

"Said you one of the smartest people he ever talked to."

Rafiq blushed.

Hank continued. "He know Barbara too. They about the same age. Says he used to be...uh, what you call it? An 'sistent pastor up in her church in North Oakland. Said the head pastor, name of...let me think...Joseph Brown would sometimes let him do the service. He seem like a good man, so I invited him to come Friday."

Rafiq thought inviting a relative stranger to the house was a bad idea considering the circumstances, but he didn't object.

"OK, Dad. Fatima and I will be there. Hope we can talk more about it then."

"I don't feel sick, son."

"Not yet, but it's coming," Rafiq thought.

13

REVEREND GREEN STOOD outside his small church waiting for people to show for Bible study. It was a crisp autumn afternoon. The sun was beginning to set as the wind blew leaves and trash in a swirl around his legs. Ricky took a deep breath and exhaled slowly.

"What a beautiful afternoon," he thought as he peered outward. A gold tinge filled the skyline—the kind of vivid gold that seems to happen only in the fall around sunset. He took a deep breath and felt grateful to be alive in this time. In this moment. His serenity vanished as he thought of his son, Reginald. He always thought of Reggie. Thoughts engulfed his brain involuntarily. Inevitably. Almost four years had passed since Reggie was gunned down. No reason. Waiting for his father to pick him up from the mall. Broad daylight.

Ricky caught himself sliding into melancholia. It was a place he never wanted to be, but especially not now, with the study group due soon. He sighed, walked into the church, and sat in a rear pew. He hoped more young men would come this time, but he had his doubts. Only a few would usually show for church functions. No reason to think more would show now. He thought back to when he was associate pastor at in North Oakland. Didn't seem like thirty years ago. More like ten, maybe. Young black men attended church in much larger numbers then. They came to Bible studies. Served as ushers. Most continued to be a part of the congregation into their twenties and thirties. Ricky sighed again.

"Not anymore," he said loudly. Same story at a church down East Fourteenth. A much larger facility that suffered from the same malady: scant young black male participation.

"Getting closer to Revelation," he thought. "Our young black men have turned away from God."

Ricky rose from the pew and walked back out. He stood for a few moments before noticing a young female walking down the sidewalk. She wore almost nothing even though it had turned cold out. They exchanged looks from a distance before the woman crossed the street.

Ricky continued to watch her. "Young lady!" he yelled stepping out into the street. "Can I talk to you for a moment?"

The young woman sped up into a trot, disappearing around the corner. Ricky couldn't keep up the pace. He stopped the pursuit. This woman was one he hadn't seen on the street before. She looked young enough to be saved. Most of the prostitutes outside his church he knew by sight. He had tried to talk to some of them. His efforts were typically returned by a "fuck you" or something worse. One of them even had the nerve to proposition him on a Sunday before noon service. He shook his head as he turned and walked back inside.

14

FATIMA AMIN WALKED briskly toward the classroom on the UC Berkeley campus. Passing through the main quad, she made a left into an open doorway and took the staircase to the third floor. Her engaging smile and easy manner made her a popular figure on campus. Not just within the Chemistry Department but also with most other students she came in contact with. Her colorful Nigerian wardrobe made her stand out among the typical blue jeans, T-shirts, and other Western-style clothing. Her fluttering voice seemed as though she were singing whenever she spoke.

Immediately upon entering room 314, she noticed professor Bertrand Adams sitting at his desk. She walked to the other side of the room, passing three students already seated.

After a few minutes, Adams rose from his chair and greeted the eleven chemistry doctoral candidates. "Good morning, and welcome back. We have a weeks' worth of catching up to do. The disturbances on campus seem to be over, unless Donald Trump decides he wants to schedule a talk."

Most of the students laughed.

"Now we'll continue with the link between chemistry and blood." He picked up packets from his desk while motioning to a student in the first row to come forward. The packets were passed out. "You will notice the title of this excerpt: 'The Anomalous Viscosity of Blood' It is a synopsis of the most definitive research ever done on the unique chemical and mechanical properties of blood. You have a week to read it. We will then discuss it in class. Afterward, each of you will write a paper correlating the properties of blood with a choice of diseases involving circulation. Each of you signed up for this course because you indicated you were interested in pursuing in-depth investigations of chemistry as it pertains to biological…no…as it pertains to human systems. This is the beginning of that section of that course. Questions?"

Fatima spoke. "Dr. Adams, will you leave the choosing of the disease to us?"

"Certainly. I'm sure each of you has your own particular interests. You may have more than one. You may want to contrast the changing properties of blood with two or more diseases. There will be plenty of latitude for your choices. The purpose is to understand the variable properties of blood under different conditions. Any other questions? Fine. Then turn in your papers from last week's assignment."

Fatima's thoughts turned to her husband as she reached into her satchel to retrieve her assignment. She and Rafiq hadn't spent much quality time together lately. Their first chance to relax in almost ten days would be at her father-in-law's house tomorrow night. She thought about her first visit there and how Hank had complimented her beauty. Rafiq had recently told her about Hank's cancer and his refusal of treatment. She said a brief prayer as she looked forward to Friday night. Maybe she could help.

As she left class, she ignored Professor Adams's intrusive stare.

15

JOSH AND RUBEN relaxed after finishing breakfast. Both had had a busy two days prior to Ruben calling late yesterday afternoon. Ruben leaned back in the comfortable thatched chair. He stared at Josh for a time, thinking. He finally said, "You feel like talking 'bout how you ended up in the joint?"

Josh didn't hesitate. "Like I told you in Quentin, my estate attorney and I cooked the books."

"What you mean by that?"

"We fixed it so that my brother's portion of my parents' estate became null and void. I'm not going to bore you with the paperwork details, but I hired this guy on the recommendation of a friend. My brother is a no-count, lazy leech who never accomplished anything on his own. The court restored part of his settlement, which he quickly spent on his drug habit. He's been down south at Soledad doing twenty-five to life. I got five to ten."

"What about the dude you hired?"

"He lost his license and got off with probation."

"Lost his license? Wonder if he's on the street now?"

"Probably not. He received one-tenth of a very large settlement."

"So you must be rich, man. How much you got?"

Josh glared at Ruben. His expression was both angry and suspicious. "Listen, Ruben. I'm here to help you as much as I can to get you back on your feet. I've got my late parents' house we're sitting in right now. The rest of the assets are tied up in real estate and a trust fund. I get a comfortable amount sent every month by the trustee to live on. There's no cash or valuables that I or anyone else can get their hands on without the trustee's written permission."

Ruben leaned forward in his chair and stared at Josh. "Hey, man. I don't want none of your money, and I 'preciate everything you done for me. Understand, I didn't kick rock and weed to just go out and jack people up. I want to get to see my daughters. Haven't seen them in years. The only chance I have is to stay straight. That's what I'm doin', and I don't have no 'tention to do anything else. I been roaming the streets for two days before I dug your number outta my coat. You the first man who done anything big for me in a long while. I ain't gonna forget that."

Josh took a sip of coffee. He pondered Ruben for a time, not completely convinced of his sincerity.

"So? What's next?" Ruben asked.

"I don't have anything happening today. I do a Bible study at a small church a few blocks from here. Just a couple days a week. What do you have going on today?"

"Got to find another job, man. It's real hard to do that out here bein' a felon. People look at you like you gonna do a pickpocket on 'em first chance you get. All I want is to work. Wanna pay my own way. Ain't gonna find a better man with his hands than me. But they scared 'cause I don't smile and laugh hardly at all. My life ain't been like that."

"I've got an uncle who has a construction company about ten miles north of here. He's always looking for good workers. Can you do concrete, drywall, that kind of stuff?"

"Man, I can do anything that has to do with buildin' somethin'. My uncle had me workin' construction back in the day, but I got fired after a few years when they started drug testin'. Learned a lot, though."

Josh paused for a long time. He was thinking of the consequences if Ruben failed and weighed them against the prospect of gaining a potential long-term headache. He decided he would contact his uncle. "OK. You sound like you're really determined to get back on your feet. I have to tell you, though, that my uncle doesn't take any backtalk. You have to follow everything he asks you to do without questions or acting out. You think you can do that?"

"If he don't mind my straight face. I ain't never had any problem follow-in' directions on a job."

"I'll call him."

"'Preciate it, man," Ruben said loudly as he stood up and extended his hand to Josh. "Got to go back downstairs. That coffee knockin' on the do'."

"Don't bother with that. There's a bathroom through the living room and to the left. You're welcome to use that."

"OK."

Ruben turned, walked several feet toward the bathroom, and noticed a family photograph on the fireplace mantel. He ambled over and stared at a man, a woman, and two children. Hanging above the photograph was a necklace.

Ruben stepped closer, focusing first on the jewelry. It looked vaguely familiar. He looked down at the photograph. "This a picture of your family?"

Josh turned in his chair. "Yeah. That's my mother, father, myself, and my little brother. Notice the smirk on my brother's face. That represents what he has been most of his life. A pleasure-seeking, self-serving rat."

"What about the jewelry hangin' from the fireplace above 'em? Looks like somethin' I've seen before. That's a symbol, right?"

"That's the Star of David, man. That belonged to my grandfather on my dad's side."

"I knew it was somethin' like that. You Jewish, ain't you? This dude at Quentin told me that a lot of cats who got names ending in 'man' are Jewish. That true?"

"Well, obviously it is in my grandfather's case, and since I inherited the Portman surname, a lot of people make the mistaken assumption I'm Jewish. I wasn't raised a Jew, my father never practiced the religion, and my mother was a Detroit Protestant." Josh laughed. "That's the reason the marriage worked. My mother never wanted to practice Judaism. She was a Christian from a strong religious family. She told my father early on in their courtship she would never convert. Dad was fine with that. His father practiced the religion, but my dad never took to it. Thought all religion was bullshit."

"So you wasn't ever really a Jew either, then. Sound like yo' mother went to church and probably took you and yo' brotha' wit' 'er."

"That's right. Although a lot of the time my brother was in Juvenile Hall. Religion never took with him either."

"Uh huh." Ruben continued toward the bathroom.

When he returned, Josh was ready with a question. "At Quentin, you never participated much during the service or with Bible study. I always wondered why you even bothered to show up."

"You forgot, man. I told you I was there for the coffee and doughnuts."

16

HANK ANSWERED THE doorbell. A tall Latino man stood at the door holding a large box of food. "How you doin?" Hank asked. "You right on time. Come on in."

"Gracias, senor."

"You can put that on the kitchen table."

The man did as Hank requested and then turned toward him. "Two roasted chickens, two large black beans, four large salads with cilantro, two large macaroni and cheese, and two large flats of tortillas, senor. That comes to sixty-two thirty."

"Are those corn tortillas?"

"Yes, senor. You said that is what you wanted."

Hank handed him a hundred-dollar bill. "Keep that."

"Muchas gracias."

"Hey. What's your name?"

"Alberto."

Hank smiled and watched as the caterer returned to his van marked Julio's Restaurant and Catering.

He stepped down off the porch and peered down the street. "They should be comin' soon."

Ten minutes later, Reverend Green knocked on the door. "Brother Hank Roberson. How you feelin' this evening?" Ricky Green extended his hand to Hank and warmly hugged him.

"Welcome to the house of Hank. You hungry?"

"Little bit. Haven't eaten since late this mornin'."

"The rest of them should be here in a minute," Hank said as he glanced at his watch.

"Listen, Brother Roberson. You know Barbara has been part of my congregation for years off and on. I should tell you before she gets here that she called me and told me about your can…your health issue. I'm very sorry to hear you declining treatment."

Hank was fuming. "Can't nobody keep a secret in this damn family for nothin'." He turned and faced the Reverend. "I done made up my mind. That's it. Ain't no need for you to discuss nothin' with me 'bout it. When yo' time is up, it's up. I trust my doctor. He told me I'm done. Don't matter what kinda treatment I get. Told me the stuff has spread into my blood. And don't be bringin' me no mess 'bout Jesus and his miracles. Already had mine. Miracle I lasted this long with all the women I had. Coulda been shot, died from fallin' down drunk, all kinda manna' a shit. I don't want to live longer than what I got left."

Ricky held up his hands. "Didn't mean to upset you, brother. I think you underestimating your value to your family, though."

Hank gave Ricky a long look but said nothing. He heard cars pulling up in front of the house. He walked over and opened the front door, watching as Barbara and Nikira exited from the car closest to him. Looking across the street, he saw Rafiq and Fatima having an animated conversation inside their car.

"Hey, Daddy. How you feelin'?" Nikira said enthusiastically, with Barbara walking close behind. Hank's daughter hugged him for a long time before turning around and facing her mother. "Momma, doesn't Daddy look good?"

Barbara looked at Hank's Oakland Raider jersey, black pants, and spotless white tennis shoes. She smiled at Hank but said nothing. Hank glanced across the street and noticed his son and Fatima were still in the car. He turned and went back into the living room. Reverend Green hugged Barbara. "Good to see you, Sister Jamison."

Turning toward Nikira, his faced lit up. "I remember you used to come to church up in North Oakland with your mother. Wonderful to see you... uh..."

"Nikira," Barbara said.

"That's right. Now I remember."

Ricky then turned toward Hank. "I didn't even notice your Raider jersey. Been a longtime fan myself. All the way back to before they moved to LA." He looked at the number 10 and the name Dickey on the back of Hank's jersey.

"Dickey? Never heard of him. When did he play?"

"Never did, really. He was the first black quarterback to ever be taken in the first round, way back in nineteen sixty-seven. Never got a real shot at playing quarterback in the NFL, though. Made him a wide receiver. Eldridge Dickey coulda been great. Broke all kinda records at Tennessee State. Could throw with either hand. Died in his fifties from a bad liver. Really died from a broken heart. But, you know, that's the way they treated brothers back then. Said we wasn't smart enough to lead a team. I wear this jersey 'cause it's about givin' honor to all the cats who coulda been somethin' if they was given half a chance. Dickey's just one of the ones nobody knows about."

Hank heard the knock on his front door. He walked over, greeting his son and daughter-in-law as they crossed the threshold.

"Hey, son." He reached out to shake Rafiq's hand.

Hank's strong handshake was returned with a weak, terse response from his son. He chose to ignore it, turning his attention to his daughter-in-law, who was wearing a full blue, violet, and gold African dress with matching shoes.

"You look more beautiful than that first day I met 'cha." He looked back at Rafiq. "You a lucky man, son. Where did you eva' find her?"

Rafiq turned and looked at his father with a glint of suspicion. "I met Fatima at Berkeley. We were having a Muslim information session there, and I happened to catch a glimpse of her sitting about four rows back."

He smiled as he looked at his wife. "I had never seen a woman so beautiful and beautifully elegant. I knew with that first contact I had to meet her. She began to leave about halfway through the presentation. I couldn't let that happen, so I said excuse me and left the podium. I finally caught up with her just outside the lecture hall. I felt during that conversation that we had a connection. We went out for lunch the next day, and the rest is history."

"I did not like your dressing style when we first met," Fatima said softly. "You resembled the manner in which many Americans dress. Much too casually. That is the reason I left early that day. It wasn't because of the content of your message, I could no longer stand to look at your shoes."

Rafiq was embarrassed but managed to not reveal it as a weak smiled appeared in the corner of his mouth. "Baby. You know you've changed a lot about my appearance since then, including my shoes."

Everyone seemed to look simultaneously at Rafiq's shoes: polished patent-leather Stacy Adams.

Hank looked over at his son. "When you want to impress a woman, wearin' loafers ain't exactly the way to go about that."

They both shared a laugh—something that hadn't happened between them for years.

Rafiq and Fatima sat on the large sofa already occupied by Barbara and Nikira. Reverend Green took a seat obliquely facing the sofa in a modest straight-back chair.

"Y'all hungry?" asked the host.

"Nikira, come into the kitchen with me so we can get everybody started."

"OK, Daddy."

Nikira followed Hank into the kitchen, leaving an uncomfortable silence in the living room.

Fatima sensed the growing ill ease and finally spoke to Ricky Green. "How long have you been a Christian?"

Ricky choked a bit on a swig of bottled water. "I apologize," he said, looking at Fatima. "Your question took a little bit by surprise. For about thirty years now."

"I'm sorry, Mr. Green. I didn't mean to be so abrupt. I have a strong interest in the reasons people commit to religion."

Ricky looked over at the Muslim couple and paused for a moment. "I've told your husband a little bit about my history and what brought me to the Lord. To make a long story short, I was living the wrong kind of life. One that was probably going to kill me. I wanted to live, so I changed."

Rafiq joined the conversation. "That doesn't make any sense on the surface of it. You must have had somebody who laid the groundwork early in your life. I mean, people usually won't commit to religion unless somebody influences them early on."

Ricky looked at Rafiq for a few seconds before he responded. "My mother took me to church up until the time I was about thirteen. Never wanted to go. She insisted, so I really didn't have a choice. Most of the time I couldn't wait to get back home. Told her once or twice I didn't like going, but that didn't help." Ricky chuckled. "Back then, all I wanted to do was play and eat. Wasn't thinking about nothing that didn't involve fun. I was almost killed at nineteen just walking down the street. Guy just jumped out from behind a car one night and stabbed me right there."

Ricky pointed to his left chest area just above his heart. "Happened just a block from the house. A policeman drove by and saw me lying there. He got out and slowed down the bleeding until the ambulance came. Took me to the hospital, and they gave me a transfusion. Quart and a half. The thing was, I didn't have my gun on me that night. Was walking back from my girl's place. If I had had it, I probably woulda shot that guy. That woulda landed me in jail, and who knows what would have happened after that. While I was healing, I thought the whole thing through and realized I had been spared that night. Not just once, but probably twice."

"That event must have been it, then," Fatima said. "So church did make you think about God after that."

Ricky let out a loud laugh. Everyone stopped and looked directly at him. He looked around the room, mildly embarrassed. "Excuse me. I'm a minister and always try to tell the truth. I really didn't get much from church growing up because I wasn't paying attention." His eyes began to glisten. "My mother always told me that God's mercy and love have no limit. I didn't learn that from church; I learned that from her. Her words were what stuck with me in the hospital. It's the core of my belief because I experienced his mercy myself. I realized I wasn't spared because of good luck. Some unseen hand was in that."

"Beautiful," Fatima said.

Hank and Nikira came from the kitchen. "This here's a buffet. Everything's ready. Y'all go ahead and help yo'selves."

The meal proceeded with typical small talk, with the sound of the Dells softly audible underneath the conversation.

Reverend Green turned to Barbara. "How's y'all's son? I remember he used to come with you to church sometimes. What's his name?"

Conversation stopped as heads turned toward Barbara. Hank rose from his chair and took his empty plate into the kitchen. Tears began to stream down Barbara's cheeks, and she sobbed for several seconds. Ricky felt immediate regret for posing the question.

Barbara spoke to him a soft, clear voice. "His name is Denard, and he's comatose in a hospital. He's an inmate at San Quentin and got attacked."

Ricky stood and gently touched Barbara's hand. "I didn't mean any harm, sister. Just hadn't seen him for years. Know he stopped coming to church with you and Nikira years ago. I remember liking his laughter and enthusiasm and was just wondering is all. I am so sorry."

"That's all right, Reverend. I know you didn't mean any harm."

"He wouldn't be in that damn hospital now if he'd stayed out the street," Hank said loudly as he reentered the room.

Barbara, now fully recovered, lit into Hank. "My son just followed what his father did. How in the world can you stand there and expect Denard to not wind up where he is? You got some kinda nerve blaming him. You set the table for that to happen."

Hank didn't try to defend himself. He had no defense. "You right, Barbara. Had no bus'ness sayin' that. I get angry over a lot of stuff, but mostly at myself. Coulda been a lot better daddy to him. Just had too much wild in me. Still do have some, but I'm old now. No way I can make up for bein' as selfish as I was, no matta' what I do. Been livin' with myself for a long time. It hurts, and I'm not talkin' 'bout the cancer."

"Dad."

Hank turned toward Rafiq's voice.

"Denard had a chance to stay out of trouble. He chose not to. You can't blame yourself for that."

Hank was surprised at the unexpected support from his elder son.

Rafiq continued. "He wanted to be out on the street with his partners. Started that in middle school. Remember, Barbara?"

Barbara gently nodded her head in agreement. She turned and looked back at Hank. "After I left you, I couldn't control him after a while. Discipline, counseling, outings together…none of it worked. I even whipped him regularly. He would never cry. He would look up at me with a kind of blank look and then just sneak out the house later that night. Put him in the Hall for a few days to scare him. Just made him worse."

She thought before continuing. "I'm thinking this boy is just too much like you. He got your wildness in his blood. You could've been the best father in the world, and it might not have made any difference."

Hank smiled weakly at his former girlfriend.

There was a loud knock on the door. Hank went over. "Who is it?"

"Gerald."

Hank opened the door for his old friend and neighbor, Gerald Daniels. Gerald was dressed up in a lavender dress shirt with white pants, coat, and shoes.

"We making too much noise for you, old man? That why you came ova' here?"

Gerald laughed. "What chu talkin' 'bout, Hank? Had to strain my ears to hear that Delfonics music you playin'."

"It's the Dells, Gerald."

"They always sounded a lot alike to me."

"That's cause you ain't never had no ear, man. We havin' a family thing. You welcome to come in and eat."

Gerald hesitated. "You musta forgot we supposed to go see B. B. King tonight, man. You had me get the tickets ova' a month ago. You turnin' into a senile motherfucka."

"Damn. Forgot all about that. I can't go tonight. It's family. You understand."

"Man, you the one who crazy about B. B. I was goin' with you jus' to keep you company. Listen, man. My sista' and her boyfriend been stayin' at the house since las' Saturday. They been askin' me if I had extra tickets. It's a sellout, ya' know. I could give the tickets to them."

"You sure you wanna do that, man?"

"I already told you, man. B. B. ain't my boy. Now if it was Bobby Bland, I woulda' had tickets long befo' you ever knew he was comin'."

Hank laughed so hard he choked. "Go ahead and give them tickets to yo' sister. Then come on back here and get somethin' to eat."

Gerald heartily shook Hank's hand. "That's exactly what I wanted you ta' say."

Hank walked back into the living room to find his son perusing a stack of CDs. "Hey, Dad. I see you got some early rap protest music here. I never knew you liked that stuff. Thought you were a blues and R&B man all this time."

"I like a lot of our music, son. Just befo' you was born, I used to listen to this radio station outta Berkeley."

"You talking about KBLX?"

"No. Befo' then it was called...let me think a second. KLE or somethin' like that. They played jazz, R&B, blues, all kinda diff'rent stuff. Musta' been way back in the seventies."

"Can I put on a CD?"

Hank looked around the room to gauge the reaction. Everyone was conversing, apparently not paying attention to their exchange.

"Go ahead." He nodded to his son. "Just keep it on the low."

"There Ain't No Such Thing as a Superman" was the first tune. Rafiq was familiar with the lyrics. He knew the song was directed toward black women: "You alone consider mercy, seems like all you get is pain. So, tell me, why can't you understand, there ain't no such thing as a superman?"

The casual conversations came to a halt as the group listened.

"Seems to me you have found the courage that others could not find."

After the song ended, Rafiq could see that his sister was agitated.

"You look upset, Nikira."

"That song has so much truth in it. Made me think about the four serious boyfriends I had. They started out almost perfect until I got to know them better. The last one didn't surprise me, though, because by then I knew to reserve judgment until enough time had passed. All of them had serious faults. Cemented my awareness that the only superman who ever walked the earth was Jesus."

"Amen, sister," Ricky Green exclaimed loudly. "That's what the Bible teaches us. I had never heard that tune before, but I knew exactly what he was talkin' about."

Rafiq shook his head, looking at Ricky. "You misinterpret the lyrics. No superman means not now, not ever. More than that, it cautions a woman about depending on a man to carry her through life. It's saying a woman has to have her own thoughts, get her own education, and try to establish some potential for a good life that's not dependent on a man providing for her. I mean, black couples break up more than we like to think about." Rafiq avoided his father's eyes as he delivered his opinion.

Barbara fidgeted in her chair. She opened her mouth to respond to Rafiq but changed her mind. She looked away from the others in the direction of the kitchen.

Fatima waved toward her. Unable to get her attention, she called her. "Barbara."

No response.

"Barbara."

The older woman slowly turned toward her voice.

"Growing up, my fata taught me the importance of self-sufficiency. My parents would not allow men to enter the house to talk with me until after my eighteenth birthday. He would not allow me to date until after I finished my first two years of university. When I was sixteen, he beat me for coming home late from school. He did not accept my explanation, so I had to take the punishment. I was very afraid of him, so I was never late again."

Barbara spoke slowly in a melancholy tone. "I think I understand what you're saying, but didn't you hate your father after he beat you?"

"Yes. Yes, I hated him, but I feared him more."

"You finished college, though. Right?" Nikira asked. "You're continuing graduate school at Cal. Do you still hate your father?"

"Sometimes, yes. He's eight thousand miles away, but he has still tried to control my life more than he should. He came out to visit years ago and tried to stop my engagement to Rafiq."

She turned and smiled at her husband. "He said my husband was unworthy of me because he had not completed university."

The group eyed Rafiq as his complexion turned once again.

Nikira continued. "What you're really saying, Fatima, is your father insisted on you being able to provide for yourself whether you married or not. Right?"

"Yes. You see, education is very important in Nigeria. Many of our youth come to America to further their studies. My mother and fata never had an opportunity to attend college. They married very young. My brother Akeem was born a year after. My fata had to work hard jobs in Lagos his entire life. He was always embarrassed because many of his friends did much better."

The muted sound of jazz played in the background. Hank stood up. "Got some cobbler in the kitchen. Y'all got two choices: peach cobbler or banana pudding."

The entire group came to life. "Oooh, that's sounds good."

"I haven't had peach cobbler in years."

"Any ice cream to go with that?" Ricky asked.

"Yeah. Y'all got two choices with that too." Hank chuckled.

"Wait. Let me guess," Rafiq blurted out. His color now restored. "Vanilla and strawberry."

Hank cracked up at Rafiq. "One out of two ain't bad, son. Vanilla and black walnut."

Everyone laughed, including Barbara.

"Be right back," Hank added.

Hank nodded at Nikira, who rose and followed him into the kitchen for a second time.

The festive mood continued as light conversation resumed. Another loud knock on the door. Rafiq called out toward the kitchen, "Dad. The door."

Hank coolly ambled from the kitchen and opened the front door. Gerald had returned, dressed casually this time.

"Hey, Gerald. Come on in."

Gerald took a seat in a vacant chair. He surveyed the room. He looked up at Hank, who was suddenly standing in front of him imposingly.

"You want something to eat?"

Gerald nodded.

"Go 'head and git it, man. Many times as you been over here, and you actin' like you fo'got where the kitchen at."

Gerald grazed Nikira's elbow as she was returning with plates of cobbler. "Excuse me, Nikira."

She glanced back and smiled.

The gathering ended a few minutes after midnight. Hank had fallen asleep in his lounge chair. Everyone had left except Rafiq and Fatima.

"Dad."

Hank didn't respond. Rafiq gently shook his father's shoulder. Hank, half dazed, opened his eyes, looked up at his son, and then slowly surveyed the room. He looked back at Rafiq. "Ever'body gone?"

"Yeah. We're getting ready to leave too. We enjoyed ourselves, and the kitchen's all clean."

Hank gave his son a weak smile as he attempted to rise from the chair. He fell back into it with an embarrassed look on his face. He successfully stood on the next attempt, letting out an emphatic "Uh huh!" Both men looked at each other for a few seconds. Rafiq reached his arms forward and gently hugged his father.

Hank hugged him back, but with much greater force.

"Boy, Nikira hugs me harder than that. You afraid I'm gonna fall apart?"

Rafiq hesitated and then backed away from his father, a sad feeling over-taking him. "Dad, I wish—"

"Boy, just take your wife and git on home. I know what you gonna say. The last thing I want is for my family to pity me. 'Specially you. You makin' a good life for yo'self. I ain't got nothing but love and respect for you. So git on outta here. We talk again befo' long."

Fatima came from down the hallway, went over, and hugged Hank. "Thank you, fata-in-law, for the nice evening. Next time you come over to our house. OK?"

Hank smiled and nodded at her but said nothing. Soon after the couple left, he went to bed and fell into a deep sleep.

17

RAFIQ'S PHONE RANG early the next morning. He looked at his caller ID: Josh Portman. He let it go to voice mail as he rolled over to touch Fatima. He tapped a little farther toward her side of the bed and felt nothing before it dawned on him.

"Oh yeah," he thought. "She's meeting her friend Iyabode for breakfast."

He lay back down, but curiosity got the best of him. "Josh Portman?"

He thought back to recent events, trying to remember if he might have met someone of that name but had forgotten. "Was it at the mosque? Maybe a contact at work? No."

He listened to the message. "Uh, hey. This is Ruben. I was just callin' 'cause you said you had a meetin' every week. I was thinkin' about goin' but forgot what day it's on. You put down the phone numba' and address on yo' card but not the day. You can call me back on this number. 'Preciate it."

"Ruben?" Rafiq took a few seconds to collect his thoughts. "Ruben? Ruben? OK, yeah. The brother on parole I met in the CD store."

His curiosity satisfied, he lay back down and went to sleep.

He woke just before ten and dialed the number Ruben had called from. The phone went to voice mail. "Hello, this is Josh. Can't get to the phone just now, but I look forward to hearing your message. I'll get back to you."

"Hello, this is Rafiq Amin. Ruben left a message from your phone earlier this morning. Trying to get in touch with him. Please tell him I'm looking forward to talking to him. Best time would be later this evening. Thanks."

Rafiq hung up the phone, walked toward the kitchen, and opened the swing door. The tantalizing smell of Brazilian coffee that Fatima had timed to be brewed filled his nostrils. "I love my wife," he said out loud. "Always thinking of me." Just as he was about to pour a cup, his phone rang.

"Josh Portman" again appeared in the window.

"Hello?"

"Hey. Is this Raf-fig?"

"Yes. This is Rafiq."

"How you doin? This is Ruben. Remember we met at that CD store…"

"Yeah, Ruben. I remember you. How you doin'?"

"Tryin' to make it, man. Just started workin' last week on a new job. Only part time, though."

"That's good, man. Glad to hear it. What's on your mind?"

"You was tellin' me you had meetin's where people could just walk in and listen or talk if they wanted to. I have a friend who's kinda' helpin' me out. Been livin' at his house for 'bout two weeks now. Good dude. He's the one who got me the job, but I don't want to be talkin' to him about all my b'inness. I think I'm ready to try yo' group out."

"That's good. We're always looking for more people to join the discussion. It's on the second and fourth Tuesdays. Our next one is in two days. You have the address, right?"

"Yeah. I just needed the time. You didn't say what time."

"Oh, sorry. Two p.m. You got a car?"

"No, man. No car and no driver's license, but I can get there. I'm off at twelve every day. I been takin' the bus all around the East Bay, so it won't be no problem."

"All right then, Brother Ruben. Good to hear from you. See you on Tuesday."

"OK, then."

Rafiq heard silence and knew Ruben had hung up.

"Wow," he thought. "I forgot to tell him the rules. I'll text them."

Rafiq finished his coffee and then ate the sandwich his wife had made.

18

BARBARA SAT AT a corner table in the quaint College Avenue café. She loved this area of Oakland. It brought back fond memories of Denard and Nikira growing up. They had lived in a Claremont Avenue apartment just off Telegraph after she left Hank. The kids had done well at a nearby elementary school, both receiving good grades and citizenship awards. As she waited for Stella Young to join her for lunch, Barbara thought about the Halloween costumes she handmade. The trips to Fairyland at the lake. She missed those times and would never forget them. She tried to avoid thinking about Denard's troubles. The troubles began when he entered middle school. She went to pick him up after school only to find him gone most of the time.

She was so deeply into thought, she didn't notice Stella approaching her table. Stella moved her hand up and down in front of Barbara's face. "Girl, you just stared a hole through that man's back sitting in front of you."

Barbara stood and warmly hugged her friend. "I was just thinking about when the kids were younger."

"You mean when y'all lived down the street?"

"Uh huh. Problem is, whenever I think about those times, my thoughts always turn to Denard. Just makes me feel so helpless. I always think there's more I coulda' done."

"You need to let that go. Denard made his own decisions. You did your best. I remember you whippin' his ass all the way home one time. He didn't have his daddy in his life, and that sure wasn't your fault either. Ain't hardly your fault he's in prison."

Stella watched Barbara's face turn morbid. She recognized she had touched a nerve. "Barbara," she said softly. "What is it?"

Barbara pulled a tissue out of her purse. She wiped a tear away. "Somebody attacked him and hurt him real bad. He's in a coma."

Stella sat with an expression of disbelief. She searched for words to console her friend. She found none. Barbara stared into her cup of coffee. Stella offered her hand. Barbara grasped it.

The waitress broke the silence. "Can I get you something to drink?" she asked Stella.

"A cup of decaf, please."

"My pleasure," the waitress said as she turned away.

Stella looked back at her friend, who was still staring at her cup.

Barbara looked up. "The worst part is not knowing whether he'll ever be conscious again. The doctors don't know. I'm praying all the time. I want to be able to talk to my son again. To know that he knows how much I love him. That's really all I'm hoping for." She began to cry softly as Stella rubbed her hand.

"Barbara. You are one of the best people I've ever met. I don't have any doubt that God will answer your prayer."

Barbara smiled at her friend as the waitress returned. "Are you two ready to order something to eat?"

"Can you give us a couple of more minutes please?" Stella asked.

"Take as much time as you'd like."

"I am so glad you're such a good friend, Stella."

"Always will be, girl. I'm lucky we grew up near each other. Went to the same schools. Fought for the same boys…"

Barbara laughed and smiled at her friend. "You always knew how to cheer me up."

"We both have that gift, girl. Do you remember Kamal Morris?"

Barbara smiled and shook her head affirmatively. "He was the finest boy at Tech. Smart too."

"Problem was, he knew that," Stella replied. "Had that beautiful, smooth skin. Real nice hair. Didn't even use Gerry Curl. Remember he told you he would take you to the senior prom, and then he ended up taking Vanessa Hill?"

"Don't remind me. Waited until the Wednesday before the dance to tell me he 'forgot' he had already asked Vanessa. He really wanted to go with you, but you were already going with Reggie."

"That's right. For a split second, I almost said yes, but that woulda been too cold. I was tempted, though. Kamal was one of the finest men I've ever seen."

"What ever happened to him?"

"He got a scholarship to some college down in Alabama to play basketball. Saw him at the twentieth reunion. You couldn't go, remember?"

"Yes. Nikira had just come out of the hospital after her ovarian cyst was removed. Had to take care of my baby for a few days."

"Anyway, he got married to a white woman he met down there. Brought her to the reunion."

"What did she look like?"

"Kind of plain. Brown hair, tall, and thin. Real nice. Talked a lot about their kids. Kamal said they lived up in Seattle. Guess both of them work for a tech company up there."

"He still look good?"

"Not like he used to. Got kind of fat and shaved off all his facial hair."

"You kidding me, girl. He used to have the cutest mustache and little goatee. I'm not surprised, though. A black man in a white-collar world with a white wife too. He's going to have more opportunities with a bald face."

"I understand all that, but damn, he used to look exceptional from head to toe. At the reunion, he still looked handsome but more homogenized. Know what I mean?"

"Yeah, girl. More power to him, though, if he's happy. You ready to go?"

"I'm ready. Glad we got together. Be gentle and patient with yourself, Barbara. I'm always here if you need to talk."

The friends hugged, then went their separate ways.

19

RUBEN GOT OFF work a half hour early and took the bus back to Josh's place. Josh had trusted him enough to give him a duplicate key. He entered the house and immediately went downstairs to the small shower stall near the toilet. He was angry at himself. He had forgotten to lay out a set of clothes to wear to the afternoon meeting.

Rummaging through a pile of his clean clothes, he found an appropriate match of jeans and a blue tee. He stopped briefly and examined his choice. "Ain't no way I'm goin' there in some wrinkled-up clothes."

He rushed upstairs and pulled the ironing board out from the hall closet. He unfolded the board and plugged in the iron.

"Damn. Coulda did this yesterday. Probably gonna make me late." He finished and dressed quickly, putting on a pair of near-new black loafers. He had nearly closed the front door when he turned back and unplugged the iron. He decided he didn't have time for the bus. BART would get him there quicker. He walked briskly the entire mile to the Ashby BART station, paid for his ticket, and waited for a Fremont-bound train. He was hoping the train wouldn't be crowded. He still felt a sense of ill ease in cramped, crowded places. The train arrived in eight minutes. He entered and was relieved to find only six other occupants in his car. Taking a seat by the window, he watched the other passengers until the train came up above ground. He enjoyed seeing Oakland's landscape from a new vantage point.

Looking eastward, he remembered the Oakland Hills fire of '91. He had stayed overnight at a friend's house after a late night of partying. The second-floor landing had a large window facing east. Ruben was awakened that morning by the cooing of pigeons outside the upstairs guest room he was sleeping in. The room was directly across from the window, and as he opened the door, he stopped dead in his tracks. The entire hillside was ablaze A strong wind was blowing smoke over the house. He knocked on the adjoining door.

"What," came the irritable response from his friend.

"Get up, man. We got to get the hell outta here."

He heard the footsteps of his friend coming toward the closed door. "What you talkin' about, man? Damn. It's only ten, and my head's all fucked up."

"Open up and look out the window."

His friend opened the door and shuffled out with his eyes barely open.

Ruben gestured toward the window. "Look over there."

His friend's eyes widened, his mouth agape. "What the fuck?"

He quickly gathered his important papers and photographs. They were out of the house within fifteen minutes.

Ruben snapped back to the present as the BART train went underground again after passing the McArthur station. Exiting at Lake Merritt, Ruben took the bus up to Foothill. He followed Rafiq's directions, walking the remaining few blocks to the meeting. No one was outside the building. He looked around for the entry, finally locating it in a small alcove. He started to knock on the door. Instead he reached for the handle and pulled it slowly open, looking cautiously inside.

"Kinda dark in here," he thought.

He noticed a group sitting on the red carpet several feet away. He walked toward them.

"Whoa, brother," a voice came from his left. "You can't walk on the carpet without removing your shoes."

Ruben looked at the figure approaching him. A tall, muscular black man with a black suit, bow tie, and confident gait stopped just in front of him.

"That carpet is clean. It's sacred. You can put your shoes in the cubicle over there," he said, motioning to the right. "But before that, I have to search you."

Ruben's expression changed to aggravation. He thought about the guards searching him almost daily at Quentin. Rafiq told him that would be done to him here but he had forgotten.

"Lift your arms up, brother."

Ruben thought about walking out but decided to comply at the last instant. After completion of the search, he removed his shoes, then rounded the corner to join the group.

Rafiq rose to greet him. "Brother Ruben, glad you could make it. Normally we insist on punctuality, but this is your first time, so let me introduce you to the group."

There were three more participants than at the previous meeting: Councilman Judy Garcia; an OPD police officer, Scott Bartholomew; and Samuel Sackman, a Jewish rabbi. Ruben felt uneasy, especially after the introduction of the white plainclothes policeman. He sat slowly while surveying the spacious surroundings. He noticed the man who had patted him down was stationed against the far wall directly across from him. Three other similarly dressed men with massive builds stood with blank expressions in front of the other three walls. He sat for a few minutes, not paying much attention to the group.

Abruptly, one of the voices got louder. "I've been telling you for months at our council meetings, and I'm telling you again here to stop voting against funding for my district."

Councilman Garcia was directing her words at Councilman Harrison. She continued. "If we're going to improve our communities, we have to vote as a unit. You act like you want to ignore that minorities are the majority in the council. The schools in the flatlands need better teachers, books, everything. I consistently vote for funding for all flatland schools, and so do the other four minorities on the council. You're the only one we can't depend on."

"Look, Judy. You've either chosen to ignore or just refuse to acknowledge my position. You need to change a lot more than just the schools for students to succeed. You know more than half of the children in East Oakland, including your district, are being raised by single parents. Most of them are women who don't have a college education. They need counseling in order to establish habits that demonstrate to their kids that education is important to them, the parent. You don't do that by telling the kid. You do that though action. Most of these parents are too tired from working, and some of those who have enough energy can't read. Others who can read don't like to unless they have to. This is where money needs to go. For parent counseling. Do you see any proposed plans in our meetings for that? No, you don't. When I proposed a referendum on this last year, the only council member who voted for it besides me was Betty Johnson."

Judy spoke again. "Nate, I've told you I agree with your position, but it's secondary to having better schools. Even with high-achieving students, most of their learning occurs in better schools."

Rafiq spoke. "You both have valid points. I remember, growing up, my late mother read to me before she died. After that, my dad's girlfriend read to me. I observed them reading on their own. Nate, your point is valid, but it has to start early in the child's development. Listen, here at the mosque's school, we teach K through eight, and our students achieve at a level in math and science that's two to three grade levels above the state average. We have the advantages of smaller class sizes and dedicated teachers who happen to be Muslim. The main factor, though, is the desire of the parents here to learn. Some are learning Arabic, for example. Their kids see them studying at night."

He looked over at Nate. "To your point, the parents have to lead by example. Demonstrate that they're interested in reading, in learning. That's more important than any other factor."

Ricky spoke up. "You know what? I agree with you about the parents. The young black men who come to my church have slacked off over the years. Most of the ones who do come are good students, though. They tell me they started learning from their parents reading little Bible stories to them."

"Bible stories or whatever. Whatever they see us doing is what they're likely to do. Pretty simple," Scott Bartholomew said.

Everyone in the group looked over at the police officer for a few seconds before Nate spoke again. "This is what I've been trying to get the council to understand. We need a comprehensive outreach program for our flatlands communities to instruct parents. You change a few habits, you put children in a better position to succeed. We've tried improving the schools several times in Oakland. Hasn't worked. We need to go into homes and have parents set aside time to read to their kids and read alone. If we can change one in five parents, we can m…"

The group turned quiet. The only sound was the audible snoring of Ruben. His nodding head rocked forward during exhalation. He suddenly sputtered, opening his eyes a second later. The entire group was staring at him.

Ruben's embarrassment quickly turned to anger. "I came here to talk 'bout how to find my kids, and seems like I came on the wrong day. Y'all talkin' 'bout schools and stuff. I need help to find my kids, dammit!"

Rafiq motioned side to side with his hand. Ruben understood right away. No profanity. He looked at Rafiq but offered no apology.

"Ruben?"

He looked over in the direction of the feminine voice.

"I can help you try to find your children," Judy Garcia said softly. "I've worked with paroled inmates before. Some haven't seen or spoken to their children in years."

"That's me," Ruben blurted.

Judy reached into her purse and handed over her card. "You can call me anytime between nine and noon. We'll set up an appointment and talk about it."

Ruben felt a surge of hope. He smiled broadly at the thin, attractive, middle-aged woman before speaking to Rafiq. "I was hopin' somethin' good would happen comin' here. I sure didn't know it be this soon, though."

He rose and gave Rafiq a firm handshake. "Have to go now. Get ready for work in the mornin'."

He looked back at Judy. "I'll try to call you 'round ten tomorrow, when I get my break."

He turned and briskly walked over to the cubicle, nearly knocking down one of the folding chairs nearby. He ran the nine blocks back to the bus stop, leaving himself winded. He sat on the bench. An elderly Mexican lady scooted away from him to the opposite end. He looked at her and smiled. She frowned, clutching her purse. Looking back toward the street, he broke out into song. "Blue skies smilin' at me. Nothin' but blue skies do I see. Bluebirds singin' a song. Nothin but bluebirds…"

He looked back in the direction of the woman. She had left the bus stop and was walking away down High Street. He stood up and did a few steps of the Electric Slide before sitting back down. He hadn't felt this hopeful in years.

20

JUDY STOOD IN her city council office talking to a wealthy investor about plans to build a new stadium for the Oakland A's.

"We've tried this before and it failed, mainly because we couldn't coordinate with Alameda County to break the lease at the Coliseum. The team is tied to that contract as long as—" Her telephone interrupted her conversation.

"Excuse me. Hello? This is Judy Garcia."

"Judy. This is Ruben Scott. Remember I was talkin' to you yesterday 'bout—"

"Yes. Yes, Mr. Scott, I remember. I found some information about your children, which I can't discuss with you right now. I'm in an important meeting. I'll have to call you back. Give me a number where I can reach you."

"I'm on my break now using another guy's phone. Won't be able to call you again till 'bout twelve."

"That's fine. I'll be here."

"OK. Thank you, Judy."

Ruben handed the phone back to his coworker.

113

"Did you get through?"

"Yeah, man," Ruben said. "Thanks. You good lettin' me use your phone like that. First thing I'm gonna do when I get paid is get me one of those."

Ruben jogged back to his workstation, elated over the news. Just before noon, he left his station and jogged back over to his coworker.

"Hey, John. Need to use your phone again, man."

John took a long swig from his water bottle and handed his cell back to Ruben. "The battery's low, Ruben, so try to keep it down to five minutes or less."

"All right, man. Thanks." He pulled Judy's card out of his pocket and anxiously redialed.

The phone rang five times before going to voice mail. "Hello, this is Judy Garcia. I'm not at my desk right now, but if you leave your name and number, I'll return your call as soon as possible. If this is another council member, call the operator and leave your code. They will contact me, and I'll return your call immediately."

Ruben cursed under his breath. "Bitch told me she'd be there. Shit." He left a message. "Hey, Judy, this is Ruben. You said you'd be at your phone now, but you not. Said you found out somethin' 'bout my kids. I don't have my own phone, but I'll be home at five thirty today. Please call me, Judy. Let me give you the number."

He left Josh's number and gave the phone back to John. "Damn. She musta' fo'got." He spent the rest of his workday thinking about what might have happened to this woman. He began to think this was another person in authority who had let him down.

After work, he rushed home, arriving at 5:18. Josh was sitting in the recliner chair reading.

"Hey, Ruben. How was w—"

"Did you get a call from a lady named Judy?" Ruben hovered in an intimidating posture over Josh, who bolted up from his chair.

"You need to relax, Ruben. Sit down."

Ruben didn't move right away. He angrily glared at Josh, who glared back. Gradually, Ruben's expression softened. He shook his head, then turned and sat down. He looked up at Josh. "I'm sorry, man. I got a temper problem. Don't mean to be mad with you. Don't make no sense. Just mad 'cause that lady I told you about said she had some news 'bout my kids. Said she couldn't talk right then. Told me she would be there on my break, but she wasn't. Told her she could call me here on your phone."

"Listen, Ruben, that woman is busy probably working on a lot of stuff. It was wrong for her to tell you she would be there, but you need to understand she may have had to go somewhere on some other city business. Whose phone did you use to call her?"

"A guy I work with."

"Did you give her that number?"

"Naw, man. It wasn't my phone."

"Well, there you go. She probably would have called you back if she had a number. You've got to get your own phone, man."

"With what? I ain't got enough dough yet for no phone. Um gonna get one come Friday when I get paid."

"All right, then. Just don't come bustin' in here again. My life is pretty peaceful. Don't need any unnecessary stress. I let you stay at my house out of kindness, and I'm beginning to see you're starting to get your life back together. You don't need to be getting mad at me for some stuff somebody else mighta done to you."

"I know, man. That shit was wrong. I won't let it happen again."

The men were silent as they gazed at each other.

"I meant ta say I won't let it happen again with you...I'll just put it on somebody else." Ruben slowly smiled, then broke into a deep laugh.

Josh continued glaring at Ruben, choosing to not react to his laughter. "Ruben, that temper can land you back in Quentin just as quick as smoking a reefer. You have got to find a way to control it. It isn't funny when you try to make a joke out of it. I'm telling you this for your own good."

"Man, lighten up. You ain't got to worry about me doin' anythin' stupid. I just got too excited, then I got let down. That would piss anybody off."

"You want a beer?"

"Yeah."

Josh went into the kitchen and came back with a couple of cold ones. They sat in silence for a few minutes.

"What time is it?"

"Five forty-eight."

"I told that woman she could call me on your phone at five thirty."

"My phone's over there on the charger. I'll take it off and see if there's any messages."

Josh walked over and disconnected his phone. He put the phone on speaker. "You have one new voice message." And then, "Hello. This is Judy Garcia calling for Ruben Scott."

Ruben stood up and moved close to the phone.

"Got your message but no answer. I'll be back in my office tomorrow at nine. Call me again during the same hours. Goodbye."

"See? She called you back. I'll give you my phone to take to work."

"Naw, man. I don't want to take your phone. Might lose it or somethin'."

"Man, just take the phone. I'm not going out tomorrow, and I don't have a problem being away from a phone for a day. I'm not a techno-slave. At least I don't think I am. You ever heard of a guy called the Unabomber?"

"Who?"

"The Unabomber. Several years ago he sent bombs in the mail to people he didn't like. Killed a few of them."

"What the hell he do that for?"

"It was his crazy way of protesting against technology. Said technology was dehumanizing people. He dropped out of society and moved to some cabin way out in the middle of nowhere and made his bombs."

"That's about some crazy shit. What happened to him?"

"They finally caught up to him. He's in a federal pen serving a life sentence. He wrote a long article they published in newspapers across the country."

"Yeah. What was he talkin' 'bout?"

"Basically, that technology would be the end of humankind as we know it."

"Man, that's bullshit. Even I know how helpful inventions are. The car, washing machine, 'frigerator. Ain't that technology? Where would we be without that kinda stuff?"

Josh hesitated and thought for a moment. "What have these inventions done for people? They've made life more convenient, easier."

"And ain't a damn thing wrong with that."

"Maybe not. Except I notice my cousin can't get her kids to talk very much about anything. If they're not watching TV, plugged into their headphones, playing video games, or staring into their smart phones, they—"

"Wait. What's a smart phone?"

"You know. The phones with the big screens. You can get onto the internet, buy stuff, watch a movie, play games, send messages to people. All kinds of stuff. You've seen them since you've been out of the joint, haven't you?"

"Yeah, I saw what you talkin' 'bout at the furniture sto' I was workin' at. Boss man had one. How come you don't have a phone like that?"

"Because I don't need it. I just want to be able to use my phone when I'm on the move. I don't want to have my head buried in a phone most of the day. Don't even like watching TV that much. It's not life. It's just kind of a fake environment created by somebody else."

"Yeah, but you do have a computer," Ruben said, motioning over to the desktop over in the corner.

Josh looked over at his computer. "Sure I do. It's good for learning and to find stuff. I pulled up other images of Jesus off my computer, off the internet. I research all kind of other historical stuff like the lives of Jews and minorities during the World Wars. There's lots of sources of knowledge. Problem is, the greater the technology, the more these computer hackers try to infiltrate systems. It can be like stealing for them if they get peoples' identities. They can sell the information or use if themselves. At some point, they may even be able to shut down electrical or water systems. All that stuff is controlled by computers now. That's one of the dangers the Unabomber was talking about. Most hackers would probably do that kind of thing for ransom. You know, 'You pay us a large sum of money, and we'll restore the system back to normal.' But some may want to do damage just to create chaos. Can you imagine having no heat living in New York during the winter?"

"Shit. I didn't have no heat sittin' on the Bay over at Quentin. I guess it might get colder than that in New York, though."

"You know it. Imagine trying to live through a whole winter with no heat. That's just one example. So you see that he might be right. As computer technology has evolved, so has the potential for catastrophic damage. That's one reason I only have a flip phone. Kind of my way to protest against 'progress.'"

"Well, hey man. You know people like new shit. If they didn't, there wouldn't be so many new cars out there. When I got out, that's the first thing I noticed. People driving around in all these nice, big cars, trucks, and shit. I thought, 'Damn, things sure have changed out here in twenty years.' I see you got an old car. What is that out there?"

"It's a '95 Volvo. Runs great. Roomy. Rattles just a little bit, but hell, it gets me around fine. It's just a matter of thinking about what's important. For me, it's not a new car. I can afford it a hundred times over, but what's the point? It's not gonna solve any problems for me or make me feel better for very long. But you're right, Ruben. People like new stuff. Autos, houses, phones. Whatever you can name. The fact that so many people gravitate to 'newness' is in itself dehumanizing, but it keeps the economy humming.

Somebody said we've conquered outer space at the expense of inner space. Just glad I found God. I don't really need much of a material life."

"I ain't really found God yet, but what I need to find mostly right now is my kids."

21

RAFIQ SAT THROUGH another tedious meeting of Alameda County parole agents. He wondered why meetings were held at all. Same review of protocol for contacting parolees, setting up initial meetings, avoiding forming friendships. All the regulations the veterans knew front and back. Rafiq had suggested to the parole administrator that the twice-monthly meetings be held for new agents only. The vets didn't need to meet formally. The department referred parolees to them via a secure website. If agents had any questions, they contacted the office for additional information. No need to spend two hours every other week needlessly. Most of the meetings reminded him of his study group in high school, devolving into a bull session without accomplishing anything tangible.

He glanced at his watch: 2:44. The meeting had run overtime again. "Typical," he thought. He was supposed to meet Fatima for a late lunch over in Alameda. He had one minute to get there. He stopped outside the hallway and called her.

"Hello?"

"Hi, baby. Just got out of the meeting. Are you there yet?"

"No. Didn't you get my text?"

"Haven't looked. What's up?"

"My professor kept us overtime. He wanted a verbal summary from each of us. It took longer than expected. He insisted I be the last to present."

Rafiq detected a vague unfamiliarity in his wife's voice. A quality somewhere between sadness and shame. "Is something wrong, baby?"

She hesitated. "Yes. I will talk to you at lunch. I'm just heading through the tunnel."

"OK. I'll be about ten minutes behind you."

"Love you, my husband."

"Love you more, baby."

Rafiq made his way down Broadway until he reached the tunnel. He was disturbed about the change in his wife's voice. He slowly passed through the tunnel, becoming more anxious by the moment. Finally reaching the restaurant driveway, he entered and caught sight of Fatima's parked car. He pulled up alongside her and parked. She had a tissue in her hand and was dabbing her cheek. Rafiq got out and moved around to her window. "Fatima, what's the matter?"

"Please. Come around to the other side and sit."

Rafiq sat down in her passenger seat, reached over, and hugged his wife, who was now clearly crying.

"Baby. Tell me what's going on."

She continued to sob, blew her nose, and then reached for another set of tissues. She held her hand up toward her husband.

"It's OK, baby. Take your time. Whatever it is, we can work it out."

She turned and looked at Rafiq with pinkish-red eyes. "It's my professor." She continued to cry as her husband rubbed her around her shoulders and gently kissed her cheek. "I should have told you earlier. He has asked me to accompany him to lunch a few times. I kept telling him I am a happily married woman and have no interest in him, but he has persisted. Today he scheduled my presentation last. When I completed it, everyone else had left. He walked over and hugged me. I could feel that his penis was hard. I tried to push him away, and finally he let go. He told me he was sorry, but he was very attracted to me, and he had lost his wife a few months ago."

She composed herself and looked at Rafiq, who was staring straight ahead at nothing. His normally pleasant face had turned into a frown.

He slowly looked back at his wife. "Baby, you should have told me about his advances sooner. I would have talked to him before it reached the physical stage."

"I thought that he would stop asking me. I do not understand men. Why would he not respect my wishes? I don't know what to do. I wish to complete my doctoral thesis, but I could never be comfortable around him again."

"When is your next scheduled class with him?" Rafiq said in a baritone tone his wife had not heard before.

She looked at him briefly. "Rafiq. I do not wish for you to become involved with this. I will go to the Chemistry Department chairwoman and file a report."

Rafiq stared straight ahead again. Not saying a word.

"Rafiq?"

"No, Fatima. Don't say anything else. You don't want me to get involved? I am involved. You're my wife, and you've been violated by someone who is supposed to be trustworthy. A professor. You know I'm going to confront him about this. You go ahead and go to a higher authority at the university if you want to. I have to do what I have to do. What's his name?"

Fatima fought against her first instinct to not reveal his name. "I wish you wouldn't. I don't want you to hurt him or get hurt yourself."

"If you had told me about this before today, I could have told you I definitely wouldn't hurt him. Now I don't know what I'm going to do. But whatever happens, I'll find him, so you might as well tell me his name."

She cringed at the thought of violence between the two men. She visualized both lying in pools of blood on the floor of the professor's office. Her hands began to shake. "My husband, please. I'm sure the situation will be resolved through the department. I'm afraid you might strike him. Will you promise me you will just talk to him?"

Rafiq looked over at his wife, his angry expression slowly softening into a more neutral look. "I promise I won't strike the man unless he strikes me first." He leaned over and gave his wife a tender kiss followed by a smile. "No violence, baby. But I'm going to put the fear of God in him."

She leaned toward him and revealed the name in a soft whisper. "His name is Adams. I think his first name is Bernard."

"Got to get back to work, baby. I'll call you later." He kissed her again and then went back to his car.

22

RAFIQ MADE HIS way toward the University Avenue exit. An accident slowed his progress, giving him an opportunity to look out toward Alcatraz and the Golden Gate. Instead he looked straight ahead, his mind in a swirl of emotion. Another man interested in his wife was not unfamiliar to him, but nothing on the order of this. He recalled when they were at an Italian restaurant. Their waiter ignored him entirely, coming back in short intervals to ask Fatima if she needed anything. Rafiq began to seethe waiting for his coffee. Before paying the bill, he wrote "It's impolite to drool" on the tip line. A flirtation by a waiter paled in comparison to this professor's actions.

He took the exit and drove up toward the university. Walking several hundred feet before finally finding the Chemistry Department, Rafiq glanced at his watch: 4:03. He stopped a tall, young Asian student walking in the opposite direction. "Excuse me. Are you a chemistry student?"

"No. I'm in premed but have chemistry classes."

"I'm looking for a Professor Adams. Do you know him?"

"That kind of sounds familiar. What does he look like?"

"He's a tall black man."

124

"Oh, sure. My brother had him for a class two years ago. He's the only black professor in the department. His office is on the third floor somewhere."

Rafiq's serious expression made the student's pleasant disposition turn suspicious. "Are you a friend of his?"

"No, no. Just an acquaintance. Thank you."

He walked toward the staircase. When he turned around, he noticed the student was watching him. Rafiq nodded before he ascended. A sign marked "Department of Chemistry"directed him to the right on the third floor. He focused on the fifth door to his left, which read Bertrand Adams.

He slowly approached the partially opened door. He knocked. A deep voice responded tersely. "Come in."

Rafiq opened the door. The man did not look up to greet him and said nothing, busy with paperwork on his desk. He had on a gray flannel sport coat with a blue bow tie crooked to one side. He wore horn-rimmed glasses much too large for his angular face. His upper body looked fit, with the outline of his biceps clearly evident under his shirt and coat. Rafiq stopped just inside the doorway.

Finally, the man looked up. "You need some help with something?"

"That depends. Are you Professor Adams?"

Adams hesitated, looking suddenly wary. "What is your name, and what is it that you want?" Adams stood from his desk chair to his full six feet four. He extended his hand. "Bertrand Adams."

Rafiq remained motionless. "You and I have some serious business to discuss regarding my wife, who is a graduate student in your class. I'm sure you know who I'm referring to."

Rafiq was surprised by how calm he felt.

Professor Adams face suddenly dropped. He took on the appearance of a caged animal. He looked off to the side, avoiding Rafiq's gaze.

"You haven't answered my question. Do you know the name of the student I'm talking about?"

Adams fearfully looked back at Rafiq. "Yes. I know who you are talking about. You must know I am very sorry and ashamed I acted in that manner."

"And what manner is that?"

"Earlier this morning, I deliberately had Fati—your wife stay late because I wanted to talk with her in private about my feelings for her. She is an exceptionally beautiful and intelligent woman. After she presented her paper, I approached her and hugged her. I—"

"My wife told me that wasn't the first time. Something about several attempts to get her to go to lunch."

"Yes, yes. I did ask her to lunch a few times."

"She told you no each time. Correct?"

"Yes, she did. I just thought that if I asked one more time, she wo—"

"Would what? Say yes?" His voice was becoming more agitated.

"You must understand."

"Understand what? That you persisted in pursuing a woman even after she told you she's happily married? A professor pursuing any student is bad enough. Even if she's unmarried. That's a violation of the rules in itself, isn't it? An immoral act, bottom line. You agree?"

"I do. I just lost my wife last summer. My life has been so lonely since. Then I saw your wife. I couldn't help myself. Please forgive me. This is the first time I've ever done anything like this. I've been a tenured professor here for twelve years. There is no excuse or explanation other than I got weak. I am so sorry."

Professor Adams lowered his head, his body slumped.

Rafiq spotted a chair next to him. He sat. "Sit down, Professor. You have violated me as a man and especially as a husband. I cherish my wife more than anything but God. How do you think you would respond if you were me?"

Adams took a deep breath now that he and his potential assailant were sitting. The sweat beading on his forehead glistened from reflected sunlight. He tried to gather his thoughts before responding. "I imagine I would be very angry. My first instinct would be to hurt the man who did that to me."

Rafiq continued to listen as Adams wiped his forehead. He looked back at Rafiq and continued. "You don't strike me as the vindictive type. The way you're handling this…you must be a principled man." Adams lowered his head again. "More principled than me, for certain."

"I respect your honestly, but that won't save you. No, I didn't come here to hurt you physically, but some types of pain are worse than lumps or bruises. My wife is thinking about going to the chief of your department. File a formal complaint. What do you think of that?"

Adams mouth gaped open. "Please tell her not to do that. That would mean the end of my teaching career."

Rafiq felt an upwelling of pleasure making this man squirm. He sat quietly for several seconds to enjoy the moment. "Even good men sometimes take pleasure in seeing a guilty man quiver," he thought.

"My wife told me it would be difficult to complete her doctorate if you remain her professor." Rafiq leaned forward in his chair. "However, I know how important it is to her. I think she'll be willing to reconsider. We don't want to ruin your career over this. If she agrees, we'll keep it quiet under two conditions. One, you keep your distance from her at all times. Two, you talk to her only when it concerns her assignments and only during class time. If you don't fulfill either of those conditions, she'll go directly to your department head and file the complaint. Is that clear?"

"Yes, certainly. You have my word."

Rafiq stood, turning toward the door. He stopped and turned back toward Adams. "One more thing. A third condition."

Adams's forehead was moist again. "Yes. Whatever you want."

"You will teach basic chemistry to our sixth- through twelfth-grade students next term. It will require a two-year commitment. You will teach three days per week, two hours per day. We'll determine the exact times later."

"Yes. Of course. What school are you referring to, Mr. Amin?"

"Our Muslim school in East Oakland. I'll give you the address later, when we fine-tune the schedule."

"Right. Fine. Just let me know. Once again, I am very sorry to have disrespected you and your wife."

"We'll let it go at that, then." Rafiq turned and strode out of Adam's office.

23

A DREARY TUESDAY reflected back at Josh through the window as he surveyed the street outside his living room. "Nothing. No change," he thought. He walked to the kitchen to check the pail he had placed near the stove. Finding it half full, he emptied it into the sink. "Should have fixed that leak during the summer."

He looked out the kitchen window, watching old Mr. Robinson next door raking leaves off his lawn. He wondered how a man over ninety had so much vigor and a willingness to perform physical tasks while wearing only a light windbreaker. Josh looked at the large circular temperature gauge on his fence. "Forty-three degrees." He looked back at Mr. Robinson and shook his head as his neighbor filled his seventh bag. He put on his large peacoat and walked outside.

"Hey, Mr. Robinson."

No response.

"Mr. Robinson," he yelled toward the old man.

Robinson stopped shoveling leaves, momentarily looking in the opposite direction, then went back to his work. Josh walked over within a few feet. "Hey, Nate."

The startled man lurched up. "Oh, damn," he said as he reached for his lower back. He turned slowly with a snarled expression directed at Josh. "Boy, what the hell's wrong with you? You oughtta know better than to sneak up on somebody like that."

"I'm sorry, sir." Josh reached over, in part to offer stabilization and in part to quell his guilt.

"Don't touch me! Jus' let me stand here for a second."

Robinson slowly bent back down again. "Shit. Been takin' care of this back for years. Ain't had no problem with it lately, and here you come."

"I called you a couple times from my driveway, but you didn't answer. I wanted to tell you how much I admire you coming out here like this and working as fast and hard as you do. Look over at my yard. I don't—"

"I know. You don't think I see how lazy you are?" Robinson said while slowly straightening up. "Got a man here old enough to be your granddaddy. I seen you watching me before. Would think you woulda done somethin' over there by now. Ain't you shame? Got an old man keeping up the neighborhood, and you ain't doin' shit."

Josh broke into a laugh.

Robinson continued to hold his lower back. "Boy, if I was twenty years younger and you hadn't jacked my back up, I would whup your ass."

"Let me help you with the rest of the cleanup."

Mr. Robinson offered a crooked smirk. "Uh huh, good. I'm almost done, and now you wanna help. Git your ass outta here."

Robinson turned and limped into his house, leaving his rake and bags. Josh watched the old man's front door for a while, then he took the bags and placed them on the curb. He leaned the rake against the porch, then walked over and entered his car.

He drove up Ashby toward the church. The usual congestion at Ashby and MLK was worse today. A man was lying on the sidewalk bordering the BART parking lot. A bright-red fire truck labeled Paramedic blocked the right lane, its red lights flashing in synchrony. Josh slowly passed, looking over in the direction of the fallen man, but the truck and bystanders blocked his view. He glanced toward the BART entrance. A diversity of humanity milled around under the eaves. Some were lying down with blankets and rain gear covering their bodies. Some who were standing wore business suits. They peered out at the sidewalk rescue scene while awaiting the next train. Josh remembered a different time before he got busted. He would drive by on a worse-looking day than this and not see nearly as many destitute-looking folks. A sure sign urban life was worsening for many.

He thought back to a key teaching from his father, a man who spoke sparingly but who would occasionally come up with some gems: "Son, in this world, there are two types of people, the haves and the have-nots. We live in a free-market economy, the best system in the world, but it's not perfect. I'll tell you a story about me. I lost my job working as a butcher at a delicatessen. I tried to find work but couldn't. You and your brother were very young. I had to feed my family, so I stole food. I got caught three times. They sent me to jail after that. Now, without someone to help me, I might not have recovered. A friend of your great-uncle Jacob owned a shoe-repair business. His name was Joseph Salinsky. Jacob told him about me. Not only did he bail me out, he also taught me the shoe-repair business. I opened my own store after a few years working for him. The same big store you and your brother worked with me at some years ago. The point is: if you get in trouble without someone who cares and has the means to help you, you're a prime candidate to end up with the have-nots. So work hard. Your mother and I may not be around if you screw up."

Josh thought about how his father's labors enabled his family to have a comfortable life. When his mother died several years ago, Josh recalled how diligent his father was, continuing to work twelve to fourteen hours a day at the shop, preparing meals for him and his brother and increasing the family wealth through investments. Anger overtook him when he recalled how his brother Isaac's consistent rebellion against authority shortened his father's life. First it was the suspensions and eventual expulsion from high school for on-the-grounds drug use, and that was followed by a seemingly endless stream of arrests. Josh began to see his father weaken. His once-brisk pace at home began to slow. He began coming home earlier from the shop, flopping into his recliner and falling asleep before Josh could bring his dinner tray. He died a few weeks after his last workday. Josh's mother died when he was seventeen and Isaac fourteen. A heart attack. Josh was convinced the constant confrontations with Isaac caused her demise.

He had begun to hate his younger brother years prior to that, for a variety of reasons having nothing to do with their parents. Isaac refused to take a shower, leaving a putrefying stench in the room they shared. He wouldn't do any chores yet would eat dessert treats his mother baked before anyone else could partake. Oh yes. He hated his brother and felt some sense of satisfaction in the thought of him being caged. At least for another twenty-four years. He mused over his own misdeed. Almost ruined his own life to get at his brother.

"Glad I turned to God full time at Quentin," he thought. "Without him, I'm sure I would still be in there." He was determined to do good in the world. Talk to more lost souls about Jesus and help his houseguest reestablish himself. He felt a sense of deep satisfaction as he parked in front of Uniteria Truth.

24

JIMMY TAYLOR STEPPED into the AC Transit bus at Ninety-Eighth Avenue and East Fourteenth Street, his anger over having his Chrysler 300 stolen blinding his usual acute vision whenever a beautiful woman was nearby. He walked right by her sitting in the first seat behind the driver as he stomped his way toward a seat near the back. The bus wasn't crowded. The lighting inside was bright, beaming off the head of a bald man sitting at the window seat in front of him. Jimmy cursed his sister. She had made him park his ride on the street. Said she needed more space in the garage for storage. Four days later, his 300 was gone. When she told him to file a police report, he looked at her and laughed. Not the kind of joyous laugh people knew him for, but a hysterical one born of anger and frustration. He knew damn well OPD wouldn't lift a finger to find it. Probably sold for parts already.

He looked out the window. The sky was beginning to show signs of blue forming over the hills. Just a few months ago, he had talked to Rafiq at his father's house. Junior had been one of his best friends growing up. Jimmy had kicked his ass a few times at Elmhurst Elementary just for the fun of it. Always seemed like Junior was out of place at their school. Real light skinned. Kinda straight hair. Glasses. Jimmy enjoyed whipping up on him. He never fully understood why he began to protect Junior from others who wanted a piece of him too. He would protect him, then kick his ass later himself. He laughed at the thought of those days.

"Things sure change when you get older," he thought. He admired his schoolyard victim for finding a life for himself. He wondered if Junior turning Muslim really had much to do with it. He thought back to several weeks ago, when he had eaten dinner over at Junior's father's house. It had been good to see him. He had been wondering if he ever would again.

Either way, Jimmy recognized he had failed at life up to this point. Regretful thoughts had become routine. He walked toward the front of the bus, intending to exit at Fifty-Fourth. As he stood at the door, he noticed the striking woman to his left. She had on a long blue wool coat. Her brown hair was braided, hanging down her neck toward her upper back. Her facial features closely resembled a movie star, but he couldn't think of who. He said nothing.

He continued to stare at her, wondering why such a classy woman would be on a bus so early in the morning. She avoided his gaze, appearing to be looking in her purse. The bus came to a halt. The door opened, and Jimmy took one step down before stopping. He turned and looked back at the beautiful woman. She lifted her head and gave him a faint smile. He smiled back, turned, and stepped off the bus. The top of the sun peeked over the hills to the east. Jimmy thought about a couple of girls he met in high school who had lived up there. So many years had passed. He remembered a jumping house party he and a couple of his partners had crashed. Big house. Old-fashioned drapes like he had seen in a couple of movies. Pop-up bar. Drank so much alcohol, he threw up before he could reach the bathroom, soiling his shirt and pants. He recalled the looks of disgust as he left. He tried calling one of the girls later. She didn't answer, and he never saw her again.

"You got anything on you, bruh?" asked an indistinguishable figure holed up in a doorway on East Fourteenth.

Jimmy snapped out of his daydream, looking over at someone shrouded in a quilted blanket. "Naw" he said tersely.

He walked another block up to Parker's store and looked in the window for old man Parker. An inside light dimly shone behind the counter. Jimmy knocked on the door and waited. No response. He knocked harder. Behind the counter a metal door opened, and a frail older man with a white short-sleeved dress shirt and a bow tie appeared. He wore thick wire-rimmed glasses, and his receded hairline revealed only small, white tufts on the sides. The back of his head was hairless. Intermittent patches of white and brown skin created a bizarre pattern. Mr. Parker's hunched frame slowly moved around from behind the counter. Reaching the front door, he peered out and unlocked it. "Mornin', Jimmy."

"Hey, Mr. Parker."

"That shipment s'pose to come through at seven thirty. Meantime, keep on with the inventory you was doin' yesterday."

"Aw-ight." Jimmy retrieved the inventory sheet and clipboard from a drawer behind the counter and went to work.

25

ARTURO PEREZ TOOK the Fifty-First Street exit off the 24 and drove up Shattuck Avenue. Several years had passed since his wife and infant son were killed in a fatal car accident. He had met dozens of women since, mostly in connection with his work as a bilingual teacher in Oakland's public school system. Few of the women sparked any interest in a long-term relationship. The two who did were already married with families. Most of the rest didn't speak Spanish, even the one from Puerto Rico. Various dating websites he perused showed some promise, but he never attempted to contact anyone. He preferred to wait, hoping that with patience, the right woman would come into his life.

He still missed his wife and the physical intimacy they had shared. He had often thought about seeking out a loose woman for sexual servicing. He came close a few times. He struggled to avoid masturbating as much as he could, but when the urge became unbearable, he would relieve himself, knowing a feeling of emptiness would follow. He could still hear his mother's voice when she had caught him a couple of times growing up. Masturbation was "the devil's way to corrupt boys from having healthy relationships with girls." Arturo always thought that was nonsense. Better to relieve yourself than go knock somebody up. It had become an indispensable part of his life. Especially since Marta was gone.

He turned right onto Alcatraz, crossed Telegraph, and parked in front of Nikira's building. His hands had a thin layer of sweat on them. He took a deep breath, exited his car, and walked one flight up to apartment 203. The loud noise of cars passing and a group of kids playing in front of the building muffled his hearing. He thought he heard someone call his name from the street. He turned and looked briefly but turned back toward the door, thinking he had imagined it. He raised his hand to knock.

"Arturo" came again from behind him. He turned again and saw a beautiful brown-skinned woman dressed in a long skirt and knitted red sweater walking toward the building. His heart jumped. He leaned on the rail watching her as she walked to the base of the walkway and motioned for him to come down. He smiled broadly and then rushed down the stairs to greet her. They hugged for a few seconds.

"I had to run up to the service station for a second. Hope you weren't waiting long."

Arturo was rendered nearly speechless by Nikira's radiant smile. He managed a few words. "No, no. I just drove up a minute ago."

"You didn't tell me where we're going."

"I wanted it to be a surprise. Are you ready?"

"Uh huh. Need to go up and close my curtains, though."

"OK."

As Nikira came back down the walkway, three teenagers walked by. "We should take that punk out," one of them muttered under his breath. They slowly walked past, two of them glaring back at Arturo as he and Nikira stood in front of his car. Arturo watched as the group rounded a corner and disappeared. He was angry but tried to hide it.

Nikira noticed his expression. Nostrils flaring a bit. His light-brown face showing a twinge of red. "Don't worry about that, Arturo. They're just boys, and you know how boys act sometimes when they get in a group. Trying to be bad."

Arturo smiled, then muttered under his breath, "Glad I'm not white. They might have tried something more than just talk."

"We don't need to be thinking about that kind of stuff. You said you had a surprise for dinner. Let's just think about that."

Nikira took a step closer to him, smile beaming. They drove to the Good Vegan restaurant on a downtown corner. Nikira laughed in surprise. "I've heard about this place since I moved to Berkeley. I've been wanting to come for weeks! You must be telepathic. How did you know I wanted to come here? I never mentioned it to you."

Arturo grinned. "You're right, Nikira. I am telepathic."

He had overheard her discussing the restaurant weeks ago, listening from an adjacent room as she talked with a coworker. Arturo was still smiling as he opened her door.

She looked up at him with a suspicious expression. "Uh huh, you're telepathic. Huh. Don't think so. I do think you have exceptional hearing, though. Leticia peeked around the corner twice when she was talking to me about this place. That must have been you she was looking at, right?"

Arturo kept smiling, looking innocently upward. "I know nothing about any such conversation. Who did you say you talked to? Letrina?"

"Uh huh. Gotcha."

"Yeah, OK. I confess."

She pointed her finger at him. "Just remember. Nikira knows everything, and if she doesn't know, she finds out. You don't lose any points for trying, though, and I'm very happy you brought me here."

She took Arturo by the arm as they walked inside. It was Saturday evening, and the place was packed. After a short wait, they were seated in the back-corner window booth. Light music played softly in the background. Arturo continued gazing at his date throughout. He barely heard or remembered a word either of them had spoken, and when his knee accidentally touched Nikira's, she didn't seem to notice. He was glad she didn't move as the electricity ran up his leg and through his spine. He wanted to tell her how he felt. Instead he held back, afraid she might consider it too early for him to mention "love." Instead, he glowed in the moment, content just to be near her. On the way back to her apartment, he nearly ran a light fantasizing about a long good-night kiss.

After he screeched to a halt, Nikira looked over at him with a puzzled expression. "What happened, Arturo? You trying to get us both killed?"

He looked at her but couldn't speak. What was he going to say? The truth? On the way up the steps to her apartment, he spat out a delayed, weak reply. "I'm sorry. Guess I just got distracted."

She searched in her purse for her key, saying nothing. Finally she turned toward him with a more relaxed look. "I had a nice time. That close call almost spoiled it, but I'm feeling better now." She leaned toward Arturo and gave him a light kiss on the mouth.

He gently placed his arms around her and kissed her back with a passion that she began to return.

Suddenly, she stopped. "That's enough. I'm not ready for a relationship based on passion." She smiled weakly and continued. "I committed all my emotion into my last relationship, and it turned out the guy was a cheat. I hope you understand. I really like you, but I need more time. You were holding something back when you got distracted on the way home. Something distracted you, but you didn't share it with me. I really need to trust the man I—"

"I was thinking about kissing you," Arturo blurted out. "You're so beautiful, it's hard for me to think straight. Like tonight, I don't think I remember much of our conversation during dinner. I was too busy being wrapped up in the electricity running up my spine when my knee touched yours. But I understand how you feel. It can be dangerous to allow passion to dominate a relationship early. I get that, but I've never been attracted to another woman the way I am to you. Not even my wife ever stirred up that kind of emotion in me." Arturo felt his eyes begin to mist as he was talking.

Nikira looked back at him with kind, peaceful eyes. She leaned forward and gently kissed him. She turned the key, opened the door, and faced him once more. "As I said before, it's too early…but I like most of what I see so far." With that, she said good night and closed the door.

Arturo turned and walked to his car.

26

MR. PARKER HANDED Jimmy his weekly pay just prior to the end of his shift. Jimmy reached down to pull up his pant leg, then shoved the envelope of cash into his sock.

"Thanks, Mr. Parker."

"You doin' good work, son. The girl I had before you just had a baby. She called me yesterday and told me she ain't comin' back, so I can give you some more hours startin' next week if you want."

"How many more hours you talkin' 'bout?"

"You working twenty-four a week now. I can give you another day. That's the best I can do."

Jimmy didn't hesitate. "I'll take it. You want me to come in Tuesday or Thursday?"

The old man scratched the back of his head. "Oh, I don't know. The deliv'ry schedule changes sometimes, so I don't know when they coming till 'bout Wednesday. So it'll prob'ly change from week to week. You all right with that?"

"It don't matter to me. You just tell me when, and I'll be here."

Mr. Parker smiled, showing Jimmy his gold and silver crowns throughout his mouth. "Good, then." He reached out his hand, offering his usual vice-grip handshake, which never failed to surprise. Years of lifting boxes and squeezing crates, along with massive hands, gave the diminutive old man a grip no one would ever expect. His physique was frail looking. His gait slow and unsteady. You wouldn't think he could lift a gallon of water.

Jimmy shook his head and smiled at his employer. "See you Monday, Mr. Parker."

"All right, son. You be safe out there." Mr. Parker thought about the dangers out on East Fourteenth. Just two weeks ago, one of his neighborhood customers had her purse and groceries stolen as she left. Parker had told her not to park her car in the alley around to the back. "You don't do that. Even in the daytime," he thought.

Parker had paid his employees in cash for years. Saved a ton of dollars avoiding the government. He had gotten away it with ever since he had opened. Auditors never came to the store or mailed correspondence. Maybe they just let it go since his store was such a small business. He wished he could pay Jimmy with a check. It would be a lot safer, especially with him having to take the bus now. He shook his head and dismissed the thought.

Jimmy walked to the bus stop and waited. He thought about his present living situation with his sister and what other arrangements might be possible. He had to find a way to get out of there. He was fed up with the constant bickering over chores, food, and his drinking.

"Hell, I only drink on the weekends and don't start no mess. Clean up after myself like a damn monk, and now my car's gone because of her."

He thought of where he might look to rent a decent room with the $500 he paid his sister each month. "Maybe I'll start lookin' downtown or West Oakland next week on my day off."

He turned his head left toward the unmistakable low roar of the bus coming his direction. He helped an old man with a cane ascend the steps and then got on himself. He took a window seat, looking around to see if anyone was watching, then reached into his sock to count his pay. He never did that in front of Mr. Parker. Didn't want the old man to think he didn't trust him. He pulled the money out of the envelope, shielding it between his legs. He counted out fifteen twenty-dollar bills. The usual amount. He wasn't surprised. The old man hadn't stayed in business all those years by not being diligent with his arithmetic. Jimmy kept his mind silent on the ride home. He didn't want to think about his sister, even though he was sure she would enjoy him moving out. Probably more than he would.

27

RAFIQ TRIED CALLING Hank for the third day in a row. No answer. He wondered if his father had been hospitalized or worse. They had been together at Hank's house less than two weeks ago.

"No need to panic," Rafiq thought.

He dialed Nikira's number. A Mary J. Blige song was playing before Nikira's voice came on: "Hi. You've reached Nikira. Please leave me a message unless your name is Leon."

"Hey, Nikira, it's Rafiq. I've been trying to call Dad for the last three days, but he hasn't answered. Please call me back as soon as you get this message. Bye." He had just walked out of Eastmont and was seated in the passenger side of his Honda. His shook his head as he surveyed the nearly empty parking lot, remembering a time when it would be full on a winter Sunday.

A loud roar from the west interrupted his thoughts.

"The Raiders must have done something."

Just as his thoughts returned to Hank, his phone rang.

"Hello."

"Hi, brother. Got your message. Don't worry. Dad had some kind of fainting spell Friday morning. I went over there to help clean up, and after a little while, he said he wanted to lie down in his bedroom. On the way there he got a little wobbly, and I had to help him get to the bed. When I asked if he was OK, his speech was slurred. I thought he might be having a stroke."

"Well? Did he?"

"They think he might have had a small one. He's better, but Highland wanted to keep him a few days for some tests. He's steady on his feet now and talking OK. No weakness or anything like that. They say he can go home tomorrow."

Rafiq felt simultaneous feelings of relief and anger. "Why didn't you call me? You know I would've wanted to know."

"I've been too busy shuttling between work and here. I saw Friday afternoon he was improving, so I thought they would probably have sent him home by now. You know Daddy. He's so stubborn he didn't want to go. Had to almost drag him to the car. Then when we got there, he started cussing at the staff. They had to restrain him in the ER and give him some sedation to calm him down."

Rafiq visualized his father dishing out hell at the hospital. He chuckled and felt a sense of relief knowing his father was probably going to be OK. For now.

"Do they know what might've caused it?"

"He hasn't been keeping up his blood pressure pills. At first, I didn't think to bring them to the hospital. I was lucky just to get him in the car, so I went back Friday night and brought them in. His nurse said he was behind schedule with the number of pills left in the bottles. They think his pressure spiked, but it's stable now since yesterday. I don't understand why Daddy would slack off on his meds. He's been good with keeping on schedule for years."

Rafiq knew the answer. He decided not to reply. Nikira probably already knew the answer herself. "Does Barbara know about this?"

"Of course Momma knows. She was the first one I called from the hospital."

Rafiq felt a modicum of regret in that moment. He wished he had made more of an effort to be a bigger part of Nikira's and Barbara's lives. The regret passed quickly. His strong sense of reason understood why Nikira would call her mother before him. "That's her mother, you idiot," he thought.

"Are you at the hospital?" he asked.

"No. I'm on my way back there now, though."

"I'll head that way myself. What room is he in?"

"Four twenty-nine."

"OK, sis. See you in a minute."

"Be good to see you, brother. Love you."

Rafiq hesitated for a moment. Saying the words to Nikira or Denard had never been easy for him. He realized he still harbored jealousy. Barbara was their mother and not his, but he had often wished she were. He knew he still had some growing to do in that area. "Love you too, my sister. On my way."

Rafiq entered Highland Hospital. A Latino woman issued his visitor's pass, and he made his way toward the elevator. Several people were turning impatient waiting for the elevator to release from the fifth floor.

"Somebody sure is rude," one man almost yelled. "Ain't but one elevator workin'. Whoever it is up there must know that."

Rafiq went back to the front desk. The receptionist was on the phone. A tall white man in a lab coat walked by.

"Do you know where the staircase is?" Rafiq asked.

The man didn't stop. Didn't turn his head as he answered. "I'm headed that way."

Rafiq followed him up the staircase, where the man promptly exited at the second-floor door.

"Hey, thanks," Rafiq said through the rapidly closing door.

"No problem" was the man's reply. It sounded as though the man was already several feet down the corridor.

The directions on the fourth floor led him left toward 429. He passed several patient rooms. Most of the doors were fully open, allowing any passersby to see clearly inside. He reached 429. The door was completely closed, with a notice posted that read "No visitor entry without staff permission."

"Wonder what that's about?" Rafiq whispered.

He continued walking left and stopped at the nurses' station. A short, middle-aged black woman was on the phone. Rafiq waited several seconds before deciding he was going to ignore the sign on the door. He knocked, turned the latch, and slowly entered. Hank was pacing back and forth in front of the window.

"Hey, Dad."

Hank stopped walking. He turned and faced his son. "Son. You got to git me out of here. Ain't nothing wrong with me. They makin' me a prisoner."

There was a knock on the door. Nikira came in, hugging Rafiq first and then Hank.

"Baby girl, did you talk to that doctor? You know—the one that came yesterday and did those tests."

"No, Daddy. He's a neurologist. He only came here to run tests on you. The nurse says his report will be ready later today."

"Shit. I can't take no mo' of this. I feel fine. Ain't dizzy. They say my pressure been all right. Don't make no damn sense making somebody suffer like this. When my regular doctor comin' in?"

"I don't know that, Daddy. Wasn't he here earlier today?"

"Not since I been awake. He the one that'll release me, right?"

"Right. In the meantime, you need to calm yourself down. You gonna make your pressure spike again on your own, you keep carrying on like this. Come on and sit down."

Nikira motioned to a chair next to Hank. As he sat, she noticed his bed was spotlessly made. She looked over at her brother, who continued to stand, saying nothing.

"You sleep all night in the recliner?"

"Baby girl, I ain't slept hardly at all. How you gonna sleep in a place like this? Ever' time I fin'ly start to drop off, here come somebody in a white coat wantin' somethin'. Yesterday I asked for some scrambled eggs, and they brought me some shit that was white and all lumpy. No cheese, no bacon, no flavor."

Rafiq said, "Dad, like Nikira said, they're trying to keep your pressure stable. You can't have stuff like bacon and cheese."

Hank looked over at his son with a frown. "I'm gonna eat it when I git home. What they think? I got a short life left. You think I ain't gonna enjoy myself before I pop off? Shit. That would be just stupid." He turned back to Nikira. "You think you can run on down to East Fourteenth and git me some snapper? I got to have somethin' I can taste."

"Daddy, you know I can't do that. They'd be smelling the fish all the way up here."

"Then you can 'spect me to keep raisin' hell in here till I git released." Hank got up and briskly walked back toward the window. He gazed east toward the hills.

"I'll put in another call to your doctor and ask the nurse to do it too. There's a chance you'll be released later today. OK?"

Hank continued to face east, saying nothing. Rafiq and Nikira looked at each other.

"I've got to go, Dad," Rafiq abruptly said. "I'll call you at home in a day or two."

Hank turned and faced his son. His expression turned from angry to sad. "OK, son. Thanks for comin'. I'll be easier to talk with when I git home."

Rafiq hugged Nikira, then left the room. Nikira sat in a chair next to the bed. She watched her father turn back toward the window.

"It'll be all right. You'll be out of here in no time. I'll take you home and make you a big, thick omelet with whatever you want in it."

Hank turned his head a bit, clearly listening to his only daughter. "You fry me some snapper too?" He turned completely and faced her with a little grin in one corner of his mouth.

She shook her head, and they both began to laugh. "I love you, Daddy."

"I know, baby girl. You my rock."

■ ■ ■

Hank was asleep in the recliner when his primary doctor entered at 3:25. "Mr. Roberson?"

Hank's body jerked to consciousness. He sat up straight.

"Your tests were all negative, including the CT. The neurologist thinks you probably had a small stroke called a TIA. You know, you're a lucky man. The charge nurse discovered your blood pressure medication vials were too full, which means you haven't been consistent taking your pills. Your pressure was one seventy-eight over one oh six when your daughter brought you here."

Hank sat motionless with a blank expression.

His doctor stared at him for several seconds before posing a question. "Are you trying to kill yourself?"

Hank tried to contain his temper. "Nah, Doc. I guess I kinda been thinkin' a lot 'bout my family lately and just fo'got. Seem like keepin' up with medicine ain't as important after you find out you dyin' from cancer. I promise it won't happen anymo', though. I'll do whateva' it takes to keep from comin' back in here."

Nikira entered holding a Styrofoam cup of steaming brew. "Hi, Dr. Wells. You going to let my daddy go home?"

Dr. Wells looked at Nikira and then turned back to Hank, letting out a big sigh. "I've already written your discharge orders, but I want you to understand one thing. You cannot, under any circumstances, neglect taking your medication. If you really don't like it here, there's a good chance that will keep you from coming back."

"Doc, I'm gonna take my pills. You prob'ly don't want to see me again any mo' than I want to be back in here."

Dr. Wells said nothing as he shook Hank's hand, nodded to Nikira, and then turned and left the room.

"I'm glad I can discharge you in good conscience," he thought. "The nurses need a break."

28

JIMMY TAYLOR WOKE up Saturday morning to the tantalizing aroma of bacon. His sister, Malena, was having a conversation with what sounded like a young man. Jimmy didn't recognize the voice. He walked over to the closed door of the bedroom and placed his ear against it. "You can stay here until March. Carol should be recovered by then."

"Carol? She must be talkin' to my nephew Horace," Jimmy thought as he listened more intently.

"Auntie, where am I gonna sleep? You don't even have a fold-out couch."

"Why would you need a fold-out bed? My sofa's long enough for you."

There was a long pause. Jimmy had stopped breathing to hear better. He knew his nephew was spoiled. Thirteen years old and never had a worry running through his big head his entire life. Probably be the first time he would sleep on anyone's couch.

"Your uncle Jimmy has my spare bedroom, and as long as he keeps up his rent, that room is his."

Jimmy pulled away from the door, moving toward the closet. He stood for a moment, trying to decide between his black jeans and a pair of cargo pants the same color. He pulled the cargos off the hanger and a speckled gray button-down shirt nearby. He thought about the strained relationship with his nephew's mother. Carol was just a year older than Jimmy, but the gulf between the two of them belied the chronological closeness. She had always been an achiever and he a failure. A psychologist with a successful private practice in East Oakland, a house in the upscale Montclair area, and a trial lawyer husband squelched any possible commonality between them. Jimmy had avoided contact with Carol for several years. He despised wealthy folks. They always reminded him of how little he had.

He snapped out of his thoughts after putting on his black-and-white tennis shoes, then opened the door and walked toward the kitchen.

"Uncle Jimmy!" Horace flung himself at his uncle.

Jimmy hugged his nephew briefly, never looking him in the eye, then lightly pushed him away. He sat down at the table, finally looking directly at him. "What you doin' here, boy?"

Instead of answering, Horace trudged out of the kitchen.

Jimmy looked over at Malena, who was standing in front of the stove with her hands on her hips. She looked at her brother with disgust. "You about the coldest person I know. Horace hasn't seen you in almost five years, and you treat him like you never even knew him."

Loud sobbing came from the next room.

"You know what? I don't want you in my house no more. You go ahead and help yourself to what's on the stove. Take it with you and get out of here."

Jimmy walked past his nephew toward the front door without saying a word. He turned and hollered out, "I'll come back for my clothes later today."

"They'll be in the garage. Give me your house key."

He removed the key from his ring and threw it through the open front door.

152

29

BARBARA PUT THE finishing touches of her makeup on before moving to her studio bedroom window. The blue lilacs that typically bloomed in April had begun to emerge early. With all the family complexities over the last several months, she hadn't taken the time to so much as open her curtains. When she did, a beautiful morning greeted her. Bright sunshine, a pair of robins perched on the chimney of the Johnsons' house next door, and, of course, the lilacs just a few feet outside her window. She felt hopeful. Hank had put her in a position of, if not prosperity, at least future comfort after years of financial toil. She knelt down and prayed for the return of health for her son. She opened her eyes, thought for a while, and then said a second prayer for Hank. "Please spare him any unendurable pain. Amen."

She went into the kitchen to prepare a cup of instant coffee. Her phone rang. She turned and picked it up off the bed. "Hello. This is Barbara."

"Mrs. Jamison? This is Dr. Rubenthal from Marin County Hospital." Barbara's heart seemed to leap up into her throat.

"I have some very good news for you. Your son has regained consciousness as of late last night. He is sitting up in a wheelchair for the first time."

"Oh my goodness. Is he talking? Can he eat?"

"Well, no to both questions. We still have him on tube feeding. The speech therapist will try to introduce soft foods on Monday. He's trying to speak but can't form words yet. The therapist started trying a communication board with him earlier this morning. He can see and understand words like *water, food, yes, no,* and some others, which is good news, but he doesn't understand anything said to him yet. He has what's called aphasia."

"Thank you, God; thank you, Doctor. You don't know how much and how hard I've been praying for Denard to come back to life."

Barbara began to cry tears of joy.

"Please, Mrs. Jamison. He's not back yet. We don't know how much residual brain damage he's going to have. Only time will tell how much independence he'll be able to recover. He helped the nurses with sitting up and moving into the wheelchair, and the reflexes in his legs are normal, but there's little right leg movement. He also doesn't move his right arm. He'll be getting therapy at least five days a week. We'll just have to see how it goes. OK?"

"OK, Dr. Ruben."

"Rubenthal."

"Thank you so much for calling, Dr. Rubenthal. We were coming to see him today. Now I can't wait to get there."

"I am surprised and happy with his recent progress. Goodbye, Mrs. Jamison."

"Goodbye, Doctor."

Barbara let the phone drop back on the bed without hanging up. She danced around the apartment singing "Ain't No Stoppin' Us Now."

After a few minutes, she went back to her phone. She dialed Nikira. A sleepy voice answered. "Hello."

"Niki. Denard woke up, baby! He's in his room right now sitting in a chair."

Nikira's lethargic voice came to life. "What! Are you sure you not dreaming? How did you find out?"

"I just finished talking to his doctor. Get dressed, Niki. I'll pick you up in fifteen minutes."

"I can't get ready that quick."

"OK, twenty, then."

"Momma!"

Barbara disconnected, rushed down to the garage, and jumped into her car.

Nikira answered Barbara's hard knock on the door. "That you, Momma?"

"Well, it ain't Yahoudi."

She opened the door and then stepped back, allowing her overexuberant mother to enter. They hugged briefly.

Barbara looked her daughter up and down. "It's been almost a half hour, and you not even half dressed."

"I've been going as fast as I can, dear Mother."

"It ain't fast enough. Throw on some jeans and a blouse. You wearing these shoes next to the bed?"

"If you give me a chance to put them on. Momma, you have got to slow down. I'm excited about my brother too, but you rushin' too much."

Barbara sighed and sat down in a chair near the front door. "I know. You're right, baby. But my baby is awake! Can you imagine that? Bad as he's looked every time we saw him."

"Did you call Daddy to let him know?"

Barbara's mood started to darken a bit before she checked herself and returned to a more cheerful demeanor. "No, I didn't, baby. I'm going to leave that up to you."

Nikira slipped on her multicolored blouse while frowning at her mother. "You know you should be cuttin' Daddy more slack. No reason why you shouldn't be calling him about Denard."

"There's really no way you can understand how I feel. Your daddy did a very good thing leaving me his house and investments. I forgive him for every negative thing he did years ago. Problem is, I can't forget. It's painful for me to even think about him most of the time. I pray for him, though. Just finished praying for him earlier this morning."

Nikira sat down edge of bed to put her shoes on. She did not immediately respond.

"You understand what I'm saying to you, Niki?"

Nikira looked up. "I understand you are the best person I've ever known. I understand you are godly. I do not understand how a godly person can hold a grudge for years. You say you've forgiven him, but I don't think so. If you had, you would understand that Daddy is in pain mainly because you avoid him. You doing that even now that he's putting you in a position for a more comfortable life after he's gone. Tell me how that makes you a good Christian."

Barbara looked away. She didn't want to think about Hank. Instead, Nikira was forcing her to think about herself. She wasn't liking that just now either. Nikira stood and began walking toward the door, avoiding eye contact with Barbara. "You ready, Momma?"

Barbara stood and reached forward, grasping her daughter's arm. She swung Nikira around to face her. "Give me a little time, baby. When God finally gives me the courage to talk to him again, I want it to be in the right spirit. Want him to sense I'm glad to be talking to him. Without that, it won't be good for him or me."

Nikira dislodged her arm from Barbara's grasp before turning back toward the door. They exited the apartment and started on their way to the hospital.

30

"GOOD MORNING," JOAN Davidson cheerfully said with a smile.

Mother and daughter looked at each other with the same thought: "Is this the same woman who rudely took our information the first time we visited Denard?" They glanced at the name tag attached to her smock: Joan Davidson.

Ms. Davidson looked directly at Barbara. "I want to apologize to you for my behavior two weeks ago. I hope you will forgive me. It's no excuse, but I was going through a particularly rough patch then." She continued to smile as she spoke.

"We don't hold grudges," Nikira said with a sarcastic glare at her mother. "I'm sure I speak for my mother when I say we forgive you. You're right, though. There's no excuse for someone acting the way you did. Hospitals are supposed to a place of comfort for patients and their families. You made a bad situation worse, and now it looks like you're overdoing it in the opposite direction."

Joan's face dropped momentarily. The smile turned into a businesslike expression. "I have your paperwork on file from last time. You're a few minutes early. Please have a seat. Officer Bartholomew will accompany you upstairs shortly." She nodded in the direction of a plump female guard stand-ing next to the elevator doors.

Within a few minutes, they were upstairs walking briskly toward De-nard's room. The same guard who was on watch with earlier visits stood outside. He smiled at the two women as they approached, then gave them a thumbs-up. They entered the room and saw Denard lying on his back snor-ing. The facial contortions and puffiness had noticeably subsided. He still had the feeding tube down his throat but no respiration mask. The women looked at each other and then sat down in chairs on either side of the bed.

"Do you think we should wake him up?" Nikira whispered.

Barbara shook her head. "No, let him rest. The doctor said this was his first day out of bed. He's probably exhausted."

She began to lean back a little, and then Denard turned his head slowly toward her, opening his eyes. He stared at his mother. His gaze was expres-sionless, with his left eye deviating outward. Barbara leaned forward, put-ting her head over the bed rail. Her son's mouth moved, but nothing came out. She reached forward, touching the less battered side of his face. She gently stroked him as he continued to stare. "I love you, baby."

Tears flowed freely down her cheeks. Denard's mouth moved again, emitting a small, unintelligible sound. His left arm shakily rose and moved toward his mother's face. She leaned farther forward, allowing his hand to reach her forehead. She felt his fingers trembling before he softly sighed, moving his arm back down to his side. He closed his eyes.

Nikira watched her mother and brother throughout their exchange. Bar-bara looked over at Nikira, who provided her with tissues. Both women wiped their faces.

"Do you think he recognized you?"

Barbara nodded back. Denard resumed snoring, his deep reverbera-tions shaking the bed.

Nikira looked over and smiled. "I remember when we were teenagers. I used to have to get up and go into his room to turn him on his side. Once a snorer, always a snorer."

They laughed. A deep, unspoken weight of relief lifted. They rose, went around to the foot of the bed, and hugged warmly.

"I'll be right back," Barbara said as she started toward the door.

"Where you going?"

"I've got something to do."

She made her way past the nurses' station to a quiet corner. Reaching toward her purse, her hands shook with excitement. She managed to pull out her phone and dial. On the fourth ring, a deep, sleepy voice answered. "Hello."

"Your son woke up and got out of bed this morning," she blurted out.

There was silence on the other end followed by a long coughing spell. "What you say?"

"I said Denard woke up. We've been here about thirty minutes. Doctor said he was up for a while in a chair earlier."

"Lord have mercy," Hank nearly screamed into the phone. "Two miracles already today."

"Two miracles? You win the lottery or something?" Barbara chuckled.

Hank's coughing resumed, only stronger and longer this time.

"You all right, Hank?"

"I'll be all right. Just seem like this coughin' happenin' mo' late..." Before he could finish the sentence, he started again. "Wish I woulda stopped puffin' when I quit hard liquor. I can hardly believe Denard woke up, but you know what's more unbelievable than that? I never thought I would eva' answer the phone and hear you talkin' to me nice the way you doin' right now."

"I just felt like I wanted to call and break the good news to you. He opened his eyes and reached toward me, Hank. He touched my forehead. One eye is cocked off a little, but he knew who I was."

"Y'all gonna be there awhile? I'm gonna call Gerald and see if he can ride me down there."

"You stop driving?"

"Yeah. I've had a little trouble seein' from time to time. Yo' daughter persuaded me to stop. Even took the keys to my Eldorado for a minute. She make me so damn mad sometimes, but I know she lookin' out fo' me."

"You know Nikira loves you to your core, Hank. She always has from the time she was a baby. Anyway, we'll be here for about another three hours. Nikira has a meeting at her school later."

"I hope y'all be there. Sho' am excited. You talk to his doctor ta'day?"

"No. It's Saturday, and he's already been here. Nurse said he'd be back tomorrow morning."

"OK, then. Thank you fo' callin'. You just don't know how good I feel right now."

"Bye, Hank. See you soon if not today."

"Bye."

Barbara walked back into her son's room. He hadn't changed position or expression and continued to snore loudly. Nikira had her headphones on and was leaning over the bed rail with her back to the door. As soon as Barbara came around, she looked up and took off her headphones. "You called Daddy, didn't you?"

She smiled at her mother. Barbara smiled back, saying nothing.

"He coming here?"

"He said he's coming if Gerald can give him a ride. Why didn't you tell me you advised him to stop driving?"

"I didn't advise him. His doctor did."

"Well, he said you did."

"You know Daddy doesn't like anyone telling him what to do. Even if it's for his own good. And I haven't told you everything because I didn't think you were interested."

Barbara frowned and looked away to the other side of the room. Then she turned back toward Nikira. "I'm interested now. You going to tell me what's been goin' on."

"Daddy had a little stroke and had to go to Highland for a few days. They discovered he hadn't been keeping up with his pills. He's OK now. Doctor told him if he didn't keep his pressure under control, he was going to have to go back in. You know that's the last thing he wants."

Denard stopped snoring for a few seconds. A long squeaking sound came out, interrupting the continuous snoring. The women were quiet for a long time. They stroked his body and listened to his loud, irregular breathing.

31

GERALD DANIEL SAT back in Hank's Eldorado, humming softly to "Ain't No Love in the Heart of the City." Gerald was leaning over toward Hank as he drove up East Fourteenth toward Ninety-Eighth. His cool "gangsta lean" was a lifelong habit. He glanced briefly at his friend. "Thanks for lettin' me put in this Bobby Bland CD, man. I know B. B.'s yo' boy, but you know he can't bring the cool like Bobby. Man, I can listen to him all day."

"Go ahead an' enjoy it, Gerald. I like Bobby, but I can't hardly listen to him for hours. Can't even do that with B. B. But you go ahead, man. Understand, though, that on the way back from the hospital, Bobby got to go back in his case."

Both men laughed as Gerald steered onto the 880N on-ramp.

Gerald hadn't seen Hank's younger son in years. He tried to picture Denard in his mind, but all he could recollect was a young boy riding his bike up and down 105th. The boy was almost always laughing. He would look over at Gerald working in his yard but never speak, never respond to his "how you doin?"

162

Denard hardly ever came over to Hank's after becoming a teenager. Barbara wouldn't let the boy stay overnight with his father, and it seemed to Gerald he was gone almost as soon as he showed up. He wondered if he would recognize him at the hospital.

Hank sat back and relaxed. That is, until they reached the Richmond Bridge. Riding over water always produced mild anxiety in him. The sensation was worse today. He fidgeted in his seat, finally slumping down a bit.

This didn't go unnoticed to Gerald. "What's the matter, man? We gone places a few times wit we me at the wheel. You turnin' scary on me or somethin'?"

"Man, just go ahead on. I'll be all right." He slumped farther down.

A light went off in Gerald's head. "Ooh. Must be goin' ova' this bridge that's gettin' to ya."

Hank didn't answer.

"That don't make no sense, Hank. 'Memba back in the eighties, we went back and forth to Frisco, seem like eva' month. You neva' had no problem back then. Must be somethin' else."

He looked over at his anxious friend. "Gerald, eva' time we went ova' there, I was drivin'. Rememba?"

Gerald thought for a few seconds. "Yeah, I got it. Matta' a fact, this the first time I been behind the wheel in a while with you in the car."

A rumble was palpable as tires hit the raised lane dividers. Gerald corrected, moving back into his lane.

Hank rose up and looked over at his friend. "That's why you hardly eva' driven us anywhere," he said with a straight face.

"Your drivin' worse than yo' ear fo' music."

Hank's mind wandered for a few seconds. "'Member Benny's party up in Richmond?"

"Yeah, I rememba'. Your head was all tore up. You was drinkin' Jack, 800, eva'thing you could get yo' hands on. Then when I asked you fo' yo' keys, you threw a hook at me. Memba' that?"

"Naw. I don't rememba' that part."

"Yeah. You missed, tho'. I saw that punch comin' a week befo' you threw it. You ended up on the ground. When you was down there, I took the keys out yo' pocket. You knocked yo'self out when yo' head hit. Me and Benny picked you up and laid yo' ass in the back seat."

Hank shook his head. "Don't rememba' any a that except the next three days I was sick as a dog. Only time I rememba' missin' work. Kept throwin' up. Neva' got drunk again afta' that. Make a left at the next light."

Gerald turned the Cadillac into the hospital parking lot. They stopped at the lot's security station. A thin, dark, younger man dressed in a gray uniform leaned out the window. He momentarily stared at Gerald with a suspicious expression. He lowered his head a bit farther, looking around Gerald to the passenger side. When he saw Hank, a smile of recognition revealed a beautiful set of teeth, marred only by a rather large gap in his upper fronts. "Mr. Roberson, how are you?"

Hank smiled back at the guard, who wore a large gold name tag over his left breast that read Tariq Armatrage. "I'm doin' all right for a man who can't drive his own car anymore. How you doin', young Mr. Armatrage?"

"I'm good. You kinda had me confused for a minute. I thought I recognized your car until it pulled up with someone else at the wheel." He nodded at Gerald.

"Gerald Daniels."

Armatrage reached out and engaged Gerald in a brief handshake. "So are you going to be driving Mr. Roberson out here from now on?"

"Sometimes. He's got family who can do that as much as me, but they already here."

Armatrage looked back at Hank. "Something happen to you, Mr. Roberson?"

Hank looked back at the young security guard with a quizzical expression.

Armatrage continued. "I mean, you don't have to answer."

"Naw, it's all right. I had a little stroke, and my doctor told me to stay out from behind the wheel for a while. That's all."

"Are you better now?"

"I'm fine. Just got a little dizzy, but nothin' lately. I'll be drivin' again befo' long."

Armatrage nodded but did not respond. He looked back at Gerald. "I need your identification, Mr. Daniels."

"What you need that for?"

"We require registration for everyone who comes out here to visit an inmate."

Gerald frowned but complied with the request. He handed over his driver's license.

"It's not as unnecessary as it sounds. Three months ago, an inmate came out here from San Quentin for an outpatient procedure. As he was exiting the hospital with the usual two prison guards, three men jumped out of a nearby van and shot one of the guards. The other guard wounded two of the attackers, who were hospitalized here and convicted later. The prisoner escaped but was found a few hours later."

Gerald listened intently, shaking his head. "I don't understand what that's got to do with me. I mean, those three dudes didn't register, did they? They probably said they was here to visit a regular sick person, right? Then they just hung out and waited in the parking lot."

"Well, yes, that's right. I guess I stated the wrong example. Something did happen here, though. I heard it happened several years ago before they started requiring parking registration. Was told it happened right in the hospital."

"Seem like eva'body should be registered then, regardless who they vis-itin'."

A horn sounded behind the Eldorado.

"That's a good idea, Mr. Daniels, but the administration doesn't want that. I don't think they want everyone around here to know that this hospital houses inmates."

The horn sounded again.

"Good to see you, Mr. Roberson, and nice to meet you, sir."

Gerald nodded at the attendant and then steered into a nearby parking slot.

After the required registration, the men made their way up the elevator and toward Denard's room. Nikira quickly stood from her bedside chair, moving toward her father as he approached the open door.

"Daddy!" She shared a warm, lengthy hug with Hank before turning toward Gerald. "Hi, Mr. Daniels."

Gerald nodded. "Nikira."

Barbara was standing near the bed. Hank looked at his son lying asleep before glancing over at his former girlfriend. Before he could speak, Barbara walked over toward him and kissed him lightly on the cheek. Her unexpected display of affection froze him momentarily.

"Our son is back," she said enthusiastically.

Hank directed his attention to the side-lying figure. There was no respirator, but the feeding tube was still attached through his nose.

"You say he was up outta bed ta'day?"

"Earlier this morning. His doctor says they're going to try to introduce soft food tomorrow."

A tall nurse entered the room. She had a natural hair style, black with gold flecks. She said "Hi" to no one in particular, moving in a businesslike fashion toward the feeding tube pole. She detached the nearly empty bag and quickly replaced it with a full one before moving toward the door.

"Thank you," Barbara said.

"Sure," the fast-moving figure replied as she exited.

Gerald was looking at her point of departure from his seat near the window with his mouth half-open. "I thought nurses was supposed to be friendly. I ain't been in a hospital for ova' twenty years. Never rememba' one of 'em bein' short like that."

"Nurses don't have as much time as they did back then, Mr. Daniels," Nikira said. "She's probably just too busy to socialize. I wouldn't read anything into it."

A loud, long groan seemed to rise to the ceiling. The group looked at Denard and saw his face change from peaceful to a grimace. Barbara rushed over to Hank, grasped his arm, and directed him over to the side of the bed their son was turned toward. Denard's eyes slowly began to open, wider than earlier, the cockeyed left eye still deviating toward the ceiling at nothing. The right eye focused on Barbara as she sat bedside in her chair. She watched the good eye track her as she scooted side to side.

"Hi, baby. I love you," she said tenderly.

The remnant of a smile disappeared from Denard's face as quickly as it had appeared. He tried to speak again. The sounds weren't words. Instead, "Aaaarahaaarah" was repeated several times, the last very loudly in frustration. Barbara knew her son was aware his attempt was futile. She stroked his head as he closed his eyes for several seconds. He opened them again, his left eye focused on her as before. He began to move his mouth again, opening it as if practicing to say something. He closed his mouth for a few seconds, then opened it, letting out a long "Maaaaaaaaaaaaa."

"Yes, baby, I'm here. I'm listening. I know you want to speak, and you will. You will speak. Do you understand?"

Denard slowly opened his mouth again, letting out "Maaamaaaa." He smiled a crooked smile with the right corner of his mouth while the left side remained limp.

"Yes, baby. I am your momma, and I always will be."

She continued to stroke his face lightly.

"Your sister, your daddy and Mr. Daniels are all here to see you."

Nikira brought her chair around for Hank. He sat next to Barbara.

"Look who's here. Your Daddy."

Denard continued his half smile at his mother until Hank leaned over closer to her. Denard did not divert his eye toward Hank.

"I'm right here, son. Can you see me?"

Denard slowly looked toward his father. His smile dropped as he looked at Hank for a short time.

"Do you see your daddy?" Barbara said softly as Denard turned back toward her voice.

His smile returned upon seeing his mother's face again.

A different nurse entered the room. "Visiting hours are over, folks."

Gerald spoke out. "The hours on the front door say they ain't over till eight. It's only six now."

"Those hours are for regular patients, Mr. Daniels," Nikira explained.

Gerald looked at her. "What 'chu mean regu…oh, yeah. OK. I got it."

Barbara stroked her son and kissed him on the cheek. "I'll be back to-morrow, baby," she whispered in his ear.

Denard had fallen back asleep.

32

RUBEN WOKE MONDAY morning to a loud sound that seemed to be coming from across the street. He looked over at the clock: 8:37.

"No need to rush," he thought. "Glad I was able to get today off."

His thoughts turned back to his two estranged daughters. He hoped Judy Garcia would be in her office. He would call sometime after nine. He put on an old robe and slippers that Josh had provided, took care of his morning hygiene, and then walked up the stairs into the living room. The din that had awoken him was louder. He peered out the front window, briefly checking out a few utility workers drilling concrete on the other side of the street. He turned and noticed Josh had placed his cell phone on the ottoman.

"He said I could use his phone today," he said softly.

His stomach growled as he made his way into the kitchen. Dishes were still stacked in the sink. He opened the cabinet underneath and pulled out the liquid soap and bleach containers. He turned on the hot water faucet and moved toward the upper cabinet. It usually took at least a minute for the water to heat up. He reached up and pulled out an individual packet of instant coffee, a cup, and spoon, and then he went back to the sink to fill the cup. The water was still cold. He would heat it in the microwave. With his black coffee prepared, he washed the dishes and then grabbed a bowl of granola. As he was sitting down, he heard a faint yawn. Josh was moving toward him, still apparently half asleep.

"Hey, Ruben. Morning."

"Didn't know you was here, man. Thought you mighta been up and gone down to the church again."

"No, not today. Didn't you see my car out there?"

"I didn't even think to look," Ruben said as he took another heaping spoonful of cereal. "They jackhammerin' across the street. I'd still be sleepin' if that didn't roll me out."

"I didn't think you'd be here either. What happened? You take today off?"

"Yeah, man. I hope I can talk to Judy Garcia today. Thanks for leavin' your phone out. Did you think I was gonna take it to work?"

"That's why I left it there in plain view."

Both men looked at each other in silence for a time.

"You a good man, Josh. I really 'preciate everything you done for me."

Josh rose. "Ruben, you don't have to thank me. I know you appreciate it, and I know you understand why I'm doing it. Five years ago, I would have never even thought about helping anybody like you."

"What you mean 'anybody like me'? You mean anybody black?"

"No. Just anybody in need. Black, white, green. Nobody. God changed my heart, man. I just want to act as much like Jesus as I can."

Ruben chewed more slowly, thinking about Josh's statement. "Do you really believe Jesus saved the world?"

Josh hesitated. "Not in the sense that most Christians think. Jesus sacrificed the pleasures of his human life to devote himself to mankind. He would give people food and water and not take any for himself, even though he was hungry and thirsty. Can you think of anybody who would ever make that kind of sacrifice?"

"My momma did that for us growin' up. She the only one I knew who actually did what you talkin' about."

"Right. But she's your mother. I'm sure millions of mothers have done that for their kids, but Jesus did it for people who weren't his kin. He did that for total strangers."

Ruben finished his last spoonful of cereal. "You right. But you asked me if I knew anyone who would ever make a sacrifice like that, and I told you. I understand what you sayin', though. It don't matter whether Jesus was taking his orders from his daddy or not. It take more strength than most men have to do that. I guess probably only a few people in hist'ry have had that kinda strength. 'Specially if they didn't know where they next drink or bite was comin' from."

The cell phone rang. Josh walked over to the ottoman. "No. This is Josh. Ruben's right here. Hold just a second." He turned toward Ruben, who was already standing with an anxious expression etched across his face. "It's Judy Garcia," Josh whispered to him while handing the phone over.

"Hello."

"Hello. Is this Mr. Scott?"

"Yes. Yes, this is Ruben."

"Ruben, this is Judy Garcia. I believe I have found one of your daughters."

Ruben was so excited he dropped the phone, catching it just before it landed on the ottoman.

"Hello. Judy? You still there?"

"Yes, I'm here. Can you come down to my office this morning so we can discuss this further?"

"Oh, yeah," Ruben almost yelled. "What time do you want me to get there?"

"I'm going into a meeting now, but I'll make sure to be available for you at eleven. Can you make it by then?"

Ruben glanced at the kitchen clock: 9:23. "I'll be there, Judy. Thank you, Judy. Thank you."

"OK. See you at eleven, then."

"OK…wait! Which of my girls did ya find?"

"Ayama."

"OK. Bye." Ruben dropped the phone and ran downstairs. "She found one my girls, Josh," he yelled as he scurried down.

Josh heard a loud bump, then "Shit."

"You all right, Ruben?"

"Yeah. Just banged my knee on the wall. It'll be OK."

Josh smiled and made his way to the kitchen.

33

"DON'T FORGET THE phone, man," Josh yelled at Ruben.

Ruben picked up Josh's phone and then speed walked to the BART station. He would've run had his contused left knee allowed him to.

The station was relatively quiet, most of the commuters having already made their Monday treks to work. Ruben removed the BART ticket from his tattered light-brown wallet, which had morphed into various shades of dark brown to black. A piece of the wallet's corner dropped onto the floor. He picked it up and tossed it into a nearby garbage can. "Um gonna get a new wallet after I get my phone."

An elderly Asian lady at a nearby ticket station was staring at him. He felt a twinge of embarrassment, realizing his spoken words were loud enough to be audible twenty-five feet away. He walked over to the ticket station next to her and placed his ticket into the machine. He added two dollars.

As he removed his ticket, he was startled to see the woman standing next to him. In her outstretched hand was a ten-dollar bill. "Take this. You should be able to get a good wallet with that."

He gently pushed her hand away. "Lady, I don't need no charity from you. I…"

She smiled broadly and then reached forward with her other hand, pulling his hand toward her. She opened his fingers, placed the bill in his hand, and then turned and walked away. He quickly stuffed the bill into his wallet and walked down the stairs toward the trains.

Downstairs, he looked up at the tickertape sign: "Fremont-bound train in seven minutes." He sat down. Josh's cell phone read 10:09.

"Plen'y a time," he thought.

The Asian lady came down the escalator from the opposite direction and sat down on a bench several feet from him. She looked straight ahead. He felt strangely ambivalent. Part of him wanted to walk over to thank this generous stranger. The other part, the prideful part, was humiliated from having accepted unnecessary money.

"I got a job. Woman prob'ly think um homeless or somethin'." He was still thinking about the incident when the Fremont train pulled up. He took a seat at the far end with his back against the wall. He had heard about a Mexican man and his wife getting stabbed on the train the week before. They had been assaulted from behind. Both victims were sent to the hospital. "If it can happen to them, it damn sure can happen to me," he thought.

"Oh shit," he whispered, pulling out his wallet.

"I don't even know where um 'spose to get off." He frantically searched for Judy's card: 1400 Broadway, Suite 601.

He exited at Twelfth Street.

Ruben approached the main entry of the Broadway address. He stopped before entering, looking up in awe at the sheer immensity of the structure. Reflected sunlight from a southeasterly facing window shone directly into his eyes. He looked down at the huge, golden-framed double doorway, seeing four doors instead of two.

He blinked a few times, clearing his vision, and then walked through. A security guard eyeballed him as he made his way past a group of men in dark-blue suits. He pushed the up arrow before looking back at the now-disinterested guard, his head buried in a newspaper.

The elevator door opened. Two well-dressed women were engaged in a heated conversation. They didn't seem to notice him as the door closed. The women continued. One moved her hand across her face in a wild gesture, smearing lipstick on the outside of her mouth. The two exited on the fourth floor. As the door closed, the tainted one seemed unaware of her mishap. Ruben smiled. The scene was so utterly entertaining. Two good-looking businesswomen arguing like street women, and one of them kind of looking like one as she exited.

The door opened on the sixth floor. Ruben saw County Assessor 609. He went left down the corridor. Room 611. He turned and went back until he reached Judy Garcia's office. Cautiously opening the door, he saw Judy standing there talking to a seated older woman at the front desk. Ruben took a few steps toward her before she noticed.

"Ruben." She smiled broadly.

Ruben smiled back. "Oh, hi, Judy. I'm here."

"You're early by about a half hour. I'm just finishing up a meeting. I'll be with you in less than fifteen minutes. Please have a seat."

Judy disappeared past a series of desks. Ruben heard a door close toward the back of the room. He sat and waited nervously. An official government clock showed 10:33. "Looks jus' like that clock they had in the parole-hearin' room," he thought. He briefly remembered the joy he had felt when his parole was granted. That emotion was short lived. Within a week his parole money had almost run out. Then they decided not to hire him after his on-the-job probation period ended.

"Motherfuckas," he whispered.

Judy's unexpected quick return snapped him out of his negative pondering. "Come on back to my office, Ruben. Let's talk."

Ruben stood up quickly. Too quickly. Pain shot through the inside of his knee. He groaned as the pain buckled him back down into the chair. He slowly stood back up and took a few cautious steps toward the swinging short door Judy stood near.

"Can you make it all right? Take your time."

"I'll be aw-ight. Just got up too fas'." He followed Judy back to her office and sat down in a chair opposite her desk. The excitement of hearing about his family made him forget about his bad knee.

Judy looked at him and smiled again. "As I told you during our phone conversation, I've found one of your daughters. By law, I had to contact her before providing you with any information. She could have refused, but she consented. Ayama Grant is married to Devonte Grant. You have two grand-children: Jamal, nine years old, and Jakara, six years old. They live here in California. Ayama teaches. Her husband is a truck driver. They have been married for ten years."

"Did she say whether she want to see me?"

"She does."

Ruben smiled and began to tear up. Embarrassed, he covered his face while reaching for the tissue box on Judy's desk. He wiped his eyes and recovered quickly. "I'm sorry. Just was scared I would never hear anything 'bout my kids again. Then I was mo' scared they wouldn't want anythin' da do wit me. I mean, they neva' answered my lettas, neva' came ta visit. This is better than I could of eva' hoped. Did she say whether I can call her or come see her?"

"You can call her right away, but she didn't want to decide on a visit just now. She knows you're working. You understand. She just wants to know you've established a stable life. That's why I can't give you her unlisted address."

"Well, when did she say you can give it to me?"

"I won't be the person giving it to you. If she wants you to have it, she'll give it to you herself."

"What about pictures? Do you have any?"

"Yes. But I can't provide you with those either. She doesn't want you to try to track her down."

Ruben thought for a while before responding. "I guess I understand. I'm just glad I can call her up."

Judy smiled at him again. "Ruben, I hope you understand your best chance of establishing a relationship with her is by being patient and following what she wants you to do."

Ruben nodded as Judy handed him a piece of paper with Ayama's name and number. Ruben took the paper, stood, and extended his hand to Judy. He embraced her hand with both of his, then turned toward the door. "Wait, Judy! What about Naima, my other daughter?"

She turned back toward him. "I couldn't find out anything about her."

Ruben frowned and began to turn back toward the exit before she spoke again. "But Ayama says she knows where Naima is." Judy's expression suddenly turned sad. "She also said Naima doesn't want to have any contact with you right now."

Ruben turned back toward her. He stood dumbfounded, not knowing how to respond. She flashed a weak smile before turning back toward the open expanse of the oversized room. He hardly noticed her. He stared beyond her retreating image toward an uncertain yet more promising future. A neatly dressed woman pushed the door open from behind, bumping his shoulder. "Oh, excuse me."

"S'awright," he said, barely looking at her while moving through the partially open door and down the corridor.

34

BERTRAND ADAMS DROVE across the Bay Bridge toward Oakland. He was ten minutes behind schedule this Saturday as traffic began to back up near the span's end. He cursed under his breath. Whatever was causing this slowdown would only make him later. The involuntary twitching of his left eyelid became more annoying. He thought he had had his last bout with that over three years ago when his wife's cancer began to worsen. He let out a long breath as the traffic picked up again. As he made the swing onto 880, his hand slipped on the steering wheel, causing his Acura to swerve into the adjacent lane. A blaring horn from his left and behind caused him to panic. He overcorrected to the right, nearly losing control. His tires screeched loudly as his suddenly spastic foot applied the brakes. The huge semi truck passed him, blaring its horn again on the way by.

"What in the hell is wrong with you?" he said to himself. "It's not like you to lose your composure like that." Streaks of sweat ran diagonally across his face. He cursed upon noticing this, reached for a tissue, and wiped the sweat from his brow.

Bertrand had lived in San Francisco for the last fifteen years. He had met and married his wife there. They had decided right away children would not be a part of their life. After all, they were both professionals, he an associate professor of chemistry and she a longtime manager of a high-tech company. They loved the urban excitement of San Francisco. Its theaters, restaurants, and jazz clubs were close to what Bertrand had experienced as an undergrad in New York. Close enough to feel at home. The commute on BART back and forth to the university was easy enough most of the time, but he was uneasy this morning. He had delayed getting ready for his volunteer orientation at this Muslim school. Today was a first. He had never been to Oakland. Never wanted to. He had read about the gang-related crime and decided very quickly that San Francisco and Berkeley had everything he needed. Why risk going someplace with such a bad reputation unnecessarily? But today he had no choice. He cursed again, knowing he had put himself in this position. He took the High Street exit off 880 and followed his GPS to the mosque.

Rafiq was conversing with the spiritual leader when Bertrand drove up. He excused himself and walked over to the Acura. He glanced at his watch. "Professor, you're fifteen minutes late."

Bertrand exited and walked over to Rafiq. They shook hands. "Couldn't be helped."

"Five minutes later and our principal would've been gone. She's not one to tolerate lack of punctuality. Don't you insist on your students coming to class on time? I bet you've established consequences if they don't," Rafiq said with a serious expression.

When the professor didn't respond, Rafiq raised his eyebrows.

Bertrand gave a nearly imperceptible nod.

"Let's go the main classroom. Our principal's in there." Rafiq walked toward the school building, which sat adjacent to the mosque. Bertrand followed with a less-than-enthusiastic gait. They entered through the sculptured double doors and headed down a short corridor to a large, half-open door on the left. Bertrand stopped suddenly to read the inscription on a plaque overhead, which read: "Seek knowledge from the cradle to the grave." Arabic calligraphy surrounded the perimeter of the plaque in beautiful dark-green and blue hues.

Rafiq turned back toward the chemistry professor. He did not disturb him. Bertrand was clearly fascinated and continued to thoroughly examine the plaque. After a few minutes, he lowered his gaze, appearing startled to see Rafiq facing him a few feet away.

Bertrand shook his head. "I've seen examples of calligraphy in various textbooks, but…" He looked up again. "I've never seen an actual inscription until now. This work is so beautiful, it looks as though a person couldn't have done it."

"It's beautiful because a person did do it," Rafiq replied. "A machine could never produce the humanity you feel coming down from there." Rafiq joined his guest in admiring the profound beauty. The blue and green hues seemed interwoven yet distinct.

"Do you know the artist?" Bertrand asked, still looking upward.

"No. The artist was a student here in the early nineteen eighties. Clara Rashad has been the principal here for over thirty years. She knew her well. Said she was a brilliant science student. Went back east to Princeton and became a physics professor at some eastern university. Sister Clara said she lost touch with her several years ago. You said you've seen calligraphy in textbooks? What kind of textbooks?'"

"I took a course in college called Scientific Achievements in the Muslim World. A rendering of a scientist in Egypt…I can remember his name was Ibn…his last name started with an R. Underneath the drawing of him was Arabic calligraphy in black and white. The lettering was smeared. No surprise. It was from a book published in the early nineteen hundreds by some British author. Anyway, Ibn was at the forefront of gains in physics, astronomy, math, and medicine sometime during the eleventh century."

An elderly woman dressed in a blue-and-white hijab tapped Rafiq on the shoulder. He turned to face her.

"Brother Rafiq. *As salaamu alaikum.*"

Before Rafiq could return the greeting, she continued. "This has to be the professor you were telling me about."

"Yes, Sister Rashad. This is Bertrand Adams, professor of chemistry."

Clara Rashad regarded the newcomer with a cryptic expression before lighting into him. "We regard timeliness as a key sign of good character in the individual. We insist our students be punctual. They understand if they violate this rule, there are unpleasant consequences to that violation."

She continued to stare directly at Bertrand, who avoided looking directly at her. He tried to think of an acceptable excuse. There was none. "I won't let it happen again," he said softly.

"I don't believe you will," she said, turning back into the empty classroom.

Bertrand wondered how much this woman knew about his encounters with Rafiq's wife. He decided he would ask him when they had a private moment.

Rafiq motioned Bertrand to enter the classroom. "I'll leave you with Sister Clara. She'll go over the specifics of what she expects from you in the way of instruction."

Rafiq gave the chemistry professor a brief nod, which was not returned. He turned and left Bertrand in the classroom. Sister Clara was standing against the far wall with her back toward him. She was reading what appeared to be a manuscript of some kind. Bertrand leaned to his left to catch a better view.

"Please have a seat, Professor Adams," she said to him in a commanding voice with her back still turned.

Bertrand briefly surveyed the room. Student chairs with accompanying desks were arranged orderly, in typical classroom fashion with one notable exception: there was a considerable variance in their sizes. Bertrand took one of the larger ones, very close to where Clara was standing. He sat quietly, watching her in anticipation. He sat for what seemed to be a few minutes while Clara stood without motion, still reading the manuscript. He noticed Arabic inscriptions etched into the front cover.

Finally. she turned and faced him. He thought he saw the hint of a smile coming from what had been, up to that point, an all-business persona. She closed the manuscript and placed it on Bertrand's desk. Bertrand examined the Arabic inscription on the cover and noticed a similar style to the design over the door. He raised his head to meet a broader smile this time from Sister Rashad.

"You're wondering if it's the same person."

Bertrand nodded.

"I'm impressed with your perception. Yes, it is the same person who did both inscriptions. She also wrote the syllabus for our chemistry class in 1985. Taught the class for a time before she went east to college. We had a high school chemistry teacher from Oakland High teach it for years using the principles and methods from this very document."

Clara picked up the syllabus, thumbed through it, and placed it back on the desk.

Bertrand checked the date on the inside cover: 1985. He looked back up at Clara and spoke slowly. "This syllabus is thirty years old. Most of it is probably still relevant, but not all of it. I'll look at it and make the necessary revisions."

Clara smiled at him again. "I know you will."

Her confident, almost smug tone sealed it for Bertrand. He knew Rafiq must have told her of his misdeeds with Fatima. He looked away from her and then abruptly stood, holding the syllabus in one of his oversized hands. "I'll take this with me and make the necessary revisions before class starts next Tuesday."

"Oh no you won't." Clara reached out her hand for the syllabus. A puzzled Bertrand reluctantly handed it over. She turned and placed it in a bookcase on top of other manuscripts. She slowly walked over to the front desk and picked up a much newer manuscript. She walked back over to

Bertrand and placed it in his hand. "The syllabus I just placed back on the shelf is the original. It stays here. I've given you a copy minus the front page. You will make your revisions from that. I trust you will teach in good faith. You'll find our students eager to learn." She smiled warmly at the chemistry professor, who turned and took one step toward the door. "Professor Adams."

He turned slowly toward her.

"In your verbal contract with Brother Rafiq, you promised two hours per session from the time you arrive. Today that time was two fifteen. It is now two fifty-four." She raised her eyebrows at him and waited for a response.

"I have to go to my car to get my laptop." He turned and walked briskly out of the room.

"I'll be right here, Professor," echoed behind him.

Bertrand clenched his teeth as he walked through the school's double doors and out into the sunshine.

35

JIMMY TAYLOR SLOWLY walked up the steps of the West Oakland boarding house. The dilapidated grayish-white structure was forty years beyond its last paint job. The upper portion of a railing hung limply, barely clearing the last step leading onto the porch. He reached the front door with strong second thoughts about the verbal altercation he had had with his sister five days ago. He was dog tired, having worked two straight overtime shifts at Mr. Parker's store. That wasn't the main reason for his fatigue. He shared a room with an older man suffering from apnea whose loud snoring woke Jimmy whenever he drifted off. He dreaded going through another night in this building where eight men shared one bathroom. The stench in there made him breathe through his shirt.

He pulled his keys out of his pocket, inserted the door key, and began the now-familiar process of readjusting its position several times before it would finally turn the lock. Two residents were watching TV in the living room. The younger one sitting in his wheelchair was always friendly. Jimmy tiptoed quietly toward his room at an oblique angle. It didn't work.

"Hey, Jimmy! How was your day, man? Come on and watch the A's with us. They gettin' ready to close out Frisco again."

"Naw, Rupe. Y'all go on and enjoy it. Um whipped."

"All right, then. See ya tomorrow."

"Yeah."

As he turned down the hallway, he could hear the old man snoring. He opened the door to their shared room. The snoring shook the tattered blinds covering the window next to his bed. The huge man was lying on his back with one leg dangling toward the floor. "Damn. I would try to turn this motherfucka, but he just as loud on his side." He grabbed his towel he had hung under the window, his soap bar, and a pair of dime-store shower shoes and headed toward the bathroom. Entering, he held his breath while turning on the water. He hung his clothes over the door and stepped into the hot stream. "That's the only thing good about this place. Water get hot right away."

Refreshed, he put on a fresh set of underwear before slipping into bed. The old man's snoring had subsided. Jimmy fell into a deep sleep within seconds. He dreamed about the beautiful woman he had seen on the bus a week ago. They had left a swanky restaurant down in Jack London. He opened the passenger door. Instead of getting in, she turned and passionately kissed him. After the kiss, she smiled lovingly at him. She turned to sit, and he gently turned her around for another kiss. She began to kiss him with even more emotion than the first. They drove to her house, went inside, and began to undress in her bedroom. She lay down and began to respond to another deep kiss.

Abruptly the bed began to shake. He woke lying face down with his arms wrapped around his funky pillow. He buried his face, wrapping the pillow around it. The old snorer had done it again. This time, though, he had awoken Jimmy from a dream of a lifetime. That was it. He rose from the bed, grabbed his pillow, and leaned directly over the top of the old man's face. He began to lower the pillow, stopping inches away from the slumbering man's nostrils. He stood in that posture for a few seconds before pulling the pillow back and throwing it onto his bed. He put his clothes on and headed down the street to a corner liquor store a few blocks away.

"That's it. I ain't neva' goin' back there," he muttered. "I'll find a place to sleep out here somewhere tonight and look for someplace else to stay tomorrow."

He was a block away from the liquor store when he heard a deep voice behind him followed by the cocking of a trigger. "Stop there, motherfucka."

That voice sounded vaguely familiar. Jimmy couldn't quite place it. The man moved slowly around in front of him six feet away. Jimmy's jaw dropped as a nearby porch light shone on the man's face. The man smiled. "Yeah. You recognize now, don't you, bitch?"

Jimmy's head dropped. He said nothing.

"I told you, if the police get us during a job, the rule is nobody turns snitch. You rememba' that?"

Jimmy raised his head. "Yeah, TJ. I rememba'. But they was gonna give me eight to ten, and all I did was drive. You and Al the ones who went in, stole his stash, and shot him. I didn't have nothin' to do with any that. The public defender dude told me the most I should get would be two to three, but he told me the DA was gonna give me more unless I named you and Al. I didn't have no choice, man."

TJ's laugh was more cynical this time. "Talkin' 'bout you didn't have no damn choice. Al down at Soledad for another twenty years befo' he even eligible for parole. You pretty much fucked up his life." TJ inched closer, waving his gun menacingly. "Only reason I'm out, didn't have no felonies on me and Al pulled the trigger. Can't get no job. Been lookin' for three years. Been lookin' for you too."

TJ moved around and jammed his gun into Jimmy's back.

"Go on down to that alley over there." He gestured with his free hand to a dark street offshoot a hundred feet away. Beads of sweat trickled down Jimmy's face. At the entrance to the alley, he quickly turned. Searing pain shot through his right shoulder blade. The second shot was more muffled. He dropped to the ground, never feeling the impact. Before his heart stopped, he thought about the argument with his sister and how that quarrel had brought him to his end.

36

IT WAS A sunny, warm day in early February. Nikira and Barbara had walked from Barbara's Lake Merritt apartment to a small café on Grand. After brunch they walked a couple of blocks to a bench next to the lake. Barbara noticed her daughter was in a particularly upbeat mood. They watched the geese waddle by. Joggers regularly passed in front of them, as well as a father with his young daughter in a paddleboat. The young girl waved at the two women as the small boat came back to the dock.

They were quiet for several minutes. Barbara looked over at her daughter. She couldn't hold back any longer. She had to say something. "You've found a new man, haven't you?"

Nikira laughed. "I can't keep any secrets from you, can I, Momma?"

"It's not much of a secret the way you've been beaming all day. You want to tell me about him?"

"I met him at work. He's a bilingual teacher."

"He speaks Swahili?"

Nikira looked over at her mother and matched her deadpan expression. "No. Arabic."

Barbara continued in a anxious voice. "Seems like just a few months ago you broke up with that bisexual guy. Is this serious?"

"I didn't know he was bisexual, remember? When I found out. I broke up with him."

"Don't get upset, baby. I'm just worried about you going head over heels with some new man when you don't know enough about him."

Nikira's daylong upbeat mood changed. "Momma, you know I'm not stupid. I learn from my mistakes. This one is solid. He lost his wife and child about ten years ago in a car accident. He's never remarried, and he's been with the district for more than fifteen years."

"So, you think he's the one. Right? Bet you've only known him a few months."

"I've interacted with him at work for more than a year. We've gone on a few dates, and he's been wonderful."

"He's Mexican?"

"Puerto Rican."

"You know anything about his family?"

"He's got two sisters. One in New York and the other here in Oakland. I met the one here, and she's very sweet. Treated me like family right away. She's got a grown son in college and a daughter in high school."

"Have you met them?"

"Haven't met the son. The daughter was kind of standoffish at first. She was better the second time, though."

"Well, that sounds good overall with one of his sisters. What about his parents?"

"His father died a few years ago, and his mother lives with his other sister in New York."

Barbara continued looking at her daughter, not speaking for a time. "You know Puerto Ricans and African Americans don't always get along."

"That's Puerto Ricans and Mexicans, Momma."

"Yes, I know that, but the Puerto Rican culture has some of that color prejudice thing in it too. There's a tendency for some of them to feel above darker-skinned black people. Even among themselves."

A small plane crossed overhead. It appeared a bit low but managed to clear the downtown buildings to their right.

"Have you ever noticed that high government people in Caribbean countries seem to be dominated by lighter-skinned blacks?"

"Of course. That's not something that's specific to Puerto Ricans, though. Besides, Arturo says—"

"That's his name?"

"Yes. Arturo says his family has always interacted with people of all shades. Says he has relatives in Puerto Rico darker than me."

"I hope so, baby. The test will be when you meet his mother and the other sister."

"Arturo says they'll be fine. They just want him to be happy."

"That's easy for him to say. He's a man. Was his wife Puerto Rican?"

"Yes, Momma."

Barbara raised her eyebrow. "Does he love you?"

"I've never felt so loved or desired."

"I already know you love him. Has he popped the question?"

"Not yet. We've had a general conversation about marriage and children."

"Have you talked about the responsibilities that come with children?"

"No. I've told him I love kids, but that's as far as I went."

"Do you have his picture?"

Nikira pulled her wallet out and showed her mother Arturo's photo. Long wavy black hair. Complexion about Beyoncé's tone. A large smile with dimples, medium-wide nose, and small ears barely visible under his hair. Barbara studied the photo for a while before handing Nikira's wallet back to her. "Handsome. If he's as much in love with you as you say he is, don't wait too much longer. If you know you really love him, I'm for it. Have you told your daddy about him?"

Nikira hesitated. "I'm not sure I want to talk to daddy about my love life. I'll let him know when I think he's ready."

37

RUBEN SCOTT SQUIRMED on his downtown barstool. His first time in a public venue that served alcohol in over twenty years. That wasn't what made him uneasy. He pulled out his wallet and handed the barmaid eight dollars. She stared at him for a moment. He watched her walk away toward the opposite side of the bar, gently rolling her shapely hips inside a sequined short skirt. "Damn. Eight bills light for one beer? Shit done changed out here."

A tall, casually dressed Asian man sitting next to him heard Ruben's muffled complaint. "She's not happy with you."

Ruben turned his head toward the voice and thought for a few seconds. "'Cause I didn't drop another dollar or two in her hand?"

The man nodded.

"That's a damn shame."

He finished his brew and quickly left the bar, walking down Telegraph toward BART. "Eight dollars for a beer. Last time for that. Next time I'll just go to the liquor sto' and take the shit home."

He felt his phone vibrate in his pocket. "Hello."

"Hey, Ruben. How you doin'? This is Rafiq."

"Hey, man. What's up?"

"Remember when we first met? You said you liked old-school jazz."

"Uh huh. I said that."

"A brother at the mosque is tight with the manager at this jazz club down in Jack London. He can get myself and a guest in tomorrow or the next night. You interested?"

"I don't know, man. Got to get up and get to work all week. What time they start?"

"Two sets each night. Seven thirty and nine."

"OK. How 'bout the first show tomorrow night?"

"That's fine. I'll talk to my friend and get the tickets from him later tonight."

"What's his name? Anybody I would know?"

"Ibrahim Al-Salaam. He's a drummer who plays at local clubs sometimes."

"Neva' heard of him. What's the name of the group that's playin'?"

"The Buster Williams Trio."

"Damn. Buster still playin'? Must be at least eighty."

"Oh yeah. Just as bad as ever. Can still do it all. Pluck it. Strum it. Bow it. Still one of the best. I'll pick you up at six. Text your address to me."

"I just got my own phone, man. Don't know how to do that yet."

Rafiq wrote down Ruben's address. "See you at six."

"OK. Buster Williams. Damn."

■ ■ ■

Rafiq drove down Ashby and around the corner onto Martin Luther King, stopping at Ruben's address, a well-lit single-story bungalow-style house. He exited the car and walked up the weed-covered sidewalk toward the front door. He looked around the perimeter of the doorway. Failing to find a doorbell, he gave a solid couple of knocks.

A tall white man with long hair answered. "Hey. You must be Ruben's friend." Josh extended his hand. "Josh Portman."

Rafiq smiled as he shook Josh's hand. "I recognize your voice from your cell phone greeting. Rafiq Amin."

"Come on in. Ruben had to run downstairs for something."

Rafiq took a seat on the sofa. He quickly noticed the rendering of Jesus hanging in the breakfast nook but said nothing. Josh came over and sat in the recliner. "Heard you guys are heading out to see some jazz."

"Uh huh. You a fan?"

Josh laughed. "No, no. Afraid not. I'm more of an old-school rock guy. I like some country. Gospel. Just never really understood jazz, so I basically stopped trying."

Ruben opened the door to the main floor entry. He had on a pair of black cargo pants, a long-sleeve white dress shirt, a mixed-gray sport jacket, and black dress shoes. Rafiq tried to hide his surprised expression. "Wow, you look good in that outfit, Ruben. Kind of makes me look plain," he said as he glanced down at his corduroy pants and casual loafers. "You ready?"

"Hell yeah. Pocket kinda light, though'."

"Not a problem. I got this."

Both men nodded at Josh, then made their way to the door.

"Good meeting you Josh Portman," Rafiq offered.

Josh responded with a smile. "Likewise." He had forgotten Rafiq's name and was too embarrassed to ask.

As Rafiq drove down Ashby to the freeway, a thought occurred to him. "Listen, Ruben. You know Muslims don't imbibe alcohol, right?"

Ruben thought about the question for a bit. "You mean you don't consume alcoholic beverages," he said in a gruff tone. "But you don't mind if your company drinks, do ya?"

"I would prefer you don't, but if you decide you want to, that's your choice."

With that, Ruben understood Rafiq would not pay for any alcoholic drinks at the set.

Rafiq glanced over at Ruben. "Yes, I know what you're thinking. When I told you 'I got this,' that doesn't include alcohol. You're on your own with that."

"'S'awl right, man. I understand. We goin' to hear a jazz master. That's enough for me."

Ruben reached his hand over, and Rafiq responded with a fist pump.

They exited on Broadway and entered the spacious parking lot opposite the movie theater. In the elevator, Rafiq pulled out his wallet and handed Ruben his ticket. He glanced at his watch. "Seven oh two."

Entering the front door, they made their way toward the usher standing beyond the ticket booth. A Japanese woman took their tickets, smiling at both men. "You may sit anywhere where there is no reservation sign."

They made their way down to a small table directly in front of the stage. Three well-dressed black women sitting at the adjacent table were having a lively conversation. One looked over at the men and smiled. Ruben looked to the far-right wall at a line of photos. He looked back to his left at Rafiq. "Those got to be jazz photos."

"Yeah, man. Some of the greats. Most of them have appeared here."

A waitress stopped at their table. "Can I get you gentlemen started with anything?"

"I'll have cranberry juice. Ruben?"

"A Coke is good."

"You like sweet potato fries?" Rafiq asked.

"Hey, that's sounds real good."

"We'll have two orders of that as well."

"You got it." She turned and made her way to the next table.

Ruben leaned over and whispered, "I didn't know they made fries outta sweet potatoes."

Rafiq smiled. "You got to get out more, brother."

Ruben looked at him with a blank expression. He turned back toward the stage.

The MC grabbed the mic and began the introduction. "Ladies and gentleman, you're in for a special treat tonight. We present a man who cut his teeth with Thelonious Monk and anchored the fabulous group Sphere during the nineteen eighties, as well as playing with a host of many other great musicians since. Please put your hands together for the Buster Williams Trio."

A loud, lengthy applause followed. Buster acknowledged with a bow. As the music began, Ruben turned to survey the room. He leaned over toward Rafiq. "Most of these people in here younger than me. How they know 'bout Buster Williams?"

"Let's talk later about that. I don't want to miss a note of this."

"Aw-ight." Ruben leaned back. His stomach growled.

"Wonder when those fries gonna get here?" he thought.

Within a minute, their fries and drinks arrived. Ruben watched as Rafiq handed over a twenty and a ten. The smiling hostess nodded agreeably at Rafiq, who didn't seem to notice, his head and foot moving in unison to the music.

Ruben went to work on his fries and drink, alternating his attention between the snack and the music. He suddenly stopped in midbite. Buster had pulled out his bow and was performing a mesmerizing solo of "Emily." Ruben sat motionlessly as Buster dropped the bow and began to strum the upright instrument, playing chords with precision and soul Ruben didn't remember hearing on his recordings. The crowd was quietly engaged, aside from an occasional "yeah" and "damn" coming from a booth way back in the upper section of the club.

When Buster finished his solo, the club erupted as he and the group finished the tune. The people at the tables adjacent to them stood, shouted, and applauded. Rafiq turned toward Ruben and saw a look of pure joy etched on his companion's face. Ruben was shaking his head. A broad smile. Shiny eyes. The kind of eyes one might see from a child opening presents on his birthday.

After the last tune of the set, a tribute to Buster's daughter called "Christine," the crowd rose for one final applause. The musicians bowed before exiting the stage. Rafiq turned toward Ruben and asked a question. "Well, what do you think about that?"

"Man, I expected this shit to be special, but it went way past that. My daddy used to play jazz records at home whenever Momma wasn't there. I hadn't eva' heard no upright player pull out a bow and play like that. Then he started strummin' that motherfu…that thing like a guitar. Damn. Um gonna be hearin' that shit in my sleep."

Rafiq smiled at him. "Glad you enjoyed yourself, brother. You just heard one of the greatest jazz bassists to ever walk the face of the earth."

"Yeah. No doubt. Thanks for askin' me to come, man, but I gots to git home and git ready fo' work in the mornin'."

They walked briskly back to the car and drove back to Josh's place. Ruben opened his door and began to exit.

"Hey, Ruben."

"What's up?"

"Josh have a CD player in there?"

"Yeah, man. But he be playin' shit that's too white for me."

"You got any CDs?"

"Nah, man. I ain't had the time or dough to be thinkin' 'bout buyin' my own shit."

"You don't have to. I can burn you one of Buster's CDs if you want. Will Josh let you play your own tunes?"

Ruben thought for second. "I neva' asked him. Don't think it would be a problem, though."

"All right. Tell you what. If I don't hear from you in a few days, I'll just drop it in the mailbox."

"Coo'. Later, Rafiq."

"Good night, my friend. Have a good week."

Ruben walked up to the doorstep, then turned around to watch the Honda drive down Martin Luther King and into the distance. He felt good as he inserted the key and turned the knob.

38

NIKIRA WAS STILL at work. It was 5:48 p.m. Friday. It had been a busy week. Extra tutoring after school for three students who had fallen behind. Frustrating sessions with the students' mothers. Two of the single mothers were simply too busy to provide enough structure at home for their kids to study. The remaining mother had stopped trying. She sat in Nikira's empty classroom looking exasperated and dog tired. She had large, shapely lips. The left lower corner of her mouth drooped. Sagging dark-brown bags under her eyes contrasted against her light-brown complexion. Her husband was a construction worker who, according to the mother, was physically abusive.

"Mrs. Jackson?"

"Oh, please. Right now I'd prefer you call me by my first name, Josette."

Nikira smiled. "Sure. I asked you here because Ernest isn't doing well with his classwork or getting along with other students."

Nikira paused as Josette reached into her purse for a Kleenex.

"He not responding well to after-school tutoring either. Is there a problem at home?"

"His daddy keeps arguing with me that school isn't important. Says our son will work with him on his construction jobs once he gets old enough. I keep telling him there might not be no construction jobs in another ten years, and our son needs to get an education so he can do something else. Whenever I bring it up, he gets mad and just ends up drinking more."

"He's an alcoholic?"

"He drinks at least a half bottle of whiskey every night after work."

"Does he get physical with you?"

"He's slapped me a few times. I don't know how much more I can put up with. I mean, he makes good money. We have good insurance. A nice house."

"How long y'all been married?"

"Ten years."

"Did you tell him I'd like to talk with him about your son?"

"I brought it up a couple of times. He's got a bad temper about stuff he doesn't want to hear."

"What you said earlier—about construction jobs becoming more diffi-cult to get and keep—is true. I have the statistics to prove that. Do you think me sending him a letter about that would help?"

"I think he'll get mad and take it out on me or my son. He hollers and cusses 'bout every day, and I think I've had enough. He wasn't like that when we first started going together."

"Our principal has gone into some parents' homes for counseling. May-be your husband would rather talk to a man."

The tired woman shrugged. "I don't think anything's going to help at this point. I would have taken my son and left, but I really don't have any-where to go. I want a better future for him than what he's seeing right now, and the last thing I want is for him to turn out like his daddy."

"Do you work?"

"No. I've never worked since we've been together."

"Maybe you should consider looking for work."

"My husband won't let me. Says he makes enough money."

Nikira inhaled deeply, then slowly reached into her desk. "I'm going to give you the name and address of my County Employment Agency contact person. My recommendation is that you begin to seek employment." She handed Josette a business card.

Distraught over her situation, Josette began to sob. "Thank you, Miss Roberson. I guess I don't have a choice."

Nikira nodded in agreement. "Once you get a job, you can begin to apply for housing assistance immediately. If you start to apply without employment, you'll only get frustrated because the County Housing Authority is already backed up with applications. Once you start working, you can seek out housing on your own. You might have to go outside the county, though. You have your own car?"

"Yes. It's in my husband's name, though."

"Doesn't matter. Try the employment agency first. You might also want to begin looking on your own."

Josette continued to wipe tears away. "I'm so scared of what my husband might do if he found out. Even if I get a job and a place, he'll come looking for me and my son. I don't know what he might do."

"I wish I could suggest something different, but you're right. You don't have a choice. You've got a husband who's basically holding you and your son captive. I can understand your fear. I'd be afraid too. You just have to remember your son's future is at stake. Yours as well."

Josette placed the tissue back into her purse as Nikira rose from her chair and approached her. Josette began crying again as Nikira hugged her warmly. "You can do this, Josette. Keep Ernest enrolled here until you find a job and a place to stay. Work during the day when your husband's at work. Get a PO box. As soon as you get established, get an attorney to help you file papers for support and maybe a restraining order. It's even possible your husband will agree to counseling with you once he understands you're serious."

Josette rose from her chair and slowly made her way toward the classroom door. Nikira stared at the door until the sound of Josette's footsteps dissipated into the distance. She walked back over to her desk and buried her head in her hands.

Nikira made her way up Seventy-Third toward 580. She missed the 24 off ramp and had to take the West Street exit instead. Up MacArthur to Telegraph and eventually home. Her phone rang as she was unlocking the door to her apartment.

"Hello, Momma."

"Baby. You sound so tired. You still want to go see that movie?"

"I don't want to do anything right now but sleep. Crazy week at school. Can't remember the last time I was this tired. Maybe tomorrow."

"OK, baby. You get some good rest now. I'm going out to see Denard tomorrow. You think you might want to go?"

"I don't know right now. Has he gotten any better since last week?"

"They got him walking a few steps in his room, and he's spending more time out of bed. They say he's eating a soft diet just fine. I can't wait to see him."

Nikira sighed, still feeling the weight of the evening's classroom encounter. "I don't know. I think I might need to just stay here in bed the whole day. I'll call you late in the morning."

"Call before eleven, 'cause I'm leaving by then."

"OK."

"Good night, Niki."

"Good night, Momma." Nikira went into the bathroom, plugged the tub, and ran the water. She poured a glass of cabernet, returned to the bathroom, undressed, and slowly lowered herself into the barely tolerable hot water. Her telephone rang.

"Probably Arturo," she thought. She started to get of the tub to retrieve the phone she had left on the bed. Quickly changing her mind, she eased back down. She took a couple of sips of wine and then placed the glass on the edge of the tub before falling asleep seconds later.

39

THE PHONE RANG on the bench where Hank had placed his gardening tools. He had harvested the bounty from his tomato plants and was enjoying the warmth of the noonday sun beaming onto the back of his neck. He didn't attempt to respond to the phone call. Wouldn't have been able to raise up out of his low squatter chair and get there in time anyway. He continued to linger there. Every now and then he moved his right foot up and down, which would temporarily stop the buzzing running down to his ankle.

"Wish I knew what the hell is goin' on with that," he spoke out loud. He wondered if the cancer was beginning to break down his joints. The doctor had informed him he might have any number of sensations as the disease spread through his lower spine. Maybe this was the first of them. He stopped thinking about it, stood up, stepped, and put weight on his right leg. The buzzing got worse. He grabbed his cane off the picnic table and put it down next to his foot. Hobbling for the first few steps, he went over and picked up his phone: "1 voice mail." The annoying sensation eased up as he turned and walked toward the house.

By the time he got to the back door, he didn't need his cane. The buzzing was gone, for now.

"I hope this shit doesn't come back later tonight," he thought. "Tired of wakin' up all the time. Either got to piss or shake my damn foot."

He continued to mutter to himself as he walked over to the kitchen table, sat down, and listened to the message: "Hank. Hey it's Barbara. Going to the hospital pretty soon. Thought you might want to come out and see your son. Let me know. I should be out there around noon. Bye."

Disgusted, he dropped his phone on the table. "How the hell I'm supposed to get there? Doctor okayed me to drive again, but now, with this foot actin' up…and Gerald in Arkansas."

His pride kept him from calling Barbara, Nikira, or Rafiq. He cussed up a storm right there in the kitchen. Suddenly tired, he went into the bedroom to lie down. His eyes closed for almost a half hour before the buzzing in his foot woke him. He cursed and in a fit of anger threw his body up to a seated position. Not waiting for dizziness or the buzzing to subside, he stood without his cane and nearly fell forward before gaining his balance. The sun shone through a small crack between his bedroom blinds against the opposite wall. He took a couple of steps, then stopped. A large reprint of a photograph taken in the sixties caught his attention. He hadn't looked at it for several months. Muddy Waters after a show at the Oakland Auditorium. A horizontal sliver of light from the window gleamed off Muddy's eyes, giving him a surreal look of wonder and power. Hank had owned the photo for over forty years but had never seen it portrayed like this.

He stood for several seconds until the afternoon light rose up to Muddy's forehead, eliminating the temporary effect. During the interlude, his anger had subsided even though the buzzing in his leg hadn't. He shook his head, continued toward the living room, and sat in his recliner next to the house phone.

"Um gonna eat what I wanna eat from now on."

Within forty minutes he heard a knock.

"Who is it?"

A confident female voice responded. "Oakland Fish Market. I got your order here, sir."

"The door's open. Come on in."

A thin, medium-brown woman entered. She held a large bag in one hand and what appeared to be a Taser in the other. Hank noticed the aroma of fried sand dabs as soon as she entered. He looked at the woman's right hand. She placed the Taser she had been holding into a pouch pocket attached to her waist.

Hank laughed. "Guess I must look kinda harmless fo' you to put that thing away so quick."

The cheerful caterer walked over to the large end table and placed the bag of food next to a lamp. "I can usually tell if I'm in any danger. You don't look like you'd start any mess."

"You mean 'cause I'm old?"

The woman hesitated for a moment, searching her mind for a diplomatic response. "Well, yeah. That's part of it. The other part is you have a neat house. I deliver sometimes to folks that just don't have no decency like that. Most of them are younger or closer to my age. Got keep my Tase out for a minute with them, but I get in and out OK almost all the time."

She looked at Hank waiting for a response. None was coming. "Four pieces of dabs, a large collard greens, four slices of wheat bread, and a large banana pudding. That comes to thirty-five eighty-seven total, including the ten-dollar delivery fee, Mr. Robinson."

"Roberson."

"Oh, sorry, Mr. Roberson."

Hank pulled a fifty-dollar bill out and handed it over. "Keep that."

She looked suspiciously at the bill. "Sir, we don't normally accept bills larger than a twenty, but you don't look like the type who would cheat."

She placed the bill in the same pocket as the Taser, said her thanks, then left.

Hank took the bag off the end table. The aroma of the fish was so delicious, he wanted to take the food out and eat it right there at the kitchen table. But he noticed it was lukewarm. "Can't eat fish 'less it's right."

He turned on his toaster oven, grabbed a metal pan, and placed the sand dabs across it. Turning back toward the kitchen table, he picked up the last remnant of hot sauce and sprinkled it on two of the four pieces before it emptied.

"Damn. Got to be some mo' 'round here somewhere." He search through every cabinet and came up empty. He opened the refrigerator. Same thing until he looked over at the door shelf. There sat a full bottle of hot sauce. He pulled the bottle out and finished sprinkling a liberal amount on the remaining two pieces, then added more to the first two. He placed the pan in the oven and the collards into the microwave. He sat, waited, and wondered. "How in the hell did that hot sauce get into the house?"

He walked back over to the refrigerator, opened it, and lying flat underneath where the hot sauce had been was a note: "Thought you might be wanting some more, Daddy. Love you, Nikira."

Hank reached in and retrieved the note. "That's my baby girl lookin' out as usual."

He sat back down holding the note in his hand. While he waited for the timers to go off, he dialed his daughter. The rings went to voice mail. "Thank you, baby girl, for the hot sauce. You always was sneaky. I was gettin' ready to drive up to the corner sto' but sho' didn't feel like it. Bye."

The microwave had stopped, but he hadn't heard it. Five minutes later, the toaster oven signaled his meal was ready. His foot was acting up again, but the sumptuous flavors overrode the discomfort. He hadn't enjoyed a meal like this since before the hospital.

40

BERTRAND ADAMS GAZED out his living room window toward the Golden Gate. The afternoon fog had obscured his view. The top of the span's nearest tower moved in and out of view as the fog blew from left to right. He turned his attention toward the East Bay Hills. The last remnant of sun shone brightly through intermittent patches of fog.

"There's El Cerrito," he thought.

His Monday had gone reasonably well at Cal. Still, he was in a foul mood. He thought of excuses to avoid going back to Oakland. He couldn't avoid it, but maybe he could postpone it somehow. He could fake an illness or accident. He slumped into a large leather recliner and gazed out the window at nothing, his mind occupied with escape. There was none. Tomorrow he was due back at the mosque at two. He would have to show. His career depended on completing the commitment.

"Two years," he whispered.

He thought of his favorite student at the university, Fatima Amin. Since Bertrand's encounter with her husband, she would participate in classroom discussions but would no longer communicate with Bertrand one-on-one. Whenever he looked at her, she would lower her head to avoid eye contact.

He rose from his chair and walked to the fireplace mantel, staring at his wedding photo. For the hundredth time he posed the same question out loud: "Why did you have to make us go through such agony?"

He knew there would never be a response. He was locked into a misery that seemed to have no end. He cursed his weakness again. "Why didn't I go on those dating sites after Rita passed?"

A rhetorical question. He knew he wasn't interested in anyone other than his wife. That is, until he laid eyes on Fatima. He blinked, dismissing the thought, and then made his way to the refrigerator. An open bottle of Pinot stared back at him. He poured, took out the brie, cut up a Roma apple, and grabbed the crackers from the pantry. Sibelius's second symphony provided the background as he eased back into his chair. He filled his mind with random thoughts. Any thought having nothing to do with tomorrow was fine.

He arrived at the mosque the next afternoon at one thirty. The double doors leading into the school building were open. Sister Clara was sitting and reading from a large book. He noticed the inscription on the cover: Holy Quran.

He cleared his throat. "Ahem."

Sister Clara turned, smiled, and greeted him. "As salaamu alaikum, professor. You're early."

"Yes. I wanted to have time to prepare a bit more, since this is my first official class with the students."

Clara continued to smile but did not respond.

"Where are the students, by the way?"

"They're in the mosque making prayer. They should be back shortly."

Bertrand opened up his briefcase and began to organize his presentation. "I meant to ask the grade level your students are working at."

"Six through twelve. Most have already had some instruction in basic chemistry principles. Again, I think you'll find them eager learners."

"How many students?"

"Fourteen."

"OK." Bertrand pulled out fifteen copies of the periodic table. He walked over to Clara, handing her a copy. "This is where I'll begin instruction. Have your kids had any exposure to this?"

Clara smiled broadly at him but did not immediately respond. "We'll see," she said after a lengthy pause.

Bertrand heard footsteps coming down the hall. Several footsteps but no voices. Kids of different sizes, shapes, and shades quietly entered the open door of the classroom and took their seats. They looked back and forth between Bertrand and Sister Clara.

"Class, this is Professor Adams. He's teaches chemistry at UC Berkeley and has volunteered to be our instructor here for the remainder of the term." She turned toward Bertrand and nodded. "Professor?"

He walked from the window toward the front of the blackboard, stopping behind the main desk. "Hello. I've taught general and advanced chemistry for a number of years. Before we begin, let's go around the class. I would like each of you to tell me your name, age, and what subject is your favorite."

After the introductions were complete, he asked one of the students to pass out the unlabeled copies of the periodic table. He paused for a short period before speaking again. "Can anyone tell me what this handout is?"

Several hands raised. A tall, thin, girl in the front row appeared especially anxious to answer. She looked to be around twelve years old and wore a blue-and-white scarf with a long dress of the same colors. Bertrand pointed to her. "What is your name again?"

"Ahmadia. These are all the elements scientists have found on earth so far. I forgot what it's called, but I remember we studied it for a little while two years ago."

A boy near the back with thick plastic-rim glasses raised his hand. He looked to be nine years old.

"What is your name, son?"

"Samad. It's called a periodic table," the boy said confidently.

Bertrand hesitated. "How old are you, Samad?"

"Ten."

"How do you know about the periodic table?"

"My parents took me up to this place up in Berkeley. They had a big copy of it out in the lobby down from where the dinosaurs were."

"You must mean the Lawrence Hall of Science. Was it up in the hills?"

"Yes, sir."

"That's very good, Samad. Now, does anyone know what the primary element of human life is?"

Several hands rose. Bertrand pointed to a tall young man in the back corner who wore a sports shirt with a vest. He remembered his name. Similar to his favorite poet. He also remembered chemistry was his favorite subject. "Yes, Gibral?"

"Carbon is the element common to all life. Not just human life."

Bertrand tried to not let his embarrassment show but managed to not avoid glancing down before answering. "That's very good, Gibral. Everyone turn their page over to the blank side, please."

The students followed as instructed. "Now, can anyone name a gas found in the table?" All the students raised their hands. Bertrand called on new students. Five answered.

"Oxygen."

"Hydrogen."

"Nitrogen."

"Helium."

"Argon."

Bertrand looked over at Clara who smiled at him.

Class ended an hour later. The students left the classroom as Bertrand had seen them enter: quietly. He gathered his briefcase, nodded at Clara, and then turned toward the door.

"Dr. Adams."

He turned toward Clara, who was standing near the far window.

"How do you feel about your first day with our students?"

Bertrand gently shook his head. "I'm surprised." He turned and walked toward the exit. "See you Thursday."

On the way back across the bridge, he thought about what had transpired and what it meant. He had never considered finding anything encouraging in Oakland. He was alone. Alone and embarrassed.

41

RUBEN WOKE UP in a sweat. Same recurring nightmare. Police separating his hand from Ayama's. His oldest daughter crying out "Daddy" as he was cuffed and deposited into the back seat of a squad car. His former wife, Reatha, pulled Ayama away while his baby girl, Naima, stood on the porch watching stoically. Ruben wiped the perspiration from his face and then turned over to the clock: 2:39 a.m. He walked over to the commode cursing at himself. "Stupid motherfucka. You was making good money. Had a family. Didn't make no sense to be at that party with Luther snortin' that shit. You saw him put it in his pocket, then you rode back to yo' crib wit' him and got busted."

That was his third strike and the last time he saw his family. Reatha wrote a short letter to him. She had had enough and was filing for divorce. He lay back down, looking up at the ceiling and reliving that event. It was fitting that Ayama would be the child giving him a chance to reconnect. She was always daddy's girl, right up until her fifth birthday. Ruben was arrested three days later. Naima, on the other hand, was always into her own little world. She talked sometimes to her sister and mother but rarely to Ruben. It didn't surprise him when she just stood on the porch while he got carted away. It didn't upset him much when Judy Garcia informed him Naima wanted no contact with him. He recalled how, when he used to sit her on his lap, she would squirm away and run off somewhere. Never could figure out why she was like that. Just must have been born that way.

He thought briefly about his night at the jazz club. Couldn't remember most of the tunes, but he could still feel that bass vibrating through his body. And Rafiq? Couldn't figure him out. Seemed so damn nice. Why would someone like that extend himself to a con? Josh was different. Ruben had known him at Quentin. He was surprised Josh gave him his phone number and even more surprised Josh took him in. He had learned to trust Josh. But this Muslim? His mind shot back to the Muslim brothers he had encountered in the joint. Not just at Quentin but Soledad and Folsom too. Always telling him he should come to Friday prayer service. Talking all that intellectual talk about how Christianity had brainwashed people of color. How it had been used as a tool for control. He never believed any of that stuff. The brothers he met inside treated him worse than white boys did. He knew only one brother at Folsom that he kind of trusted. The others were trying to get whatever they could. One cat borrowed two packs of smokes, then transferred the next day. Guard said the man knew he was being transferred a week before. Hustled. He wondered what this Muslim's hustle was. Could it be he's just a good man? At least he hadn't asked him to come to any of their services. That counted for something.

He turned on his side, slowly drifting back to sleep. The alarm seemed to sound as soon as he closed his eyes. Six a.m.

"Another day gettin' paid beats any day in the joint," he thought as he rolled out to the aroma of freshly brewed java.

42

NIKIRA AND ARTURO'S date at the Paramount was their first together seeing a live show. Keith Sweat had always been one of Nikira's fa-
vorites, and he didn't disappoint. One romantic ballad following another
had the majority-female audience swooning. The performance garnered
only secondary attention from Arturo. He deliberately pressed his thigh
against Nikira's throughout, electricity coursing through his body. They
had visited New York two weeks earlier, meeting Arturo's other sister, Ame-
lia, who was reserved toward Nikira initially but warmed gradually within
a few days.

After the show, they stopped at an all-night diner around the lake. Arturo directed her to a booth in the rear.

"Wow, Merritt restaurant," she exclaimed. "My mother used to take us
here when we were growing up. Haven't been here in years."

Arturo smiled broadly, proud that his choice pleased her. "Does it still
look the same?"

Nikira turned around toward the entrance and briefly surveyed the
room. "Hasn't changed at all from what I remember. Still the same large

neon clock behind the counter. The seats have been refurbished, though. Wonder if they still have that good ol' fried chicken?"

She gave Arturo a strange look. "Why do you keep looking down in your lap and then back up at me?"

He flashed a sheepish grin toward her and then pulled out a diamond-studded ring box, placing it midway between them. Looking up, he reached forward with both hands. Nikira lightly grasped them. She waited for him to speak.

"Nikira, I love you beyond anything I could ever say to you. I never thought I could feel as much for any woman as I do for you. I have since the first moment I saw you. I'm asking you to spend the rest of your life with me."

Nikira smiled, yet she hesitated. They continued to hold hands even though he noticed a film of perspiration had formed on his forehead.

After what seemed to be an eternity, she answered. "Arturo, I love and trust you as much as anyone I've ever known, and that includes my mother. I'm thirty-four years old, and I think I've had more than my share of disappointments with love."

Arturo felt her hands trembling in his.

"I would be lying if I didn't tell you I'm scared."

Arturo released one hand, took his dinner napkin, and wiped his forehead. He reached back for Nikira's hand.

She continued. "I'm scared, but I'm as sure of my love as I've ever been with anything in my life. I was hoping you'd ask me soon. I just didn't think it would be tonight. I can't imagine ever being any other man's wife but yours."

Arturo opened the box and placed a gold-and-diamond engagement ring on his beloved's finger. He rose from his chair, walked around, and gently kissed his fiancée. He tasted her joyful tears, happy Nikira had been so deeply touched. After the kiss, Arturo peered into the eyes of his beautiful woman. They were dry and clear. He continued his gaze, which had turned blurry. Nikira wiped the tears from his eyes and cheeks.

They decided on a late-summer wedding. It would be outdoors at the lake. Nikira's old high school friend from Tech, Danielle, agreed to be the maid of honor. Arturo's cousin, Julio, would be best man. It would be a small gathering of family and friends. Nikira talked to Barbara the day after the proposal. It was Barbara who convinced Nikira that a summer outdoor wedding would be lovely. She already knew her daughter was no longer involved with the church and decided to forgo the idea of trying to persuade her to have the site be the North Oakland church they had regularly attended years earlier. Besides, Barbara had fallen in love with the idea of an outdoor venue since seeing Mia Longley get hitched up in the Redwood Hills a few years earlier.

Barbara would handle the logistics: making the reservation with the Oakland Park and Recreation Department, ordering the flowers, having the altar delivered, and cordoning off the area with a festive colored border. She had eight more weeks. For now, though, her immediate concern was to help her daughter find a wedding dress. They were at their third dress shop that Saturday, and Nikira had yet to find something suitable. Barbara eyed a dress she was sure her would finally fill the bill.

"Nikira! I think this is it. Take a look."

Nikira walked over, took the dress, and held it up against her body. She frowned. "Momma, this is just like the one at the first shop. Remember, I said I didn't want a lot of lace across the shoulders."

"Yeah, baby. I already know that, but this one has a lot less, and it doesn't extend down the arms like the other one."

Nikira's expression didn't change. She sighed, reached into her purse, and pulled out a photograph she had cut out of a magazine. "This is what I'm looking for. I showed this to you before we started today."

She handed the photo to her mother, who was now frowning herself. "This looks almost exactly the same as the one I just showed you."

She went back to the rack and pulled it back out. She held up the dress next to the photo. "Now tell me they don't look alike."

"They don't. That doesn't have lace around the breast area."

"But the lace around the shoulders is exactly the same."

Nikira took both items for another comparison. She handed them back to her mother, letting out a long sigh. "OK. I don't want any lace around the shoulders, period. I want curved lace below the breast line, just like in the photo."

Barbara took a deep breath. "I know, baby. But we haven't been able to find that yet. Let's just stop for today, and I'll look online. We might have to go to Frisco or Sac to find it. I'm tired. Let's go get a cool drink."

"I'm tired and disappointed. Thought we would've found it by now. OK. Where do you want to go?"

"Let drive over to the juice bar on Grand."

"OK."

They walked out onto Broadway, making their way toward Nikira's maroon Subaru parked in a lot near Eighteenth and Telegraph. Nikira paid the attendant before heading toward the lake.

They drove in silence for a few blocks before Barbara spoke. "You forgetting something?"

Nikira briefly glanced over. "No, Momma. Oh, wait! You mean my sense of direction? My sanity? What?"

"Your daddy. Don't you think you should talk to him soon?"

Nikira sighed but didn't respond right away. "I've been thinking about the right time. I'm just afraid he's going to overreact again. You remember that time I told you about when I brought my boyfriend over to his house, and th—"

"You mean that bisexual one?"

"No. Before him. His name was Earl. You met him over at your friend Stella's house about five years ago when I came to pick you up. Remember?"

"Oh yeah. The guy wearing coveralls and smellin' like grease and sweat."

"He had just gotten off work, Momma. He's a fireman, remember? And he hadn't had time to clean up."

"Hm. Hope he didn't look and smell like that when you went over to your daddy's with him."

"Please. The time at Daddy's house was prearranged. When I brought him over to Stella's, that wasn't part of the plan, but I was already late picking you up, so I had no choice."

"You could've taken more time. All you had to do was call and let me know the situation. You must have not cared about the first impression he was going to make on me. Should have taken him home, then picked me up."

Nikira was quiet. They pulled up in front of the juice bar with neither in a good mood. After ordering, they took a seat at a front window table. Sitting in silence over peanut butter/chocolate and strawberry/banana smoothies, they began to feel a sense of rejuvenation.

"Do you want to talk about your visit to your daddy's with this man? You said he overreacted."

Nikira began to recount the meeting. "Everything went real well at first. You know how Daddy likes the blues, fixing cars, and sports. Well, so does Earl. So they started having conversations about that. They went and sat down at the kitchen table. Then Daddy asked Earl if he wanted something to drink. Earl said he'd drink whatever Daddy was having. Daddy went in the cabinet and pulled out a bottle of whiskey. The conversation started getting louder and loud—"

"Where were you all this time?"

"In the living room watching TV with the volume turned down low. Anyway, Earl told Daddy that he loved me and I was the prettiest woman he had ever been with. Well, Daddy took that the wrong way. He stood up over Earl and said, 'What do you mean "been with"?' He didn't even give Earl a chance to respond. Told him to get out of the house. I think he was so drunk by then that he forgot I was even there. He gave me a kind of surprised look. Then when I got up and left with Earl, I looked back at him, and he had this look of shame on his face."

"Did you ever talk to him later about what happened?"

"I tried, but I think he's too ashamed to. Turns out Earl wasn't my type anyway. His habits are too much like Daddy's with the alcohol. I don't think I could completely trust a drinking man to be faithful over the course of a marriage. Wouldn't want to be around it all the time anyway. Learned that from being over at Daddy's on some weekends after you left him. He'd have Gerald and some of his other friends over. They'd get drunk and start cussing loud. I'd go to my room, but I could still hear them. Denard would go outside. Much as I love my daddy, I never wanted a man like him. Always been looking for one who's more…you know, refined. That's what I know I've found in Arturo."

"You know your daddy has always thought of you as his crown jewel. The way you used to cling to him when you were little. He knew you were his little girl and looked up to him despite his shortcomings. It's just the kind of attitude some men have for their daughters where no man is ever going to measure up. Barack Obama wouldn't be good enough for you in his eyes."

Nikira chuckled as Barbara touched her hand. They looked at each other for a long while, sharing a silent understanding until Barbara continued.

"It's more than that, though. It's possession. Think about Hank's life. He lost Julia, his first wife. That is, if you include me as a wife. He probably felt guilty behind that. Out there running the streets when they were married. Maybe he thought he caused her cancer. Then there's Denard. He felt like a failure toward him. I did too. Just couldn't keep him out of the street. You said Denard went outside when Hank and his friends got drunk. You think Hank didn't know the kind of life he was living was influencing his son the wrong way? I just don't think he had the strength to change. I bet sometimes he wanted to."

She took a tissue out of her purse and dabbed the tears from Nikira's face. "He feels guilt about the way he treated me too. The only person left of his family that he doesn't feel guilty about is you. That's why whenever he sees you, talks to you, or thinks about you, he feels good."

Nikira nodded. She wiped the tears with her own hand. "I know what you're saying is true, Momma. That's why I try hard to see after him. I know he needs me in his life, but that's why I'm worried to introduce Arturo. That man is the best man I've ever met, and I know he's going to love me and be faithful for the rest of our lives. But I'm scared. I almost feel like I should wait…this is going to sound terrible, but I should wait until Daddy's gone before I jeopardize my relationship with either one. That's why I've waited this long. Daddy's probably not going to last even another few months."

"Have you talked to Arturo about him?"

"Yes. But not about any of the emotional vulnerabilities Daddy has about me."

"Well, it's time you did talk about it with him. Otherwise, maybe you shouldn't until you're sure Arturo can handle the kind of reaction your daddy gave you about your last boyfriend. If there's any doubt, maybe you should postpone getting married."

"I'll talk to Arturo in more depth. I don't want to risk hurting Daddy, though, so I'll see how he feels about postponing the wedding. I think he'll be OK about it after he understands more. All he knows now about Daddy is that he has cancer. My man is a good man. He cares about others' feelings, and if he doesn't know how much Daddy means to me, he will after we talk."

43

RAFIQ AND FATIMA took the downtown route toward Fourteenth Avenue. Fatima left her car in the parking lot close to Rafiq's office at city center. Several weeks had passed since their failed attempt to enjoy lunch together, when Fatima dropped the news about Bertrand Adam's attempts to take her out. They had recovered but had been too busy for a meal date, with Fatima working on her doctoral thesis and Rafiq saddled with several new parolees. Finally, they had a chance to sit down and enjoy a meal together. Fatima had heard about Lady Sakalee's weeks ago and was eagerly looking forward to dining on West African cuisine. This restaurant, according to her Senegalese classmate, was so popular that patrons had to make reservations days in advance.

Rafiq drove down East Twelfth and made the left onto Fourteenth Avenue. The small parking lot was packed. Customers were lined up outside twenty deep. They excused themselves as they waded through the crowd to the reservations desk. A short, bespectacled black man with glasses too large for his pockmarked face greeted them with a formal Nigerian accent. "Do you have a reservation?"

Fatima said, "Yes. Amin."

The man frowned as he perused the reservation book for an extended time. The longer he looked, the deeper his brow furrowed. "You said Amin?"

"Yes. I made the reservation earlier this week. On Monday."

"I cannot find a reservation under Amin. Are you certain it is not under a different name?"

Rafiq stood by his wife silently, trying to mask his anxiety. Fatima said, "Yes. I am certain of the name. It is the name of my husband and myself."

"Please excuse me for a moment." He briskly walked toward a staircase, unhooked the rope blocking access, and then made his way up the steps.

"I wondered what happened?" Rafiq whispered to his wife.

She didn't turn to answer but instead whispered under her breath.

He strained to hear but couldn't. "What did you just say?"

Fatima put her mouth to his ear and whispered, "Is this not some shit?"

Rafiq bent over and laughed so loudly, some of the nearby diners looked over.

The man came back down the stairs and handed over to Fatima what appeared to be a voucher. "The owner instructed me to give this to you. It includes two free meals of your choice for another time. He wished to express his apology for the trouble. If you would like, I will take your reservation for any time after next weekend. I am sorry. We are booked until then."

They decided on two o'clock the Saturday after next. They walked past the waiting crowd of would-be diners toward Rafiq's car. Fatima lightly touched her husband's arm. "I'm so sorry. I thought we would finally have quality time together. It seems like a year since—"

Rafiq pulled his wife toward him and kissed her tenderly. "Baby, I don't care about that. The important thing for me is that I'm with you. We can always sit down in a restaurant."

She gazed deeply into his eyes.

"I love you, Fatima. God brought you to me, and I'm grateful every day, even though when I first saw you, I thought you were running away from me."

She smiled. "I wasn't running away from you. I was running away from your ugly shoes. Remember?"

As they kissed again, his stomach growled loudly.

Fatima chuckled. "You may be grateful, but right now you're hungry. Yes?"

Rafiq raised his eyebrows. "I have to get back to work, baby."

"What you will eat, though?"

"I'll get a sandwich on the first floor when I get back."

They drove back toward downtown, taking the freeway this time.

44

RUBEN'S HANDS WERE sweating as he sat alone at home. A Buster Williams CD that Rafiq had placed in the mailbox was playing softly in the background. He grabbed the CD player remote, turning down the volume to a whisper. He had wanted to call Ayama weeks earlier but never seemed to be able to muster up enough courage. He wasn't even sure he could do it now. He hadn't talked to his older daughter for over twenty years. Even though Judy Garcia had discovered Ayama's whereabouts and obtained permission from Ayama, he still was hesitant. What do you say to your child who never returned your letters or visited you in the penitentiary?

He wiped his sweaty hands on his T-shirt and dialed. The phone rang five times before a soft female voice answered. "Hello."

"Hello? Ayama? This yo' daddy."

There was silence for a few seconds, which seemed like an eternity to Ruben. "Hello, Daddy. How are you?"

"Um, good. Been workin' regular and tryin' to save some money. How you doin'?"

"I'm good. I've got a good husband. Two daughters. Teach school. Life is going really well. You say you've been working? What kind of work?"

"Construction. Workin' full time now that all the rain stopped."

"You got that job from where? The parole office?"

"No. No. Parole gave me some kinda job in a secondhand sto'. That one didn't work out."

Silence again.

"Well? How'd you get to work construction? Somebody had to help you get that."

"Somebody did, Ayama." He told her about Josh.

"A white man helped you with all that? I never heard a story like that before."

"It's true. He just a good man. Wasn't for him I'd prob'bly be out on the street right now. Or dead. It a strange world, Ayama. Sometimes the place where you think help'll come from, it don't. Sometimes it just come out the blue."

"I talked to my husband about you. He's OK meeting for a short visit in about a couple of weeks. The plan is for us and the kids to drive up there and go out for a meal with you."

"Oh. OK. I thought maybe I could come down th—"

"No. Maybe later. We want to reconnect up where you live. Talk and get to know each other a little better first."

"OK. I'm very happy you kept the do' open for me, Ayama. I know I messed up bad, but I always loved you. Naima and yo' momma too. How she doin'?"

"She remarried two years after the last time you got arrested. He's a good man. Owns his own computer store. Has treated Momma real good all these years."

Ruben struggled with mixed emotions, the most prevalent being shame. "He must be a good daddy to y'all, then."

"Yes. I'm very lucky to have had him guide me through childhood. He helped me in so many areas, including my schoolwork and staying away from the wrong kind of boys. I love him very much."

She heard a deep sigh on the other end of the line.

"He and Momma never wanted us to have any contact with you, though. I kept asking if we could go visit you. Even before she met my second daddy. She didn't want to see you anymore, even though I did, and Daddy just went along with her about that."

"'Saw-right, Ayama. I get it. I wouldn't a wanted to see me either if I was her. What about Naima?"

"She's up in Seattle working with some tech company. I don't talk to her that much. She's making good money and sounds happy."

"She married?"

"No. She's got a girlfriend, though."

Ruben coughed into the phone. "'Scuse me. Naima was always off to herself. I just neva' thought…it's aw-ight, though. Long as she happy."

"I've got to go pick up the kids. It's good to talk with you, Daddy. I always wanted to, but circumstances with Momma, and later when I got married…I guess I decided to just concentrate on my own life and family."

"That's aw-ight. Glad you got a good life goin' for yo'self. I'll be happy when I can see you and meet yo' family."

"I'm praying that you stay straight, Daddy."

"Been straight, girl. Now I got reasons to be even stronga' with that. Bye, Ayama."

"Bye."

He sat motionless for a few minutes, thinking about the fear and anxiety he had heard in Ayama's voice. His oldest child. The one he had been closest to. He smiled, having felt the undertone of love that had come through. Forgetting his painful knee, he quickly rose and turned the volume up on Josh's CD player.

45

"WHAT?" HANK'S FOREHEAD began to sweat as he hollered into his phone. "Nikira, you know you ain't had no kinda luck with men in yo' life. Now you gonna get married all of a sudden?"

"Calm down, Daddy. I've known this man for over four months now. He's the best ma—"

"Four months? Four months ain't nothin'. You sure you not rushin' things? I know you probably gettin' nervous 'cause you gettin' a little older an' ain't hitched up yet. Lotsa women get anxious like that if they ova' thirty. That's it, ain't it?"

"Daddy, you're overreacting. Arturo is the one man I've met wh—"

"Arturo? Sound like a Mexican. You ain't gettin' ready to marry a—"

"He's Puerto Rican, and like I was going to say before you interrupted me, he's the best man I've ever known."

Hank was quiet for a time.

"Daddy? You still there?"

"Yeah, I'm still here. Listen. Are you sure about this?"

"I'm as sure about this as I've ever been about anything in my life. I'm having a get-together this Friday at my apartment. I want you to come over and meet him. Rafiq said he'll come through and pick you up."

Hank didn't answer.

"Daddy?"

"Yeah, OK. What time I'm 'spous to be ready?"

"Around seven."

"Who else gonna be there?"

"Momma said she's coming. So it'll be you, Momma, Rafiq, Arturo, and me."

"Uh huh. OK, I'll come. You happy now?"

"Yes, I'm very happy. And Daddy? Please be nice when you come over."

"I ain't makin' no promises. How the hell I know how um gonna be? Ain't never been in this situation befo', but I'll tell you one thing. I'll try, but if I see somethin' I don't like, don't 'spect me to bite my tongue."

"OK, Daddy. See you Friday."

"Bye, baby girl."

After he realized he had been standing in front of the recliner for the entire conversation, he flopped down into the awaiting chair. The buzzing sensation in his right foot a few weeks earlier had expanded upward to his midthigh. He balled his fist and pounded the outside of his leg in frustration, which only served to replace the tingling with searing pain. He felt satisfied. "I'd ratha' feel that than that damn vibrator," he thought. Pounding the leg had become a common reaction as the frequency and intensity of the annoyance had increased. He reached over for his glass of Jack and Coke. The ice had nearly melted, leaving a watered-down, flavorless taste.

"Shit."

He returned the glass to the reading lamp table, contemplating whether he should make the effort to go to the refrigerator for a fresh one. Disgusted, he raised the legs of the recliner, knocking his nearby cane onto the floor.

He leaned over the side of the armrest and laid the cane down in the chair. The doorbell rang.

"Who is it?"

"Gerald."

"Come on in, man."

Hank heard the doorknob turn back and forth.

"Musta locked the door, Gerald. Go 'head and get the key from inside the porch light."

Several seconds passed before Gerald entered. "Hey, man. Called you twice from Little Rock. How come you neva' called me back?"

"Man, you know how sometimes you just don't feel like talkin'."

"Yeah, I do. But you could at least call and say you don't wanna talk. We been friends for how long? 'Bout forty years? At least I'd know everything coo'."

"Listen, man. My leg been messin' up mo'. Shit goin' furtha' up, and mos' the time I don't feel like talkin' to nobody. If you wanted to know how I was, how come you didn't call Nikira? You got her number, don't cha?"

"Not no more. Musta lost it or it dropped from my phone. Anyway, I neva' thought I'd need to call somebody else."

Hank took out his phone and pulled up his daughter's number. "Here it is." He handed it to Gerald. "How long you been back home?"

"Late las' night." Gerald took a good look at his friend. He had never seen Hank look so miserable.

"You need me to git you anythin'?"

Hank looked over at his friend standing a few feet away. "Yeah. You can make a run down to the fish market and get me some sand dabs. I'm almost outta Jack and Coke too."

Gerald hesitated. "You shouldn't be drinkin' hard liquor, man. That shit might be makin' yo' leg worse. Might be gout or somethin'."

Hank glared angrily at his friend. "Gerald, I don't give a damn if it is makin' my leg worse, 'cause it makes the rest of me feel betta'. Don't start talkin' to me like some damn doctor man. I'm gonna eat and drink what I like till I can't do either one anymo'."

Gerald raised his hands defensively. "All right, man. You want anything else with yo' fish?"

"Yeah. Get some collards, sweet potato fries, white bread, and banana pudding."

"All right."

"Get some money out my wallet. It's on the nightstand in there." Hank gestured toward the bedroom.

"Naw, I got this." Gerald turned toward the door. "In a minute."

Hank listened futilely for the sound of Gerald's Dodge pickup before realizing he had probably walked over from his house. The pain in his thigh subsided and he drifted off a few minutes later.

46

Nikira peered down at Alcatraz Avenue from her living room window. She hadn't expected to be this nervous. Barbara calmly observed her daughter from her vantage point on the end of the couch closest to the window. She shook her head before speaking. "Baby, your daddy isn't going to get here any sooner than he gets here. Sit down and relax. Get a glass of wine. You starting to get me nervous."

Nikira released the curtains, then turned toward Barbara. "It's already seven twenty. He was supposed to be here at seven. I'm going to call—"

"You gonna do no such thing. Get your glass of wine, then come back over here and sit with Arturo."

Nikira did as her mother requested, coming back into the living room with two glasses of red wine. She handed one to Arturo before sitting next to him. Arturo brought the rim of the glass toward his mouth. A drop of perspiration rolled down his forehead and splattered into his glass. Nikira reached across him and pulled out a tissue from the end table. She gently wiped his brow, half relieved that someone else appeared to be as nervous as she. They sat silently for what seemed to be an hour but was, in real time, only a few minutes. They heard the sound of slow, weighty footsteps coming up the stairs and then down the second walkway toward the apartment. A knock on the door. Nikira all but leaped from her seat on the couch before composing herself. She looked through her cloudy peephole, barely recognizing the shape of Rafiq's head.

"Is that you, brother?"

"It is. Myself and Dad."

Nikira opened the door. Her brother was smiling warmly. Her father was leaning over the rail with his back to them. The siblings briefly hugged before Nikira turned her attention toward Hank.

"You OK, Daddy?"

Using his cane for support, Hank slowly turned around. He forced a smile. His eyes weren't happy, though. Bags had formed underneath, and they were more bloodshot than Nikira had ever remembered. His normally pristine complexion had developed stress lines along the lateral contours of his face. Nikira stepped forward and warmly hugged her father. He returned the hug, which was clearly weaker than usual.

"Come in and meet Arturo," she whispered in his ear.

Rafiq had already entered and was talking softly with Arturo. Both men were standing facing the door as Hank entered, followed by Nikira. Hank stopped and stared directly at Arturo, who stood motionless, trying to avoid what he interpreted as intimidation.

"Daddy, this is Arturo. Arturo, this is Hank."

Arturo cautiously moved forward, finally extending his hand. Breaking his stare, Hank reached forward and shook hands.

"I'm pleased to meet you, sir."

Hank relinquished a brief nod before releasing his hand.

"Your daughter has told me so many good things about you."

Hank raised a quizzical eyebrow. "Like what?"

Barbara moved closer to Hank, standing just a few feet away. "Daddy, come on and sit down."

Nikira motioned toward the recliner chair facing the window. Before Hank moved, Barbara came forward and hugged her former boyfriend warmly. His dour expression masked the joy he felt. He returned the hug. As they separated, Barbara smiled before returning to her seat. Hank limped over and sat in the recliner. His propped cane fell on the floor.

"I got it, Dad," the still-standing Rafiq said eagerly.

Hank's stare stopped Rafiq in his tracks. "You think I'm helpless, boy? Um always pickin' this thing up off the flo'."

He reached over with his long right arm and easily retrieved it. The satisfied look of "I told you so" on his face made Rafiq laugh.

"Yeah, Dad, you're right. I should know by now you're a do-it-yourself man."

"Damn right."

"Daddy? Can I get you a glass of wine?"

Hank looked over at Nikira. She was snuggled up tightly against this man he had just met. Mixed emotions coursed through Hank. Mostly jealousy and worry that he might be losing the one person who had bothered to look out for him all these years. His beloved Nikira.

She repeated her offer. "Daddy? Do you want something to drink?"

"You got any beer, baby girl?"

"Sure. Be right back. Oh, do you want a glass?"

Hank stared at her before understanding it was a joke. "You got any of those beer mugs? You know, the ones they call steins? I got to have class. Matches my personality."

Everybody laughed except Arturo, who leaned over and whispered to Nikira, "What's a stein?"

Nikira whispered into his ear, "It's a container with a lid. I think it was Germans who introduced steins a long time ago, for beer drinking." Her disappearance into the kitchen was followed by a brief, awkward silence.

Arturo looked over at Hank, who was examining his cane. His future son-in-law broke the silence. "Mr. Roberson?"

"Hank. Just call me Hank."

"Do you like baseball?"

"I like the A's. Ain't been to a game for a while, though."

Nikira handed the beer bottle to her father as Arturo continued. "Maybe we could go see them play sometime. I've been going ever since I moved to Oakland. My uncle played for them for two years before they moved from Kansas City."

"Yeah? When?"

"Nineteen sixty-five through nineteen sixty-seven."

Hank briefly nodded toward Arturo before responding. "My days of goin' to see baseball all ova' now. Too much climbin'."

Arturo thought he would ask if Hank would mind going in a wheelchair but changed his mind.

The group continued casual conversation for several minutes. Hank came back from the bathroom and turned toward Arturo. "Come on out-side with me," he abruptly commanded. Arturo looked first at Nikira, then at Barbara and Rafiq before following Hank outside. Hank walked over to the rail and turned sideways as Arturo turned to face him. Hank gave him a stare that lasted longer than Arturo could tolerate. He turned away and faced the street.

"Is there something you want to tell me sir?"

"Look back ova' here at me."

Arturo shuddered imperceptibly as he turned back to face the older man.

"You know my daughter is the person I love mo' than anyone else in this world, don't 'cha?"

"I know that. She had a long talk to me about your relationship."

Hank pushed down on the rail and stood straighter. "Oh, she did, huh? What she tell you?"

Arturo took a deep breath. "She talked about how your son—"

"You talkin' about Rafiq?"

"Yes. How the two of you didn't get always get along and that your other son was in prison. She said she was the only one who was in your life regularly."

"She told you all that? Ain't that a bitch!"

As Hank reached for his cane, Arturo moved a few steps back. Hank gave him a mean look, then broke into a belly laugh. "Boy, come on back over here. I ain't about to bust you with this thing. Just needed it to kinda' balance myself after you sprung that shit on me."

Arturo stepped back over but a bit farther away from Hank than before. Both men stared out onto the street for a time collecting their thoughts.

Without turning to look at Arturo, Hank continued. "She tell you about some of her other boyfriends?"

"Yes, sir."

"Dammit! Don't call me sir no mo'. My name is Hank. I'm just gonna tell you straight. I don't want my daughter goin' through any more pain when it come to her relationships with men. She done been through too much already. You understand what um sayin?"

"Yes I do."

"Well, you betta'. I 'spose she told you about me dying pretty soon too, huh?"

"Well, she didn't say it like that, but yes, she did tell me you were sick."

"She say you love her. Lookin' at you today wit her, I believe that's true. But that can change. Um tellin' you that no matta' what happens, um puttin' it on yo' shoulders to love her from now on."

"You don't have to worry about that. I know how deep my love is. There's no chance that will ever change."

"It betta' not. I don't have all that much time left, 'cordin' to my doctor. But look ova' here at me."

Arturo turned back toward Hank.

"I will come back from my grave and take yo' ass out if you eva' mistreat her."

Arturo held Hank's intimidating stare, unafraid this time.

Hank continued. "You believe what I say is true?"

"I believe you love your daughter so much, you would do anything in your power for her."

"Damn right."

Arturo dared not share his thought: "But you're not coming back from the grave."

47

ARTURO AND NIKIRA were married at the lake on one of those perfect late-summer days. Hank presented his daughter to the groom. He had been experiencing a functional remission over the last several weeks and was getting around better for short distances without his cane. After he kissed his bride, Arturo glanced over at his father-in-law and was pleased to see a broad smile. He had never witnessed an outward appearance of joy coming from Hank before. At the Lakehouse reception, the families dined and danced to salsa and old-school R&B. Hank danced with his daughter. Both smiled and chatted throughout. It was one of the most memorable days for the Roberson clan, and Arturo's family expressed open affection for Nikira. Following the ceremony, the happy couple drove to their oceanfront lodging in Monterey and spent a full week enjoying the sights and sounds. Arturo had refurbished his house in Oakland's Diamond District in preparation for married life. A gifted carpenter, he had built a redwood deck extending around to the back and both sides of the second floor. Nikira grew to love the northerly view of the large nearby park. The joyous sound of children frolicking made her thoughts of starting a family more frequent.

Three months after the ceremony, Arturo prepared an exquisite dinner of blackened salmon, cheese garlic mashed potatoes, stir-fried zucchini, and cornpone. They sat on the carpet in front of the large fireplace enjoying the aroma of food, wine, and pound cake cooking in the oven. Arturo finished his meal, then stood to check the cake. When he returned he announced, "Not done yet—about ten more minutes." He looked lovingly at his wife, her facial hues and contours flickering from the fireplace light. She was chewing her food in her usual sedate way but with a broad smile simultaneously gleaming from her face. Arturo leaned over to kiss her but stopped as his bride began to laugh.

"Baby, what's so funny?"

"I'm so happy tonight being here with you. Did I tell you that you are the only person I have ever been completely relaxed around?"

"No. You've never actually spoken those words, but I've felt it most of the time." He began laughing so strongly he nearly knocked over his wine glass.

Nikira smiled, tilted her head, and looked at him with a puzzled expression. "Now you've got me guessing. Tell me what's so funny."

Arturo continued to laugh, finally composing himself to answer. "You never answered me. Why should I tell you first?"

Nikira jumped up, came around behind him, and put a fake choke hold around his neck. "Arturo Perez, you are going to tell me right now what you're laughing at, or I'll just have to strangle you."

He continued laughing more hysterically before finally relenting. Nikira sat back down.

"Do you remember our first date?" he asked while wiping the tears from his eyes.

"All of it. I'll never forget it."

"You just said you've always been completely relaxed around me."

"You know you always make me relax. How could I ever…oh, yeah. I guess I forgot you almost got both of us killed."

"Uh huh. But I had a very good excuse. You distracted me."

Nikira knew what he was referring to but continued as if she didn't. "I distracted you, huh? I wasn't even sitting close to you in the car or talking. You just had a brain meltdown."

"I couldn't control myself. In the restaurant, you shouldn't have pressed your knee up against mine. It caused a shock to go through my spine."

Nikira laughed. "And that shock lasted all the way through the drive back to my place?"

"Yes, it did. It just kept running up and down my spine and continued for the next two days," Arturo said with a straight face.

Nikira laughed so hard she fell over on her side. No longer able to keep his deadpan expression, Arturo broke down, his laughter causing him to brace his elbow on his plate. He lifted himself up, first wiping the smear of mashed potatoes off and then the tears from his eyes for a second time.

Nikira took another forkful of food into her mouth. "Aren't you forgetting something?" she asked in a sensual tone.

Arturo's face was a blank slate.

She continued. "You're forgetting I didn't answer your question. You wanted to know why I was laughing."

"Baby, we were just having so much fun I forgot. I hope we'll always be like this. OK, what were you laughing about?"

"Do you know the empty bedroom your sister used to live in?"

Arturo stopped chewing his food. A goofy look appeared across his face. Right then, he knew. He smiled. "Your mother wants to come live with us, and we need to fix it up for her."

Nikira smiled but didn't laugh. A child was something she had wanted for most of her adult life. "We've got some time, but let's start planning on what kind of a nursery we're going to have."

Arturo sat down next to his wife. They hugged warmly and, for once, he wiped tears from eyes other than his own.

48

RUBEN PACED NERVOUSLY in the living room he shared with Josh. Today was the day. His daughter, son-in-law, and grandkids would knock any moment. He looked at his reflection in the hall mirror, straightened his pastel striped tie, and checked if any food was trapped between his teeth. He blew into his hand to check his breath even though he had just brushed minutes before.

He heard car doors closing. Sounded like it was coming from directly in front of the house. He rushed to the kitchen window. A maroon SUV was there where Mr. Robinson's daughter was usually parked. He heard footsteps coming up the walkway. Turning quickly toward the front door, he tripped over a kitchen table leg and almost fell before regaining his balance.

"Calm down, man. You actin' like a damn child."

He heard the doorbell, took a deep breath, walked over, and slowly opened the door.

Ayama was taller than he expected. Next to her stood her husband, shorter than she by a full four inches and thin. The two children stood behind them.

"How you doing, Daddy? You looking good," Ayama said with an un-smiling yet pleasant expression. "This is my husband, Devonte, and our two children, Jamal and Jakara."

Abruptly, Jamal jumped from behind his two parents. "You my grand-daddy?"

Before Ruben could respond, the boy was hugging him around his thigh. Surprised by this display of affection, Ruben returned the hug, then gently pushed the boy away. "Uh huh. I think it's safe ta say I'm yo' granddaddy."

His granddaughter shyly stood behind Ayama, peeking around her leg. "Y'all come on in and make yourself comfortable."

Devonte extended his hand to Ruben as he was passing, but Ruben had turned toward the room and didn't see it. The couple and Jakara sat on the couch while Jamal began exploring the room before his father summoned him. "Jamal. Come over here and sit down."

Ruben sat in the recliner before quickly standing and walking toward the kitchen. "Y'all want something to drink?" he asked.

No one responded. Ruben heard unintelligible murmuring between the two parents before Ayama answered, "Just some water, please."

Ruben turned around to face the group. "What about the kids? I got some lemonade in here."

Jakara looked up at her mother and nodded. Jamal squirmed next to his father. "You got any soda, granddaddy?"

Ruben looked directly at the boy. He was starting to dislike him a bit. Kind of reminded him of some inmates at Quentin who never seemed satis-fied with the available drinks at the snack shop. They would ask for some-thing else. If only strawberry-banana was available, they wanted orange. Ruben answered the boy with a firm "No. It's lemonade or water."

Ruben watched his grandson's head drop. He continued to wait for a response. When the pouting boy continued his quiet, Ruben retrieved the drinks, handing the bottles of water to the parents and the glass of lemon-ade to his granddaughter.

His son-in-law broke the silence. "Mr. Scott, do you know any good places to eat around here?"

"Yeah. I know a lot of good spots. Really jus' depend on what y'all want." He sat in the recliner not feeling a bit guilty for making such a statement knowing most of the restaurants he had only heard of but had never actually been inside. He continued. "I like barbecue. We have two good spots here if y'all want to go. There's all kinda otha' choices, like vegeta—"

"Momma, I'm thirsty," Jamal interrupted.

His mother did not hesitate with a response. "Your grandfather gave you a chance to have a drink. Now you just sit there and wait until you get another chance."

Jamal lowered his head again, crossing his arms over his chest this time. Ruben gave his daughter a look of admiration. He wondered if this was the way she usually handled the boy or if it was just a show.

Ayama looked over at her husband. "Baby, what do you think?"

"I'm hungry and really don't care where we go, but I sure would like some good barbecue brisket." He chuckled as he looked over at Ruben and then back at his wife. "What do you want, baby?"

"Barbecue sounds good." She looked back at Ruben. "We've decided, and we're ready to go when you are."

"Aw-ight then. Let's get on outta here."

Early afternoon on a Friday. Traffic down Shattuck was light. Good timing for some barbecue, or so Ruben thought. Devonte parked on the street, less than half a block away. A man was asleep in the doorway of a boarded-up store. He looked sharp—unusually so for a street person. He had on a red long-sleeve shirt partially covered by a charcoal sport coat. Sharkskin pants matched the coat, and his patent-leather shoes were only slightly scuffed. No container to accept money. Devonte walked over and dropped a couple of bills in his lap. The startled man lurched forward, picked up the money, and waved it at Devonte. "Tank you, but I don' need no money."

"Then why you layin' out here in the do'way, man?" Ruben said.

The man smiled broadly and pointed over his head. "I live up on the third floor. Just had a fight wit my wife last night, and she kick me out. She have a bad temper. Not the first time I hole up down here. Be all right, though. I give her a day to calm down." He handed the bills back to Devonte.

"You been out here all night?" Devonte asked.

"No. No. Not all night. Just since about four this mornin'. Not so dangerous at daytime."

The family continued walking toward the aroma two or three buildings away. As they approached, Ruben noticed a line of people outside nine or ten deep. "Shit," he whispered.

He and Jamal exchanged glances. "Didn't think that was loud enough for anyone to hear," he thought. He had been saying "shit" so often for so long he hadn't realized he had uttered the word at a decibel above a whisper.

"I better go inside to see what they have left, 'cause sometimes they run out early."

He returned with good news. "They got enough of everything, so y'all can get whatever you want."

Finally inside, they ordered and took an empty table in the corner. At an adjacent table, an elderly man with gray cornrows and a goatee stretching down to his sternum stared at Ayama through bluish-gray-tinged eyes. She looked away a few times, but his penetrating stare continued. She nudged her husband and whispered. He turned to face the man, who immediately looked away. Devonte turned back toward his wife and shrugged. Seconds later, he caught the man staring at his wife. The mysterious interloper turned away again, but not in time to avoid being seen.

As Devonte began to rise from his chair, Ayama grabbed his forearm. "Baby, let's not make a big thing out of this. Let's just change seats."

Devonte stood to his full five-foot-six-inch stature. Ignoring his wife's suggestion, he walked over to the man's table. "Excuse me."

The man ignored him, sopping what remained of his barbecue sauce with a bread slice.

"That's my wife you've been gawking at over there, and I'd appreciate it if you train your eyes somewhere else."

The man slowly turned toward Devonte. The bluish-gray circles inside his eyes contrasted against his dark skin, giving him a surreal, unworldly look. Devonte held his gaze until the man finally turned back to his food.

"She's a beautiful woman. Just don't get to see many classy women 'round here. You a lucky man."

He finished his sauce and bread before slowly standing. He reached over for his cane and began a slow limp toward the exit. Having reached the door, he turned to face Devonte, who was still standing midway between their two tables. The man raised his cane, pointed it at him, and held it steady for a few seconds before leaving. Devonte shook his head as he turned back toward Ayama. She had a huge smile on her face.

"Why are you smiling, Ayama? Did you notice how crazy he looked? Had the nerve to try to undress you with his eyes."

Devonte stared out the window and down the street in the direction the man was walking. He appeared more unsettled over the event than his wife. Ruben took this as an opportunity to observe his son-in-law. To judge his character. He remained silent throughout, only looking back and forth between the two.

"Number twenty-six!" came from behind the counter.

Ruben retrieved both trays of barbecue.

Devonte still seemed shaken, periodically glancing toward the door and out the window. "Fool might want to come back in here and start something." He looked at his father-in-law. "You see the way he pointed that cane at me and got that crazy, wide-eyed look on his face?"

Ruben smirked. He could have comforted Devonte right then, knowing what he knew about the strange man, but decided instead to let him squirm a bit. During the meal, Devonte continued to be preoccupied with looking outside.

After they finished, Ruben leaned over and touched his son-in-law on the shoulder. "Otha' than flirtin' aroun' with almost every woman that come in here, that man ain't about to do harm to nobody."

Devonte hesitated before he replied. "You've seen him before? In here or someplace else?"

"Jus' in here. Seem like almost every time I come here, ol' Chester in here, sittin' right ova' there where he was."

"You know his name. You've talked to him."

"Naw. But seem like everyone that work here know him. They be talkin' back and forth all the time."

"Really? No one seemed like they were interested in talking to him this time."

Ruben laughed. "That's 'cause they was too busy watchin' the show. They wanted to see what you was gonna do. Somebody always say goodbye to him on the way out the do'. Guess they neva' saw him turn and use his cane like it was a rifle or somethin'. Did all I could to keep from bustin' up laughin'."

Devonte was not amused. He wondered why Ruben didn't consider the actions toward Ayama offensive. After all, it was his daughter who the man was staring at. He thought of asking Ruben but held his tongue.

Ruben continued. "Manager say Chester used to own this place. Owned it for about forty years. Worked it with his daughters, but they didn't want to take it over when he got to old fo' the work, so he sold it to the manager. He live just a coupla' blocks away."

As Devonte strained to look back down the block, Ruben let out a huge belly laugh. Ayama joined him with a high-pitched giggle. Ruben hadn't heard that since she was a young girl. He looked over at his daughter and smiled. He felt good. Felt like his life was really beginning to take shape again.

49

JOSH ANSWERED THE doorbell midmorning the next day. Devonte's surprised look was quickly replaced by recognition. He smiled at the tall, pale, pony-tailed man.

"You must be Josh. I'm Devonte. Ruben's son-in-law." As they shook hands, Devonte examined Josh's T-shirt. On it was a unique rendering of Jesus bearing more of a resemblance to Bob Marley than to any traditional image. It read, "I am the truth and the light." In the doorway, Josh stood a good foot and a half taller than his visitor. He looked over the top of Devonte and saw a woman and two children in a maroon SUV.

"Is that your wife and kids out there? Why don't you tell them to come in and visit for a while? Ruben's still getting ready."

Devonte motioned toward Ayama. She and the two children were soon at the threshold. "Welcome. Come in and make yourselves comfortable."

They entered and sat in the same seats as the day before. Jamal was uncharacteristically subdued. He stared at Josh in bewilderment. Ayama thanked Josh for taking her father in and helping him find work.

Josh shrugged it off. "I'm a Christian. Before I turned to God, I was mostly angry and selfish. Did Ruben tell you how we met?"

"Yes. He told me how he went to church in prison for coffee and dough-nuts. Said he called you after he got out, and you directed him here."

Josh nodded. Music crept up the stairwell from the basement. Then si-lence followed by footsteps. Ruben entered the room looking sharp and refreshed. "How y'all doin?" He smiled at the family, walked over to Josh, and placed what appeared to be cash into his hand. He then walked over and kissed his daughter. "Good to see y'all. Did you rest OK?"

He moved over in front of Devonte. "How about you, son-in-law? You rest OK?" A big belly laugh shook Ruben's torso.

Devonte was not amused. He understood the reference and resented it.

Ruben picked up on it. "Listen, Devonte. I'm a joker. Don't take it per-sonally. I liked the way you stood up for Ayama yesterday. You supposed to protect your woman like that, and you did. Lookin' down the street after Chester left, you didn't have no way of knowin' whether he was comin' back with a gun or somethin'. You acted like a man who loves his family, and I respect that."

Devonte took a deep breath as his face assumed a more relaxed look.

They stayed for several more minutes, talking to Josh about his life in and out of the church. He told them about the hatred he had for his brother and how it was lessening the more he prayed.

Devonte turned toward him as they were leaving. "You're a good man, Josh."

"Damn right he is. If he wasn't, I'd still be on the street," Ruben said.

As they made their way down Ashby, Ruben twitched in his seat. "Y'all didn't tell me where we goin' today."

He turned around to look at Ayama, who was seated behind Devonte.

"We're going to the Marin Headlands just across the Golden Gate Bridge"

"OK." Ruben had heard of the Headlands but couldn't imagine where it might be.

A Salvadoran man named Javier at Quentin's church used to talk about it. He said he would take his family there for picnics before he was arrested. Ruben remembered Javier used to fight back tears, as though he would never return to a place anywhere near that beautiful. Ruben tried hard to remember any other details but couldn't. It had been years ago, and Javier had died not long after his sixtieth birthday.

They crossed the Bay Bridge and drove through the Embarcadero along the eastern and northern perimeter of the Bay. Ruben had crossed the Golden Gate going the opposite direction to a specialty medical appointment. The prison bus he had traveled in back then didn't afford much of a view. Today was different. He looked eastward at infamous Alcatraz Island and the vessels of various sizes sailing the Bay. Devonte exited on the other side of the bridge, doubled back under the freeway, and headed up a steep road.

"Park right there, Devonte," Ayama said.

They exited the car and walked over to the rail, where most of the Bay could be seen.

A large container ship was passing under the bridge, heading out to sea.

"Daddy, look how huge that boat is," Jamal exclaimed.

"Anything that large is not a boat, Jamal. It's a ship."

"Momma, is that the bridge we just came over?" Jakara said excitedly, pointing back at the Golden Gate far below.

"Yes. Isn't it beautiful?"

"How'd y'all find out about this place?" Ruben asked.

Ayama hesitated.

Her father looked over at her and asked again.

"Eric used to bring us here sometimes when we were little."

"You mean the man your momma married?"

"Yes."

A beautiful scene suddenly became cloudy for Ruben. He shook off the temporary low mood and decided to enjoy the day as much as he could. His low was replaced by the awareness that he, a man separated from his children by his own mistakes, was now reunited with one of them. He felt how fortunate he was.

"I'm happy to be here with y'all to see all this. I wanna thank you for bringing me here. I'm really diggin' on this view. Never seen nothin' like it."

Ayama walked over and squeezed his arm. "I'm glad you're enjoying this, Daddy. You want to see more?"

"Hel…oh yeah."

They drove farther up the hill and reached what appeared to be a dead end.

"Look like this as far as we can go," Ruben said.

"Wait a minute," Ayama said, smiling. "You're in for a surprise."

Devonte turned to the left and began to descend a narrow road.

"Whoa. Devonte! You better slow down. This road is steep."

Devonte did as Ruben suggested, dropping down to a lower gear. Suddenly, the road veered to the right, and the entire Pacific Ocean opened up before their eyes. The children talked excitedly back and forth, thrilled by the immensity of the view. They stopped halfway down the hill in front of a walk path and rolled down the windows. They quietly watched and listened. Still a few hundred feet above sea level, the distant sound of seagulls could be heard below. They heard the deep horn of the cargo ship they had seen earlier as it approached a fog bank farther out to sea. The wind rustling through the bushes made it seem like they were the only people on earth until a car passed and broke the mood.

"There any place to eat around here?" Devonte asked his wife.

"I don't know. Haven't been here for so long, but Momma used to pack us food for a picnic. We would stop and eat farther down the road where some tables were."

"I know Devonte's not the only one who's hungry, 'cause I sure am," Ruben said. He looked back at his grandkids. "Y'all hungry?"

"Yes, Granddaddy," Jamal said.

Jakara didn't answer or look at Ruben. She was afraid of her grandfather.

They continued down until the road leveled off and passed the remains of military posts, where concrete slabs echoed gun battles that had never happened. They reached a turn where a roadside food stand stood. The small food truck's aromas blew east as they rounded the corner and parked.

"Hmm. Smells like roasted chicken," Devonte said.

A man wearing a T-shirt that read Headlands Snack Truck smiled at them as they approached. "Nice day to be out. Let me know when you're ready."

"Thank you," Ayama said, smiling back.

They ordered chicken sandwiches, fries, and drinks and then sat down at a nearby picnic table. The sound of waves crashing on the shore several hundred feet away triggered a memory. Ruben wiped his eye to keep a tear away. He thought about a scene years ago when he had taken his wife and two daughters to a beach in Alameda. They spent the whole day there roasting hot dogs and listening to the waves. That day and today were the only days in his life when he had heard that sound. He thought of all the time he had squandered. All the moments he had missed.

Jamal noticed Ruben turn his head away from the family. "Granddaddy, you OK?"

Ruben turned his head away from his grandson's voice. "Yeah, I'm fine. Wind kinda strong out here. Think I got a piece of sand or somethin' in my eye."

They enjoyed their food and the atmosphere, looking around at the large hills and trees in the distance. They stayed in that one spot for two hours before leaving for the drive back to the East Bay. They pulled up in front of the house and got out.

"Daddy, we're going to on to the hotel. We've got an early start tomorrow to get back home."

"Yeah, OK. Y'all got to get back to work on Monday?"

"Yes. I do. Devonte has to go back tomorrow night." She turned toward her husband. "He'll be fine, though. He's a different kind of man. He can eat with anybody but never needs much sleep."

Ruben looked at his son-in-law walking toward him. "Well, Devonte. You ain't nothing like me, then. Got to get my eight in eva' night."

Devonte extended his hand to Ruben, and the two grimaced at one another in one of those "my grip is stronger than yours" masculine ego-tripping gestures. When they finished, Ruben massaged his hand. "Damn, man. Didn't know you had that kind of strength in you."

Devonte walked around and sat behind the wheel with a little grin of satisfaction on his face.

Ayama gave her father a warm, extended hug. "I really enjoyed our visit, Daddy. Looks like you're doing well. Please keep it up. I'll be calling you."

Ruben smiled at her. "I didn't know how much I really missed until today. You better believe I don't 'tend on missin' any mo'. Ain't nothin' for me to do but stay straight. I want you in my life. That mean eva'thing to me."

She and the kids waved as they drove off. The kids hadn't said goodbye, and Ayama had not reminded them to. Ruben didn't give it a thought. He walked through the door still hearing the sound of the ocean.

50

HANK'S EYES POPPED open. The clock read 8:14. Someone was pounding on the front door. "Wait a minute, dammit!" He slowly sat on the edge of the bed, but the pounding continued. He grabbed his cane and stood. Pain shot down the outside of his right leg.

"Shit! Who the hell would be wakin' me up this early?"

Just as he opened the bedroom door, the pounding resumed. "All right, dammit, um comin'." His leg hadn't hurt this badly in several days, which made him even madder. He looked through the peephole but didn't see anyone. He slowly opened the door and looked over to his left. Gerald was standing several feet away, peering into his bedroom through a cracked slat.

"Gerald! Why the hell you bangin' on my do' so damn early in the mornin'?"

Gerald walked over past the mulberry bush. "Man, I just don't know about you. 'Member we just talked yesterday about goin' down to the pier and doin' some fishing?"

Hank stood there with an embarrassed expression. "Damn. Well, why the hell didn't you just call me instead of tryin' to knock my whole damn house down?"

"Man, your phone is turned off. I told you I was coming by around eight, and you said you'd be ready. You still wanna go?'"

Hank really didn't, but he didn't want to disappoint his longtime friend. "Yeah, I still wanna go. Just give me a little time to get dressed."

"Look, man. Um gonna walk back down to the house. Turn on your phone and call when you ready."

"All right." Hank looked around the living room for his phone.

"Might be in the kitchen," he mumbled.

He turned on the tea kettle and slowly made his way into the bathroom. There it was. Lying on the back of the sink.

He tried to retrace his steps the night before but couldn't remember bringing it into the bathroom. He wondered if the cancer had spread to his brain. Just last week, he was late paying taxes on the house. He had never been late paying any of his bills, and two nights ago, he had left the front door unlocked.

Back in the bedroom, he put on the blue pants and striped shirt he had worn a few days ago. Using his cane, he retrieved one of his shoes from under the bed. He sat down and got dressed. Something was nagging at him. Something he had forgotten. He stood up, thinking the change of position might clear his brain. It didn't. He turned around. Lying on his pillow was his phone. Taking a deep breath, he reached over and turned it on. "You have two messages."

"Daddy. Just checking in on you. It's early. Don't know why your phone is off. Call me if you need something. Love you." He saved it. Just as he did all of Nikira's messages.

"Hank, I'm leaving the house to come over. Hope you remembered 'bout fishing. Bye."

Hank shook his head. "Wouldna' had to mess my leg up mo' goin' for the do' if I 'membered to keep my phone on," he thought.

He dialed Nikira. "Hey, Daddy."

"Hey, baby girl."

"Daddy, why don't you just write yourself a note to keep your phone on so I don't have to worry?"

"I'll do that. Gonna get the marker and paper soon as I'm done talkin' to you."

"Good. Got to go. Love you, Daddy."

"Love you too." He disconnected and laid the phone down next to him. "Guess I'll call Gerald". He picked his phone back up and dialed. "Hey, man, I'm ready."

"OK. Be right ova'."

Hank went outside as Gerald was coming up the sidewalk. Gerald had already gone into Hank's detached garage and grabbed his fishing rod. As they were getting into the car, Gerald looked over at his friend. "You know what you should do, man? Make yo' self a big note remindin' you to keep yo' phone on."

Hank didn't respond. He closed the door, took a deep breath, and then reached for the door handle. "Hold on, man. Got to go back inside. I'll be right back." Gerald watched as his friend entered the house. Hank walked into the kitchen and turned the flame off under the tea kettle.

51

BERTRAND ADAMS WASN'T sleeping well. He had tried but failed to get erotic thoughts of Fatima out of his head. The dating service he had joined had a variety of interesting professionals. He had contacted an attractive Indian woman. She was a software engineer who provided interesting conversation and showed interest in him during a lengthy dinner date. He did not call her back. Fatima had left an indelible imprint on his soul from which he could not escape. The term was winding down at the university, but for Bertrand, it couldn't end fast enough. He had succeeded in not approaching Fatima, knowing his career was at stake. Furtive glances at her were the norm during class time. His timing to avoid eye contact succeeded most of the time, as he realized she was intent on doing the same.

When he dismissed class, he would watch her at a profiled angle until she disappeared. At home, he would imagine holding her and kissing her—daydreams in which she eagerly returned his kisses. His dreams were more graphic and recurring. He would caress her breasts, slowly working his way down her abdomen to her sweet spot. She would moan for what seemed like hours before commanding in a deep voice: "Come up here now." When he would move on top of her, something in his brain triggered him to awaken. Frustrated, he would take a shower, sometimes washing the discharge off his abdomen and privates.

At the mosque classroom, he continued to experience satisfying, even joyful moments teaching the children. Ten-year-old Samad, who had shocked him by reciting the periodic table, asked him to come to the mosque for midafternoon prayer. Bertrand felt awkward, not knowing the meaning of the Arabic words or the various prayer positions. He declined further invitations from Samad until he learned the English translation and the movement sequences.

Near the end of the term, he arrived early at the mosque to meet Sister Clara and Rafiq on a Friday. He had learned weeks ago that Friday was the day for community prayer but had since forgotten. When he arrived early to get a head start on correcting final exams, he was surprised to see the number of vehicles in the parking lot and on the street. His usual parking spot was occupied, and as he began to pull off in search of another, a voice yelled out, "Professor Adams!"

He turned his head to see Rafiq walking briskly toward his car. "I saved my spot in the lot for you. Follow me, and I'll take you to it." He walked down the block to the open-gated fence, motioning for Bertrand to take a spot with green lines marking the space. Bertrand pulled in and exited.

"As salaamu alaikum. I didn't expect you to get here this early," Rafiq said.

Bertrand shook his hand and attempted to offer a feeble smile but could only manage a smirk. "Thank you for that. These must be all the people for...uh, Jama?"

"It's 'Jumah,' professor."

Bertrand turned his head in embarrassment, hoping Rafiq wouldn't notice.

"One of our students, Samad, told me you've come to afternoon prayer sometimes. He says you understand the meanings and positions. Why don't you come to prayer today with the community? It starts in about fifteen minutes."

Bertrand shifted his weight, unable to hide his discomfort. Right now, all he wanted was to get away from this man and find some solitude.

"Brother Rafiq. As salaamu alaikum."

Rafiq turned to see Sister Clara walking slowly toward them. "Wa alaikum as salaam, Sister. I'm trying to persuade the good professor here to join us for Jumah."

Sister Clara turned to face Bertrand with her usual cryptic expression. "Professor, the three of us understand the reason you first came here. We would like you to experience the beauty and unity of the one prayer of the week that brings us all together. It's not the most important prayer, as all of them are important. However, it is the one with the largest turnout, which makes it all the more beautiful."

She came closer to Bertrand, which startled him. He had never really looked into her eyes. The thought of doing that frightened him. She gently latched her forearm around his. Something in him commanded him to look at her. Her eyes were shining around the irises. Her face had a strange, faint glow. His legs began moving with hers in the direction of the mosque. Just before entering the door, she released his arm, allowing Rafiq to walk him inside.

Worshippers were removing their shoes. Rafiq and Bertrand sat next to each other and removed theirs before walking onto the crimson carpet. Some were already praying. Others were seated, waiting for the *khutba*, or sermon. Rafiq and Bertrand sat on the carpet and were silent. After the khutba was finished, a man wearing a prayer cap and a long, flowing white gown rose and began to recite the call to prayer. His voice was so high and melodic it sent chills down Bertrand's spine. He had heard the children recite the call, but never like this. The worshippers began to line up shoulder to shoulder.

Rafiq led Bertrand to an open space forward in the third row. During the prayer, the spirit of united voices with common movements filled the room, and for one of the few times in his life, Bertrand began to feel a sense of belonging. Afterward, worshippers of all colors and sizes greeted him and invited him to come back. Today, for the moment, he was not a professor fulfilling some requirement to keep his position. He was a member of a community performing a prayer in unison. He didn't know if he would study more about Muslims or even come back for another Friday prayer. He only knew he loved the way he felt that day.

52
TEN MONTHS LATER

HANK GRUNTED AS he reached across his body and rang the bell. A middle-aged, light complexioned nurse with green eyes and wavy brown hair entered his room.

"Do you need some help, Mr. Roberson?" she asked with a cheerful smile.

Hank frowned at her. "How many times I got to tell you? Call me by my first name. You been here off and on for two weeks. Ain't no need to keep actin' like no butler." He read the name tag above her left breast: "Jeanette Coleman, Compassion Home Care Services."

Her dimpled smile broadened even more. "I'm sorry. I'm so used to the formality at the house I worked at before I came here. The patient insisted I call her by her last name. I'll remember from now on."

He grimaced as he grabbed the bedrail and rolled onto his left side. The pain had expanded over the last several months. It was no longer confined to his right leg. Pain regularly shot down his left leg to midcalf. "I need for you to help me sit up and walk into the bathroom. First I need some mo' pain pills, though."

Jeanette's smile waned a bit. "You aren't on hospice yet, so I can't give you pain medication whenever you want it. Remember, I called your doctor yesterday and made an urgent request for you to be transferred to hospice care. I'll call him again now."

Hank released his hold on the rail, rolling over again onto his back. He swore at the ceiling. "Ain't that a bitch! Damn cancer eatin' me up and can't get no relief."

Jeanette glanced back at her patient and continued her advance toward her phone in the kitchen. Within a few minutes, she returned. "Your doctor gave a verbal order for you to be placed on hospice immediately. I can give you morphine every hour if you want it until the end of my shift."

She went back into the kitchen and returned with the medication and a glass of water in hand. She handed them to Hank, who quickly swallowed down the dosage. He lowered the head of his hospital bed. "Do you have to go badly, or can you wait awhile?"

"I can wait for number two." He reached for the urinal hanging on the rail. Jeanette watched him for a moment. Hank nodded his head at her. A cue to leave the room.

"Oh. Sorry. Had a brain lock. Call me when you want to get up. By the way, you'll be getting an IV of morphine beginning tonight. You can take a dosage whenever you feel you need it." She disappeared, allowing Hank his privacy.

■ ■ ■

Almost a half hour had passed. Jeanette had heard Hank turn on the TV, but not another sound had come from his room. As she slowly entered, Hank jerked his hand from underneath the sheet. The discernable shape of an erect penis showed underneath. Hank's eyes were droopy. He looked at his nurse with a sheepish grin on his now-relaxed face.

Still embarrassed by her intrusion, she blushed as she smiled at him. "Anything I can do for you, Hank?"

He spoke to her in a kind of slurred stupor. "Hell yeah. I can think of a lot you could do for me. Trouble is, ain't no way I could keep up."

She stood nearby. His eyes opened a bit wider as he examined her face. "I been wantin' to ask you. You look mostly like a white lady, but somethin' tell me you got some a my people in you somewhere from not too long ago."

She had just recovered from her previous embarrassment but now turned pink again. "My great-grandfather on my mother's side was Ethiopian."

"Hmm. You sure a pretty thing."

"Thank you." She cleared her throat while turning her head away from him. She thought for several seconds before speaking. "Hank, since you're now on hospice care, some new nurses from there will be taking over starting tomorrow."

Hank raised the head of his bed. "I don't want no new nurse. You been real nice, and I'm sorry if I came off wrong. See, I'm just a ho—"

"That has nothing to do with it, Hank. Care agencies have their personnel, and hospice is separate." She thought for a moment, deciding whether to disclose more information. On balance, she enjoyed this assignment. Her patient was entertaining and motivated to get up whenever he could and walk. She made a decision. "I'm also a hospice nurse. Haven't worked for them for a few months, but I can ask if they will allow me to continue with you."

Hank smiled broadly as she walked back to her telephone. He watched her profile as she turned. "I knew it. Sho' 'nough a black booty."

53
ONE WEEK LATER

"ARE YOU SAYING you can predict he's going to be gone in less than a month? Doctors said he wouldn't last this long. What are you basing this on?" an aggravated Nikira asked.

The hospice physician, Dr. Wellman, said, "Please calm down, Ms. Roberson. I'll explain the results of the testing we did last week. The key problem is, the cancer has spread into his lungs. His lung ventilation is far below normal because the little sacs in his lungs that fill with air have mostly closed off. I've arranged for oxygen to be administered starting this afternoon. The cancer in his spine and pelvis has spread, but that's not what's presently life threatening. It would be if he didn't have the lung issue."

He heard high-pitched sobbing. Several seconds passed before Nikira spoke. "Are you saying there's nothing that can be done?"

"I'm afraid not. Lung transplants would be a remote possibility, but again, the cancer has spread throughout his lower spine, which in and of itself will be lethal sooner rather than later. I'm very sorry. I would suggest you spend as much time with him as you can."

Nikira cried and disconnected the call without responding. She slowly composed herself. The thought that her father had only mild pain was a brief comfort for her. He was even joyful and joking most of the time when she came through on her visits. She would need to talk with Rafiq, Barbara, and Arturo. They needed to make final arrangements.

54
LATER THAT NIGHT

NIKIRA SAT BEDSIDE as the nurse, Jeanette, prepared the oxygen delivery system for Hank. As she moved the cannula up toward his nostrils, he grabbed one of her hands. "Stop," he said weakly. "Thought you had a thing for me. Didn't know it was gonna start with my nose." His speech was slow and slurred. He was using the morphine pump regularly, including throughout the night.

Jeanette smiled as he released his hand. She put the cannula in, then stood up. "See? That's not so bad, huh?"

Hank nodded at her, then closed his eyes. She turned toward Nikira in anticipation of seeing an embarrassed look on her face. Nikira showed a sad expression and nothing more. "You know your father likes to have fun. The more he uses the morphine, the more comments he makes like the one you just heard."

Nikira looked at Jeanette with a blank expression. "That's my daddy. Up until the last few years, he always tried to make a way with women. He changed because of all the pain he caused my mother, but that pain medicine is taking that away. Now he's just reverting back to his old self."

A baby was crying in the next room. Nikira quickly moved in that direction, then returned with a medium-brown two-month-old boy with a full head of light-brown, curly hair. She turned her chair away from her father and pulled down a strap on her blouse, placing her breast into the baby's mouth. Hank's snoring drowned out all sounds in the room.

"Do you mind if I look at your baby?" Jeanette asked.

"Uh uh. I'm not bashful."

"What a beautiful child. And look at that hair. I can't even see his scalp!"

The child diverted his eyes away from his mother and toward Jeanette.

"Hi, little pretty baby. You happy now? What's your name? He looks a lot like my youngest son did at that age, except Donny didn't have nearly as much hair."

"How many children do you have?"

"Five, and three grandchildren. What's his name?"

"Armando Henry Perez". Nikira picked up her ringing phone.

"Sis. Hey. How's dad doing?"

"He's weaker but not in any pain. You know they gave him his own morphine machine he can use. They just started him on oxygen tonight. I talked to momma. She's going to take more time off work. It would be good if you could too."

Rafiq hesitated. "How much time did the doctor say he has?"

"He said any day now but you know Daddy. He's lasted a lot longer than they said he would already."

"Is he talking much?"

"Not a lot. He just flirted with his nurse. Tried to make it seem like she was making a pass at him with his nasal cannula."

Rafiq forced a laugh. "Sounds like he's regressing back to his old self. That the morphine?"

"You know it is."

"How's the baby?"

"He's right here. He's happy 'cause he's full now."

"OK, sis. Got to go pick up Fatima. We'll be there all day tomorrow. By the way, how's Denard?"

"Momma said he's up now, walking on his own with a cane. He's eating and talking, but his speech is slurred. They transferred him out for rehab last week."

"Wow. That's incredible after being in a coma. My brother is a strong man to come that far back."

"He's blessed. Don't know what kind of life he's going to have, but we should show him our love by visiting regularly."

"I agree. I've been kind of remiss in that area, but now that he's up… when do they allow visitors out there?"

"Only one day a week, on Thursdays. Love you, brother. Bye."

"Love you too, my sister. See you tomorrow."

55
TWO NIGHTS LATER

NIKIRA REMOVED THE plate of sand dabs and cornbread from Hank's tray. He had barely eaten anything before falling back to sleep. A pattern that had repeated over the last two days. Baby Armando woke up and began to cry loudly. His mother returned from the kitchen, lifted him from his stroller, and sat in the corner recliner for another feeding. Rafiq and Arturo sat a few feet away in adjacent chairs, which were borrowed from the kitchen. Fatima sat quietly next to Rafiq. Barbara silently prayed bedside, holding Hank's generally unresponsive hand. After praying, she wondered to herself whether she'd be in such close proximity to her former boyfriend if he were fully awake.

After a time, Hank squeezed Barbara's left hand and then opened his eyes. He turned his head slightly in an attempt to focus on her face but saw only an opaque outline. Too weak to speak, he smiled. Barbara's return smile went undetected through his blurry gaze. Nikira placed the now-satisfied Armando back into his stroller and came back over bedside to join her mother.

"Daddy? Are you in any pain?"

Hank managed a subtle side-to-side head movement, still looking at Barbara.

"Do you want to see your grandson?"

Hank didn't respond.

Nikira lifted Armando out of the stroller and carried him over.

"Here's your grandson, Daddy." She placed the sleepy baby on top of his grandfather's chest. She took Hank's right hand and placed it around the infant's left hand. The other family members stood around the bed and watched as Hank's fingers closed around his grandson's hand. The sound of oxygen running through his cannula was constant. His chest gently rose and fell, and the baby with it. The group quietly murmured unintelligible whispers to one another. Rafiq never took his eyes off his father. A short wheezing sound was Hank's last exhalation. He still held the hands of his grandson and Barbara as he passed into the unknown. Rafiq felt immediate regret. He knew he had failed. The anger of his youth had squelched any semblance of kindness he could have shown his father years ago. He would regret it the rest of his life.

ACKNOWLEDGEMENTS

TO MY WIFE Glynies who complemented the love notes I've written to her over the years. Your love and exceptional beauty inspired my creativity. To our granddaughter Zin who provided helpful feedback. To all of our children, grand and great grandchildren: seek enlightenment over entertainment. To the Latina RN at San Quentin who told me that she and other medical staff loved reading my clinical notes. Your comment confirmed their value.

ABOUT THE AUTHOR

ROBERT SPRIGGS IS a retired therapist who spent the last six years of his practice treating inmates at San Quentin State Prison. He resided in Oakland for several years.